M000191605

THIEF OF THE HEART

What Reviewers Say
About MJ Williamz's Work

Exposed

"The love affair between Randi and Eleanor goes along in fits and starts. It is a wonderful story, and the sex is hot. Definitely read it as soon as you have a chance!"—Janice Best, Librarian (Albion District Library)

Shots Fired

"MJ Williamz, in her first romantic thriller, has done an impressive job of building the tension and suspense. Williamz has a firm grasp of keeping the reader guessing and quickly turning the pages to get to the bottom of the mystery. *Shots Fired* clearly shows the author's ability to spin an engaging tale and is sure to be just the beginning of great things to follow as the author matures."
—*Lambda Literary Review*

"Williamz tells her story in the voices of Kyla, Echo, and Detective Pat Silverton. She does a great job with the twists and turns of the story, along with the secondary plot. The police procedure is first rate, as are the scenes between Kyla and Echo, as they try to keep their relationship alive through the stress and mistrust."
—*Just About Write*

Forbidden Passions

"*Forbidden Passions* is 192 pages of bodice ripping antebellum erotica not so gently wrapped in the moistest, muskiest pantalets of lesbian horn dog high jinks ever written. While the book is joyfully and unabashedly smut, the love story is well written and the characters are multi-dimensional. ...*Forbidden Passions* is the very model of modern major erotica, but hidden within the sweet swells and trembling clefts of that erotica is a beautiful May-September romance between two wonderful and memorable characters."
—*Rainbow Reader*

Sheltered Love

"The main pair in this story is astoundingly special, amazingly in sync nearly all the time, and perhaps the hottest twosome on a sexual front I have read to date. ...This book has an intensity plus an atypical yet delightful original set of characters that drew me in and made me care for most of them. Tantalizingly tempting!"
—*Rainbow Book Reviews*

Speakeasy

"*Speakeasy* is a bit of a blast from the past. It takes place in Chicago when Prohibition was in full flower and Al Capone was a name to be feared. The really fascinating twist is a small speakeasy operation run by a woman. She was more than incredible. This was such great fun and I most assuredly recommend it. Even the bloody battling that went on fit with the times and certainly spiced things up!"
—*Rainbow Book Reviews*

Heartscapes

"The development of the relationship was well told and believable. Now the sex actually means something and M J Williamz certainly knows how to write a good sex scene. Just when you think life has finally become great again for Jesse, Odette has a stroke and can't remember her at all. It is heartbreaking. Odette was a lovely character and I thought she was well developed. She was just the right person at the right time for Jesse. It was an engaging book, a beautiful love story."—*Inked Rainbow Reads*

Visit us at www.boldstrokesbooks.com

By the Author

Shots Fired

Forbidden Passions

Initiation by Desire

Speakeasy

Escapades

Sheltered Love

Summer Passion

Heartscapes

Love on Liberty

Love Down Under

Complications

Lessons In Desire

Hookin' Up

Score

Exposed

Broken Vows

Model Behavior

Scene of the Crime

Thief of the Heart

THIEF OF THE HEART

by

MJ Williamz

2020

THIEF OF THE HEART

© 2020 By MJ Williamz. All Rights Reserved.

ISBN 13: 978-1-63555-572-1

This Trade Paperback Original Is Published By
Bold Strokes Books, Inc.
P.O. Box 249
Valley Falls, NY 12185

First Edition: January 2020

THIS IS A WORK OF FICTION. NAMES, CHARACTERS, PLACES, AND INCIDENTS ARE THE PRODUCT OF THE AUTHOR'S IMAGINATION OR ARE USED FICTITIOUSLY. ANY RESEMBLANCE TO ACTUAL PERSONS, LIVING OR DEAD, BUSINESS ESTABLISHMENTS, EVENTS, OR LOCALES IS ENTIRELY COINCIDENTAL.

THIS BOOK, OR PARTS THEREOF, MAY NOT BE REPRODUCED IN ANY FORM WITHOUT PERMISSION.

CREDITS
Editor: Cindy Cresap
Production Design: Susan Ramundo
Cover Design By Tammy Seidick

Acknowledgments

Before I thank the usual suspects, I want to give a heartfelt thanks to my wife, Laydin Michaels. She's my sounding board, my voice of reason, and my truest supporter. Without her love, I wouldn't have it in me to write these stories. So, thank you, babe.

I need to thank my beta readers, Sarah, Sue, and Karen. Thank you for riding this wild ride with me and helping me turn out another book. Thank you so much for your words of encouragement along the way. *Thief of the Heart* wouldn't have happened without you.

A huge thank you to everyone at Bold Strokes Books for giving my writing a home and for their never wavering efforts to make me a better author.

Last, but certainly not least, a ginormous thank you to the readers. You make all of this worthwhile.

Dedication

To Laydin—Thank you for everything

CHAPTER ONE

The Maritime Alps glowed bright orange as the sun made its descent behind them. As the rest of the world prepared to sleep, Monaco was just coming to life. Kit Hanson woke sensing the whirls and clangs of the casino as guests began taking chances. It was a sound she thrilled to. It meant money. It meant challenge. And most of all, it meant jewels.

The sounds meant thousands of beautiful women dressed to the nines. Women in all shapes and sizes would don their very best in attempts to outshine each other. It was like a smorgasbord to Kit. One she could never resist. She'd never be able to resist.

Kit took a leisurely shower before dressing in her fitted tux. She wore purple accents that she knew brought out her blue eyes. She would be irresistible to one unfortunate woman that night. Or maybe more. Only time would tell.

It was time. She heard the church bell toll ten and knew it was time to make her move. She wandered through the streets, enjoying the reflection of the moonlight on the water. Everything was so serene for a moment. But as she wandered along, the sounds of the casino called to her anew. Her blood rushed and her heart pounded. Internally, she was churning. Externally, she was cool as could be.

It took Kit a moment for her eyes to adjust to the bright lights once inside. The noise was deafening, but she was used to it. It wasn't her first trip to Monte Carlo, nor would it be her last. As was her norm, she'd rented a house in town under an assumed name. She never stayed at the casino. She couldn't risk being recognized. She had her methods. And they worked.

She knew she cut a handsome figure as she stood just inside the front door and surveyed the room. There were couples everywhere, all dressed in their finery with the women decked out in jewels.

She pushed off the pillar and made her way through the throngs to the roulette table. Roulette was her favorite. God knew she had plenty of money to play with. She was filthy rich. She'd even begun to have thoughts about retiring. But those thoughts never stayed long. She'd miss the thrill, the taste of victory, the taste of women.

Kit was on a roll. She couldn't seem to lose. A crowd had gathered around her, and while she feigned concentration on the numbers, she really took in who was paying her the most attention. And how they were dressed.

There were both men and women gathered around her, but only a few of the women seemed to be flying solo. The rest were coupled up.

Kit's gaze landed on a statuesque blonde in a form fitting red dress. She had rows of diamonds cascading around her neck and more dangling from her ears. She reeked of money. And the way she held herself. Her head held high and arm clutching her purse. She seemed completely at ease. She was class personified. Something inside Kit flipped. She'd found her target.

She surveyed the pile of chips in front of her, wondering how much longer she'd play. She wanted to keep the blonde there and paying attention to her. She needed to draw it out just a little longer.

Kit placed another bet. And another. The crowd cheered every time she won. Which she couldn't help but do. More chips piled up. She took another breather and surveyed the crowd. The blonde was gone. Where had she disappeared to? Kit craned her neck to survey the casino beyond the crowd but didn't see her.

"Place your bets."

She heard the words through her fog of determination. Without really thinking, she moved some chips to red thirty-two. The wheel went round and round. And ended on thirty-two. Kit had had enough. She had lost interest in the game. She needed to find the blond woman.

She gathered her ticket to cash in and cut through the crowd, which was now applauding loudly. People were patting her on the back and speaking to her in several different languages. She knew they were all saying congratulations, and she smiled in appreciation. But she wasn't into it. She wanted to get her cash and find her target.

"You were very impressive back there," a woman with a thick German accent said quietly as Kit cashed in her ticket. "How much did you win?"

"Enough." Kit knew she was being short. She turned to see who was speaking to her. It was another blond bombshell bedecked in diamonds and sapphires. Her long blue dress hugged a full figure, and Kit realized she might need to recalculate.

She flashed her best smile.

"But is it ever really enough?" She shrugged.

The blonde smiled back.

"I'd think it was more than enough."

"It all depends on how you look at things," Kit said.

"And just how do you? Look at things, I mean?"

Kit shrugged again.

"I look at everything as a challenge. And I like to win."

A slow smile spread across the woman's face.

"Do you usually win at everything? The way you did tonight?"

"That all depends." She offered the woman her hand. "I'm Ronnie."

"My name is Anika. It's very nice to meet you, Ronnie."

"Likewise, I'm sure. Would you like to get a drink, Anika?"

"I'd like that very much."

Kit escorted Anika to one of the bars in the casino. It was quieter there and much less crowded. She forced herself to look into Anika's eyes and not at her necklace as she asked her what she'd like to drink.

"A chocolate martini, please."

Kit arched an eyebrow at her but ordered as requested. She ordered a rum and Coke for herself and guided Anika to a quiet table in the corner.

"Are you here alone?" Kit asked. "Or are you a casino widow?"

Anika laughed, a deep, soulful laugh that made Kit smile.

"I'm alone. I am single. And you?"

"Oh, I'm very single. Here's to no strings attached." She raised her glass and clinked it against Anika's.

"Do you live here in Monaco? Or are you just visiting?" Anika said.

"Just visiting. And you?"

"It's my first time here. It's a bit overwhelming." She laughed again.

"Where is home for you?"

"I'm from Cologne. In Germany."

"Ah, I've been there. It's quite lovely."

"Yes," Anika said. "It's a wonderful place."

"Do you go to the casinos there often? I loved the Spielhalle Schnicks."

Anika beamed at her.

"That's my favorite place to gamble."

"And when you gamble, what's your poison?"

Anika shook her head slightly.

"I'm sorry. I don't understand."

"What game do you play?"

"Oh, I play many. But blackjack is my favorite."

"When we finish these, shall we hit the tables?"

"Sure. If you don't mind."

"Not at all, Anika. Not at all."

Kit took in the sparkling blue eyes that matched the sapphires rimmed in diamonds that hung from her ears. Anika was a very attractive woman. Kit could have fun with her. And since she obviously wasn't going to find the blonde in the red dress at this point, Kit decided to relax and take full advantage of all Anika had to offer.

The plunging neckline of her dress revealed a copious amount of cleavage. Big breasted women had always been Kit's weakness, and Anika was no exception. However, Kit was a professional and would maintain her composure. She'd have fun and enjoy Anika every which way but loose. But she'd keep her eye on the prize. Her employers were expecting her to deliver and she wouldn't, couldn't disappoint.

She noticed Anika's drink was empty.

"Would you like another one? Or would you like to gamble for a while?"

Anika smiled.

"It does not matter to me. You finish your drink then we'll decide."

"Nonsense. I'll not have you just sitting there. Let's hit the blackjack table."

Kit took her hand and guided her through the crowds. They found a table with two open seats and quickly took their places. Kit wasn't crazy about blackjack, though she could count cards with the best of them. It just didn't interest her that much. So she played a few hands, broke even, and gave up her seat to stand behind Anika.

She rested her hands on Anika's satin clad shoulders. She could feel her heat radiating through her sleeves. This was a woman with plenty to offer. She'd make a great bedmate, of that Kit had no doubt.

The fact that she was beautiful and smelled divine only added to her allure. Kit had to be careful and maintain a professional distance. She couldn't let emotions or hormones deter her from her goal.

❖

Savannah Brown had been fascinated by the woman at the roulette wheel. She was on a roll, and Savannah had enjoyed watching her. The woman had been very attractive, with her short, spiked black hair and piercing blue eyes. Eyes that were accentuated by the purple accents worn with her tux.

And her smile. Every time she won, her smile lit up the whole casino. Her teeth were perfect, straight, and pearly white. Savannah had found herself drawn to the stranger. And then, the woman had looked right at her. Their eyes had met, and Savannah had felt the electricity to her core.

That was when she'd turned away. She had a job to do. And it didn't involve handsome androgynous women. Or maybe it did. She didn't know. That was the frustrating part of her job. She had to find someone who'd eluded authorities for years.

Someone many believed was a lesbian but had no proof. Many of the victims claimed it was a man who'd stolen their jewels. Others claimed to have no knowledge of who had done the robbery. Still others said it was a woman. So there she was, in Monte Carlo, searching for a specter who stole women's jewelry. Millions of dollars' worth of jewelry.

Savannah traveled the world, going from high stakes competition to high stakes competition which seemed to be where their thief hit. She was in Monte Carlo for the big poker tournament weekend. She only hoped the thief would be there, too.

Was it possible that several jewel thieves were at work? Yes. It certainly was. But she didn't believe that. Savannah believed she was looking for one person. One daring, ballsy person with one thing on her mind.

The woman at the roulette table didn't look or act like she needed to steal jewels to make money. She'd been throwing chips around like she was made of the stuff. But she had to make money somehow. And Savannah hadn't missed how the woman had eyed the diamonds she'd been wearing. Was she just being appreciative? Or had it been more sinister?

Either way, Savannah had been unable to deny her reaction to the woman's brazen once-over. She'd been on fire, every nerve ending twitching under the scrutiny. She'd needed to get away. The last thing she needed was to let her hormones interfere with her investigation.

So she'd gone back to her room, washed her face, and applied minimal makeup. She'd let her hair down so it flowed freely to her shoulders. She'd taken off the diamonds and placed them securely in her safe. Then she dressed in a nice dark gray pantsuit and headed back down to the casino.

She couldn't help herself. She walked past the roulette table, but the woman was nowhere to be seen. With a knot in her stomach that might have been disappointment or might have been residual hormones, she checked the rest of the gambling areas.

Women in jewels were everywhere. She wished she could warn them to be careful but knew it would be pointless. News of the infamous international jewel thief was everywhere. Most thought they were immune. And most were insured. So even if the thief struck, the patrons would be simply inconvenienced. Unless the jewels had sentimental value. But at this level, she doubted that was the case in most instances.

Savannah wandered around the floor, through the slot machines, and baccarat tables. She found a game of craps to watch and almost choked from the cigar smoke. She could barely see the game through the smoke. She didn't stay long, opting instead to cruise past the card tables.

She was watching a game of pai gow that wasn't holding her interest. She allowed her gaze to roam to neighboring tables. There she was. The woman from the roulette table. Savannah couldn't deny the disappointment at seeing the woman clearly enjoying herself in the company of an older woman.

The woman was also blond, and Savannah quickly racked her brain. Were most of the victims blond? Did the thief have a type? Was the dashing woman the thief after all? But, no. She couldn't remember any predominance of any kind when it came to victims. Except they were all women. And they were all rolling in dough. The thief knew what he or she was doing.

Unable to stay away, Savannah sauntered over to the blackjack table where the woman's companion was playing. She walked close to the sexy brunette who didn't give her more than a glance. Funny, she'd been ogling her like crazy earlier. But why not now? Because she wasn't bejeweled. That's why.

CHAPTER TWO

Y̲ou're very attentive," Anika said as they stepped away from the table several hours later. "I'm not used to that. You never let my drink run empty. You urged me onward every hand. I really appreciate that."

"You're most welcome. I believe beautiful women should be treated like gold."

Anika blushed.

"My husband could learn a few things from you."

Husband? Kit held her breath. She hoped she hadn't been barking up the wrong tree all night. Married women were her bread and butter, though. She hoped she'd still be able to relieve Anika of her jewels. Without interference from a meddling husband.

"Is your husband here?" She hoped she sounded cooler than she felt. "Do we need to check in with him?"

"Oh, no, Ronnie. He didn't come with me this time, but how sweet of you to inquire."

Kit was relieved, but less confident. Anika wouldn't be the first married woman she'd targeted, but she wasn't sure how seducible she'd be. Would she be open to pleasure from a woman?

"Are you tired? Shall I walk you to your room?" Kit needed to find out if she was wasting her time. But how?

"Far from it. I'm invigorated. Let's cash in my winnings and then we can get some dinner?"

Dinner? Kit's stomach growled on cue. She didn't have time to think about food. She had bigger worries. But since Anika had invited her, maybe she was curious? Maybe Kit would be able to get what she needed after all.

The deafening sounds of the casino caused Kit's head to throb. Sounds that usually brought such pleasure, such energy, were now annoying. She felt like she'd failed. And the people in charge, those waiting for jewels, wouldn't be happy. Kit had never failed before and didn't like the sensation.

"Ronnie?" Anika said. "Will you join me for dinner?"

Kit forced a smile that she knew showed off her dimples.

"Of course. I'd be delighted."

Once seated, Kit reached across the table and placed her hands on Anika's.

"So, tell me about these trips you make without your husband? What do you do? How do they play out?"

"I just gamble. My husband is in politics. That's where his heart lies and where he's his happiest. Politics bore me as a rule. So, while he works, I travel and play." She shrugged. "It works for us."

Kit took a deep breath and forged onward.

"Anika, you do know I prefer the company of women to men, don't you?"

"Well…I rather assumed."

"And you're okay with that?"

"I'm fine with that. It intrigues me, titillates me if you will."

Kit's stomach did a somersault. Her heart soared. Perhaps there was hope after all.

"Titillates? How so?"

"I've never been with a woman," Anika admitted. "Though I've always thought how wonderful that might be. I'm sure a woman would instinctively know how to please another woman. Much more so than a man does." Kit nodded slowly. Anika had a good point. "Forgive me. I'm speaking of inappropriate things. I barely know you."

Kit squeezed her hands.

"There's nothing to forgive, Anika. I'd like to please you. Later. When you're ready. If you'd like me to." She held her breath, scared of Anika's response.

"I'd like that, Ronnie. I mean, if you're serious. You're not toying with an old woman, are you?"

Kit laughed. It was genuine. She was relieved beyond words.

"You're not an old woman."

"I could be your mother."

"Possibly. But you're not."

"No," Anika said. "I am not. You do things to me. You invigorate me. Excite me. Make me feel things I shouldn't feel for anyone save my husband. And yet, you're a woman."

"Yes. I am a woman. A woman who finds you incredibly attractive."

Anika blushed.

"Stop. You must stop or we'll get in trouble."

"I've never been afraid of trouble," Kit said.

"Why does that not surprise me? Still, I don't get in trouble. To be caught with you would be scandalous. And my husband can't afford a scandal. By extension, neither can I."

"I won't embroil you in a scandal. I promise."

"Good."

They finished their meal and Kit was amped to move on, but knew she still had time to kill.

"Would you like an after-dinner drink?" she asked

"I'd love that. Let's go find a lounge."

They found one, dark and relatively empty. Kit knew it would suit her purpose. She needed Anika to relax a bit more but didn't want her too intoxicated. Drunk women turned her off. And she needed to be able to perform.

Anika had had much to drink that night at the blackjack table, but she seemed to be doing okay. Another drink or two might just ease her into relaxing enough for the meat of the evening to begin. Maybe.

Kit made sure to take a table in a far corner away from the lights and sounds of the casino. There was no way to fully escape the sounds, but she wanted to be out of the sight of curious passersby.

She got their drinks for them and seated herself next to Anika at the small table. She didn't want to sit across from her any more. It was time to ramp things up, to push the envelope a little.

She rested her hand on Anika's leg briefly. She gave it a little squeeze before putting it on the table with her other hand.

"Tell me, Ronnie. You've always been a lesbian, yes?"

Kit laughed. What a ridiculous question.

"Yes. All my life."

"I mean, you've always known."

"Right. From my first kiss with my best friend in high school. I've known."

"And are you single? Not that I have any room to talk, but I need to know."

"I'm very single."

"Why is that? Why has no nice woman made you settle down?"

Kit knew the real reason. She couldn't settle down. She was always on the move. Always searching for brighter diamonds and more expensive jewels. Like the ones Anika wore.

"I suppose I just haven't met Ms. Right yet."

"That makes me sad."

She took Anika's hands in her own again.

"Oh, no. No sadness tonight. Only joy and celebration."

"You need someone to take care of you. Someone to spend your life with. Someone who completes you."

"That all sounds lovely," Kit said. "And hopefully, one day I'll find just the right woman who'll do all those things for me."

"I hope so, too."

"Tell me about yourself, Anika. How did you meet your husband?"

"We were childhood friends. Our families planned for us to marry when we were very young. But I don't want to talk about my husband. I don't want to feel guilty. I just want to enjoy the excitement you provide."

"Fair enough."

Savannah made her way through the casino several more times, always finding herself back at the blackjack tables and the sexy, androgynous butch woman who'd captured her attention. It was early morning when she cruised past the tables again and the woman and her companion were gone. Disappointment filled her. If the woman was the thief, then she'd let her slip through her hands. If not, then her opportunity to snare and bed the gorgeous being had passed.

She did several more laps around the place, checking out the roulette tables, slots, baccarat, and all other gambling locations. The woman seemed to have disappeared. The sun was beginning to make its ascent, and Savannah decided it was time for bed. She needed a good night's sleep. Her phone hadn't buzzed to announce a robbery, so she considered the night a waste.

Sleep came quickly, and Savannah was in the middle of a dream about the handsome butch when the shrill sound of her phone awoke her. She glanced at the time before answering. It was only eight o'clock. This had better be good.

"Brown here."

"Agent, come quick. Suite 369. He struck again."

"Shit. I'm on my way."

Savannah dressed, threw her hair in a bun, grabbed her bag, and bolted out the door. She was in the elevator in less than five minutes, on her way to yet another scene. These had to end. She needed to catch this thief.

She arrived at the suite and took a deep breath, straightened to her full height, thrust her shoulders back, and knocked on the door.

"Agent Brown. Thank God you're here."

It was one of the younger agents on the case, Li Nguyen. He was young, but he was good. Savannah had the utmost respect for him.

"What do you know?" she asked.

"It was a man this time. An older gentleman." He flipped through his notes. "She'd guess he was in his fifties or so."

"How's she doing? Who's the victim?"

"The victim is one Anika Schuster from Germany. She said he followed her into her room, held a gun on her and demanded her jewels."

Savannah stepped into the room to find a distraught looking middle-aged woman crying on the bed. Her hair was disheveled, and she looked like she'd just woken up. She was wearing a plush white bathrobe. Savannah approached her cautiously.

"Ms. Schuster?"

"Mrs. I'm married to Gustav Schuster."

The name sounded familiar to Savannah, but she couldn't place it. Besides, it wasn't important or relevant at the moment.

"I'm sorry. Mrs. Schuster, please tell me what happened."

"I've already told them." She motioned to the other agents in the room. Some of whom were dusting for fingerprints, some of whom were standing still, watching Savannah.

"I understand that. And they've filled me in. But I'd like to hear it from you. Please, take a breath, and when you're ready, tell me in detail everything that happened."

Anika took a deep breath and let out a shuddered sigh.

"I was letting myself into my room when I felt something poke me in the back. Someone closed their hand over my mouth, and a man whispered into my ear to keep quiet and open the door. So I did. He held his gun on me and demanded that I give him my necklace and earrings. I feel so foolish. I know I should be grateful I'm alive and the jewels were insured, but I'm still so shaken up."

"I'm sure you are. You're doing great though. Can you describe the man to me?"

"Average height. Six foot or so. Thinning brown hair. Dark, menacing eyes. I'm sorry. That's all I can think of."

"That's okay," Savannah said. "Now, Mrs. Schuster, what did you do after this happened?"

"I took a bath to try to calm down. When it didn't work, I decided to call and report it. I almost didn't but thought I'd better. I'm sure the insurance company would have insisted."

"We don't believe this is the first time the man has struck. We'd really like to catch him. Please think. Hard. Can you describe anything else to us? What was he wearing maybe?"

"A tux."

"Anything unusual about it?"

"No. A regular black tux with a white shirt. That's all I remember." She started sobbing. "I'm sorry. I just feel so violated."

"It's okay to cry," Savannah said. "You're lucky to get out alive, but I'm sure you know that."

She stared at Anika's reddened blue eyes looking up at her. She studied them. There was fear and anger, but Savannah thought she saw something else. Shame maybe? Where was that coming from? And why wasn't her hair wet if she had just gotten out of the bath? Something wasn't right.

"I'm going to look around for a moment," Savannah said. "I'll be right back."

She walked into the expansive bathroom and ran her hand over the tub. It was bone dry. There were no damp towels either. Anika's story wasn't adding up. What had really happened? Why, if she'd been robbed by an unknown man, hadn't she called them immediately? She walked back out to the bedroom and handed Anika her card.

"Thank you for your time, Mrs. Schuster. I'm going now to begin my investigation. If you can think of anything else, anything at all, please don't hesitate to call me. My cell number is on the back. I always have it with me. The rest of the agents will finish up here as soon as they can. I don't have to advise you to be very careful now. Not only were you robbed, but you saw the man who threatened you. You're in a difficult predicament."

"I've already changed my flight. I'll leave for the airport as soon as all of you are gone. Thank you for your time. I hope you find the man."

"So do I. So do I."

Savannah motioned to the door with her head and Li followed her out.

"Where are we going?" he said.

"To my room. Don't say a word until we get there."

They got on the elevator.

"So, what do you think?" Li said.

"Sh. Not until we're in my room."

She let Li in and closed the door behind her.

"Now," she said. "Now we compare notes."

"She told me he followed her into her room. She told you he put a gun on her outside."

"Right. So her story changed right from the beginning. Also, she said she'd just gotten out of a bath. Is that what she told you?"

"Yeah," Li said. "So that part's probably true."

"Her bathtub was dry and there were no damp towels in the bathroom."

Li's eyes widened.

"Why would she lie about that?"

"That's the million-dollar question. She looked to me like she'd just woken up. Who falls asleep right after they've been robbed?"

"So what are you thinking then, boss?"

"I'm thinking she knew who robbed her. She was with them. Then she woke up alone and found her jewels missing."

"Why wouldn't she just tell us that?"

"That's another million-dollar question. Why indeed? Unless she was embarrassed by who she was with. Or if she slept with them, then that means she cheated on her husband. And she wouldn't be able to admit that."

"Why can't it be easy?" Li said. "And why can't we catch this guy?"

"I wish I knew, Li. Damn, how I wish I knew."

Chapter Three

K it sipped a piña colada as she checked the balance in her offshore account. It had a beautiful sum in it, thanks to her haul in Monte Carlo. She had a new assignment now. A new goal for the weekend. But it was only Wednesday, and she was relaxing in the sun in St. Thomas.

She had opted to lie on the lounge by the sea rather than hang out by one of the overcrowded pools. She'd be surrounded by people soon enough. She didn't need them at the moment. All she needed was the sun and the surf and a cold drink. That was it.

"Excuse me, miss," a woman with a charming accent said. "Is there anything I can get for you?"

Kit looked up into deep brown pools surrounded by tan flesh and a million-dollar smile. She checked the woman's nametag. Polly. It seemed too simple for a beauty like her. She forced herself to a sitting position, placing both feet in the warm sand.

"Polly, huh? You could join me."

Polly laughed, her eyes sparkling.

"I'm so sorry. I'm working."

"What time are you off? Can I buy you a drink then?"

Polly smiled at her.

"I'd like that. I'd like that very much. I'm off in an hour."

"I'll be here. Come find me?"

"I will."

Kit admired the sway of Polly's hips as she walked away, graceful even while walking through the white sand. Kit smiled to herself. Maybe she'd get lucky just for the sake of getting lucky that afternoon. It would be nice to pleasure a woman without having an agenda. And maybe be pleasured in return? What a novel idea.

She felt her face beginning to sting, so she rolled over to get some sun on her back. She hadn't meant to fall asleep, but she was pleasantly awakened by Polly's voice.

"Ma'am? Are you awake?"

"Hm? Oh yeah. I'm awake." She sat up. "Hello, Polly. Are you ready for that drink?"

"Sure. Do you mind if we go into town? I get enough of this place while I work."

"I don't mind at all. Come on up to my room with me and I'll put on some clothes."

"I'll wait for you in the lobby if that's okay."

"That's fine," Kit said. "Come on."

She picked up her laptop and they walked to the lobby where Kit left Polly and went upstairs and took a quick shower and donned some white linen slacks and a short-sleeved, button-down, light blue top. She slicked her hair with gel and was back downstairs fifteen minutes later.

"Sorry that took so long. I opted for a shower."

Polly must have appreciated it as she favored Kit with a bright smile. Her teeth shown white against her bronze skin.

"No problem at all. Come on. I'll drive you to my favorite watering hole."

She drove them to a lovely spot, the Side Street Pub. They sat on the patio under an umbrella and Kit felt more relaxed than she had in longer than she could remember. Polly was engaging and funny and oh-so-easy on the eyes. She'd ordered each of them a Bahama Mama and Kit had to admit, it was delicious. It was also clear that she was a local as the drink was much stronger than any she'd had there to date.

"Where are you from, Polly? And how did you end up here?"

"I'm from here. Born and raised. I'm going to school in the States, but I come back here and work on my breaks. I love my job but need more to do with my life."

"What are you studying?"

"I'm going to be a social worker."

Kit was impressed. That took hard work, compassion, and brains. Maybe she should consider Polly for more than just an afternoon delight. But no, her own lifestyle demanded she stay single. She couldn't gallivant all over the globe if she had a woman at home.

"That's great," Kit said. "But it must take a lot of school."

"It does. But it'll be worth it when I start working."

"Do you plan to stay in the States?"

"Oh, no. I already have a practice waiting for me here."

"Excellent. You're lucky to be able to live here year-round. It's such a beautiful spot. Truly paradise."

"I agree. And you? What do you do that allows you to spend a leisurely Wednesday afternoon with me here in St. Thomas?"

"I work on Wall Street, but I can do work from anywhere."

"Ah, yes. I saw you on your computer earlier."

"Yes, indeed."

"I bet that's exciting."

"It is. Not as compassionate as a social worker, mind you, but it more than pays the bills."

"We all have to answer our own callings," Polly said.

Beautiful, intelligent, and insightful. Kit set the walls around her heart in place. She was only here for fun. Besides, she'd be leaving the island soon and didn't plan on leaving a woman pining for her.

"Well, thank you for agreeing to a drink," Kit said. "I figure you must get tired of tourists hitting on you all the time."

Polly laughed her melodic laugh.

"It can get old. But you're different. You seem kind. Besides, you're not a man and that helps tremendously."

Kit held up her glass.

"Here's to lesbians."

"Hear, hear."

They enjoyed a few more drinks, then Kit convinced Polly to let her take her out for a late lunch. Polly took her to a little hole in the wall that was a favorite among the locals. After lunch, Kit broached the subject that had been on her mind since she'd first laid eyes on Polly.

"I don't suppose you'd like to go back to your place, would you?"

Polly's whole face lit up.

"I can think of nothing I'd rather do."

Polly lived in a small bungalow not far from the beach. It was cute and quaint, and Kit tried to show her admiration rather than simply salivate over Polly.

"I like your place." She fingered some seashells on the mantle. "It's homey and beachy. It's nice."

"Thank you." Polly sidled up behind her and wrapped her arms around Kit's waist. "But I don't think you came here to admire my house, did you?"

Kit turned and took Polly in her arms.

"No, Polly. That's definitely not why I'm here."

Kit lost herself in Polly's beautiful, soulful eyes before dropping her gaze to her parted, full lips. She lowered her head and brushed her lips over Polly's. There was an almost forgotten stirring inside her. She was here of her own accord. It wasn't an assignment. She could relax and enjoy herself. It was almost too good to be true.

As soon as their lips met, Kit felt a jolt in her belly. A current of electricity coursed through her body, and she held tightly to Polly to keep from falling over. The meeting of their lips was brief, but it promised so much.

She straightened up, but Polly pulled her back. She opened her mouth and welcomed Kit in. Their tongues danced, and Kit felt her world tilt. She could lose herself in Polly, forget the world, her world, and her next assignment. She stepped away again to catch her breath and Polly took her hand.

"This way." She led Kit down the hall to her bedroom. Her windows were open, and Kit could hear waves lapping the shore. It was a seductive sound, but nowhere near as seductive as the woman standing before her.

Kit pulled Polly to her and kissed her again. While their tongues tangoed, she slid her hands under Polly's blouse and unhooked her bra. She made short order of her blouse and bra before removing her shorts and thong. Polly stood naked before her and Kit was certain she'd never seen a more beautiful sight.

Polly was not only stunning, she was obviously comfortable in her own skin. She didn't squirm at all under Kit's scrutiny.

"Your turn," Polly said. "Let's see you in all your glory."

Kit quickly stripped and took Polly in her arms again. The feel of soft skin against her own caused Kit to overheat. Her need to have her was complete.

"Bed," was all Kit could manage.

"This way, stud."

They fell into bed, limbs and tongues entwined. Kit's desire was all-consuming. She wanted Polly so desperately yet didn't know where to start. Her full breasts won the debate, and Kit gently and tenderly caressed them before she lowered her mouth to take first one nipple and then the other in her mouth. She felt them grow and pucker under her attention, and it fueled her onward.

No longer capable of thinking, Kit let her instincts guide her down between Polly's legs where she feasted on her flavor. Kit couldn't get enough of Polly and continued to please her even after she'd cried out several times.

When Polly had finally claimed she'd had enough, Kit kissed her way back up her body until she could share Polly's flavor with her. The kiss lasted forever, and when it was over, Kit's whole body hummed with its need for release.

Polly proved herself as capable at giving as receiving, and she skillfully took Kit over the edge not just once but twice.

Sated, Kit pulled Polly close and held her as she felt a necessary nap approaching.

"Don't get too comfortable," Polly said.

"Hm? Why not?"

"It's about time for me to get you back to the resort."

Kit was surprised at her tone.

"Seriously? I thought we'd take a nap then have a go at seconds."

"Not today. It's been fun. Don't get me wrong. But I just think it would be better to say our good-byes sooner rather than later."

Disappointed, but understanding, Kit picked her clothes off the floor and dressed in silence.

"Will I see you again?"

"I doubt it."

"I'm here until Friday. Maybe we can have drinks again."

"Thank you, but no thanks. Look, I like you. I really do. And, if circumstances were different, who knows how this might have played out. As it is, I'm not looking for anyone right now and I doubt you are either. So let's part as friends and keep the memories."

Kit nodded her understanding. She watched as Polly put her clothes on then followed her out to the car.

"Well, thank you for this afternoon anyway. I really enjoyed myself."

"As did I. And I wish you nothing but the best in life."

No strings attached. Just how Kit liked things. So why was she so bummed?

❖

Savannah got off the plane and drew in a deep breath. The island air felt good in her lungs and she wished she was there for pleasure and not on business. But she was on a mission, and nothing, not even the call of the tropics, could veer her off course.

She turned to Li as they deplaned.

"I know it seems like all we've done is review notes, but I want to go over them again. Meet me in my room in an hour to go over everything again."

"But, ma'am, we haven't even picked up our bags from baggage claim. Will we even be at the resort in an hour?"

"I believe we will. I'm sorry to be such a hard-ass, but I can't stand the thought of someone else being robbed."

"Yes, ma'am. I hear you there."

They convened in her suite an hour later.

"What are we missing?" Savannah said.

"I hate to disagree with you, ma'am, but I think we're dealing with more than one thief here."

"You do, huh?" Savannah respected Li's intuition. He may be young, but he was good, with a keen eye for detail. "And why is that? Please convince me because I'm going out of my mind trying to find just one."

"Some say it was a man. Some say it was a woman. Could be we're dealing with both. Maybe even a tag team."

"You honestly believe that?"

He nodded slowly.

"I do. I truly think they're a couple who get their thrills robbing women."

"There's never any struggle, Li. That's what perplexes me the most."

"No. And seldom is a weapon used. Out of the twelve robberies we're looking at right now, only three claimed a weapon was used."

"True statement," Savannah said. "And what does that mean?"

"I don't think a weapon was ever used, to be honest. I think people use that excuse to cover up the fact they were duped."

"Interesting. That's very interesting. And, while we can't prove or disprove that, we'll certainly keep our options open. It's as good a theory as any we have so far."

"Do you think we'll find whoever's behind it here? At the Bahia Mar?" Li said.

"I hope so. I hope we can stop whoever's behind this before they nab another victim."

The handsome butch from Monte Carlo flashed in Savannah's mind. Could she be the guilty party? Why couldn't Savannah get her out of her head? She was obsessed with her and wanted to prove her guilty so badly she could taste it.

Or maybe she just wanted her. She couldn't deny the stirrings between her legs whenever she thought of her. If only she had time for a little fun. She really needed to get that woman out of her system. But there was no time for that.

But what if she was really the thief? Savannah could seduce her and let her steal her jewels and then she'd have her. Yes. That was definitely a great idea.

"What are you thinking about, boss?" Li interrupted her musings.

"Hm? Nothing. Why?"

"You were smiling. You don't smile very often. You should do it more often."

Embarrassed that she'd been caught fantasizing, she brought herself back to the present. She needed to focus on the task at hand and not daydream like some pathetic schoolgirl with a crush.

"I was just thinking how nice it will be when we finally catch the thief. Or thieves."

"It's going to be amazing."

"That it is."

Chapter Four

Kit made her way along the walkways to the resort. The noise, though muted, rang out on the night air. The sounds were of voices and machines and the occasional laughter. Kit tried to remember the last time she'd laughed sincerely. Or at least when she wasn't on a job. But it seemed she was always on a job. She'd damned near perfected her skills, so she was constantly being called upon.

She stepped into the casino and surveyed the crowds. The dress code was much more lax than at Monte Carlo. Kit wasn't wearing a tux or tie. She was wearing a simple white linen suit with a cobalt blue shirt underneath. It was her lucky shirt. Now she just needed to get lucky. In some form or fashion.

The big poker tournament had been going most of the day. She wasn't interested in that. She needed to find a poker widow. Just one and she could fly out a richer woman. As she glanced around again, she noticed lots of expensive jewelry adorning women's necks and wrists. Even though they weren't dressed in formal wear, it was still a competition to see who had the most bling. She smiled to herself. It should be a good night.

"You look amused," a husky voice spoke in her ear.

She turned to see a lovely older woman with chestnut hair and emerald eyes. Her eyes shone like the green jewels that clung to her chest and dangled from her ears. She was a looker, sure, but that wasn't why Kit turned on the charm.

She flashed a smile she knew showed off her dimples.

"I'm always amused," she said.

The brunette arched an eyebrow.

"Oh you are, are you?"

"Indeed. It's the only way to go through life."

"Is it now?" Her smile was radiant. "Buy me a drink and tell me more."

It really wasn't a suggestion, but Kit nodded nonetheless.

"What's your favorite spot for a drink here?" she asked.

The woman led the way out to a bar that overlooked the pool. It was a warm night and the sea breeze felt cool to Kit's excited, fevered flesh.

"What shall we drink?" the woman said.

"I'm a sucker for those Bahama Mamas." Kit's mind flashed back to her afternoon with Polly. She shook it off though. She was here for business, not pleasure.

"I've never had one. Order two while I go powder my nose."

Kit had to smile. This woman, whoever she was, was clearly used to being in charge. Kit wasn't one to complain. As long as she ended up with those jewels at the end of the night, the woman could be anything she wanted to be.

She was back and joined Kit at a small table.

"I'm Midge, by the way." She extended her hand in such a manner Kit had no choice but to bring her knuckles to her lips.

"Pleasure to meet you, Midge. I'm Randi."

"And what's your surname, Randi?"

Kit smiled slowly.

"Come now, let's save some mystery for later."

Midge laughed loud and hearty.

"Fair enough, dear Randi. Fair enough."

Midge wasn't a small woman, but that was fine. Kit didn't discriminate. She'd seduce her, rob her, and forget her. It was the story of what had become her life. And she couldn't complain. She had a feeling Midge could even teach her a thing or two. Nothing wrong with that. She just needed to drop some more hints, put out some more feelers that they were on the same page, and the fun could begin in earnest.

"Are you here with your husband?" Kit felt her out.

Midge rolled her eyes.

"I suppose you could say that. He's in that godforsaken poker tournament so it's more like I'm here alone."

"I'm sorry to hear that. It must be hard being a poker widow."

Midge shrugged.

"It's not so bad. I meet interesting people when left to my own devices."

She winked at Kit, who lifted her glass to Midge.

"To interesting people," she said.

"I'll drink to that."

Midge had finished her drink while Kit still had half of hers left. She forced herself not to show surprise.

"Must be time for another drink," she said.

"Oh, be a dear and get me one please."

"It would be my pleasure."

Kit jumped when she felt Midge slap her ass. Maybe they'd better go easy on the drinks. Nah. Kit was sure Midge could hold her own. No matter the stakes.

"Did you want to go gamble?" Kit asked when she returned to the table.

"I don't want to bore you."

"How could you possibly bore me?"

"I only play slots," Midge said.

"And what's wrong with that?"

"Nothing I suppose. What's your game? Surely you didn't come to Bahia Mar to pick up old ladies."

Kit laughed genuinely. That was, in fact, exactly what she was doing there.

"I like roulette," she said.

"Wonderful. Let's go watch you play."

"And then slots?"

"Yes, my dear. And then slots."

Once again, Kit was on a roll at the roulette table. Soon, a crowd had gathered around her and she tried to block out all the jewels she was seeing. She had a target for the night already. She didn't want to mess that up.

As she gathered her chips to wager again, she sensed a somewhat familiar presence. Then she caught a whiff of familiar perfume and her heart raced. Was one of her victims there? Should she keep her head down and hope she wasn't recognized? Or look to see danger?

She opted to look up and found herself locking gazes with the beautiful blonde she'd seen in Monte Carlo. She was stunning in a black cocktail dress. And the diamonds that clung to her neck said she was loaded.

But what was she doing there? Was it a mere coincidence? Or was Kit being followed? The thought chilled her to the bone. And, just like that, the blonde disappeared into the crowd, leaving Kit both terrified and aroused. If their paths crossed again, Kit vowed to make her her next target. Of course, she knew she'd likely never see her again. While some people ran in the same circles at these casinos, the likelihood of seeing the same person was pretty slim. At least Kit counted on that.

Savannah felt her heart leap to her throat when she looked into the stunning eyes of the stranger again. Something passed between them. Something she couldn't name but felt, nonetheless. It took her a moment to regain her composure and check the area for any woman who might be with the gorgeous brunette. But there was a crowd around her as she was clearly winning, and she couldn't tell if any woman in particular was more interested than the others.

Feeling like it was futile to try to predict the woman's next target, assuming the woman was the thief she was searching for, Savannah fought through the crowds and made her way outside for some much needed fresh air.

Damn that woman! How dare she have such an effect on Savannah? Savannah, who was calm, cool, and collected all the time. Savannah, who was the picture of professionalism especially when on a case. And yet this woman, this potential criminal, could disarm her with a mere glance.

She took a deep breath of the warm salt air and steeled herself to go back inside. She shouldn't let that woman out of her sight. She knew that. Maybe she should assign Li to follow her. But she knew she wouldn't. This was personal. She had to prove to herself that she could keep her head in the game where it belonged. She could stay focused on the subject at hand. She could catch the jewel thief who had been terrorizing some of the world's most popular casinos.

And if that drop-dead gorgeous woman was the jewel thief, well then, she'd go down like the rest of the criminals Savannah had tracked. It would be simple. It would be over. She'd be behind bars where she belonged rather than in Savannah's thoughts, waking and asleep.

The night before, Savannah had dreamed of the woman. It had been a very sexual dream, and Savannah could still feel everything the woman had done to her with her talented tongue and probing fingers. She shook her head. She didn't need to be thinking about it. Not now. Not ever.

She took one more deep breath and braced herself to go back into the casino. She'd march right back to the roulette table and pay close attention to who was around the stranger. Her next victim could have been right in front of her and she'd missed it.

But when she arrived at the roulette table, the strange woman was nowhere to be seen. She must have collected her winnings and moved on. Who knew? She could be plotting to rob another woman right then. Savannah kicked herself again for losing her composure earlier.

She made the rounds through the casino, paying close attention to the card tables as she remembered seeing the woman at the blackjack table in Monte Carlo. But she couldn't find her.

Savannah made a perfunctory round through the slots area, but the smoke was so thick she didn't pay a lot of attention. She was sure the androgynous beauty was a high roller and didn't think she'd find her at the slot machines.

She kept herself vigilant through the night, searching for the woman as well as keeping her eyes open for anyone who seemed suspicious. While she was sure the handsome woman was the jewel thief, she had no proof and had to keep her mind open to the possibility it was someone else. And she hoped in her heart of hearts that it was someone different. Then she'd be free to pursue the gorgeous one. No. She was fantasizing again. She really needed to get a grip.

It was early morning when, out of the corner of her eye, she noticed a woman moving away from the baccarat table. She was a middle-aged woman with graying hair who was bedecked in diamonds. A man was with her. A younger man who looked like he'd rented the suit he was wearing. It didn't fit him well at all. He certainly didn't look like he belonged.

She followed them at a discreet distance and, when they entered her room, she posted herself at her door to be there in case the man robbed her. And that's where she was several hours later when her phone buzzed. It was Li.

"Talk to me, Li."

"The robber struck again. We're heading to room four twenty. Meet us there?"

"I'm on my way."

Reluctant to leave her post and mad at herself for following the wrong suspect, Savannah hurried down the hall to the elevators and punched the four button. The elevator seemed to travel at an ant's pace but finally got her to the floor she needed to be at.

She knocked on the door and announced herself. Li opened it.

"What have we got?" she said.

"A woman was robbed while she slept. Husband is determined it was someone from the staff who entered the room and took her jewels. He's convinced and isn't open to suggestions."

"I'm Special Agent Savannah Brown." She presented them her identification. "I realize you've already gone over this with Agent Nguyen, but please tell me again exactly what happened, Mrs.…?"

"Rottingham. I'm Midge Rottingham. Please call me Midge."

"Okay, Midge. Now, one more time. What happened?"

"I don't know. I was tired. Jim was in the tournament and I didn't want to disturb him, so I came up to the room. I went to sleep and woke when he got back to the room. He went to put his winnings in the safe and found it empty. That's all I know."

"Thank you for that."

Jim Rottingham was a large man with an angry red face. He was livid and Savannah could understand why.

"No one has access to these rooms except the staff," he said. "I want each and every one of them questioned."

"And they will be." She turned to Li. "Get some agents on that ASAP."

"Thank you," Jim said.

"Now, Mr. Rottingham, surely you know your wife was not the first victim of a jewel thief lately."

"I've heard of the robberies. Sure. But this isn't one of them. This is a simple case of a staff member abusing their position."

"Was the safe locked, Midge? Are you sure you locked it? How would a member of the staff know your combination?"

"I thought I locked it," Midge said. "But I can't be sure."

"I'm sure she didn't. She was tired and just wanted to go to sleep," Jim said.

There was something about Midge's demeanor that bothered Savannah. Like she seemed to be lying. The way she wouldn't look anyone in the eye. And her skin was flushed, like someone who'd just had sex. Could it be she had been seduced by the jewel thief?

"Midge, I'd like to ask you some questions in my suite if that's okay? Would you come with me, please?"

"My wife did nothing wrong," Jim said.

"I don't think she did. I simply need to ask her some questions away from the scene."

"I'm coming with you."

"No, Mr. Rottingham. I need you to stay here while the agents work the scene. We'll be back shortly."

"May I get dressed first?" Midge pulled her robe tight around herself.

"Of course."

Once Midge was ready, Savannah escorted her to her suite. She had her sit on the couch while Savannah sat on a chair.

"Would you like a cup of coffee? Tea?"

Midge shook her head and Savannah saw unshed tears in her eyes.

"Are you okay?"

"I feel violated. That's all."

"I understand that. Midge, is there anything, anything at all you want to tell me that happened that might help us find who did this?"

Midge stared at a spot above Savannah's shoulder and shook her head.

"I've told you people everything I can."

"Are you certain? Your husband's not here now. You can tell me anything."

Fear registered in Midge's eyes as she finally met Savannah's gaze before quickly looking away.

"There's nothing more to tell."

"Fair enough. Come on. I'll walk you back to your room."

Savannah was frustrated and exhausted by the time she got back to her suite. She knew there was more to Midge's story. Why wouldn't she admit it? How were they supposed to solve this string of jewel thefts if people wouldn't be honest with her?

CHAPTER FIVE

Next stop on Kit's trip around the world was Les Ambassadeurs in London. She arrived a day early to get the lay of
the land. She'd rented a flat that served its purpose of providing her
a space away from the scene of her crime. She dressed in a black
Calvin Klein suit and wore a black shirt under it. Her red tie was the
only color she had on. She checked herself out in the mirror and,
satisfied, made her way to the casino to check things out.

The casino wasn't as large as the ones she was used to, so she'd
have to be careful. She wandered around and felt like she was being
watched. It was an uncomfortable feeling. She slowly turned around
and saw the mysterious blonde standing there. Sure she was being
followed, Kit remembered the old adage, keep your friends close
and your enemies closer. With that in mind, she sauntered over to
the woman.

"We seem to keep running into each other," Kit said.

"Do we?"

Was it possible the woman hadn't noticed Kit before? No. She
had seen the lust in her eyes every time they'd looked at each other.
So, she wanted to play it cool? That was fine. Kit was sure she could
defrost her.

"May I buy you a drink?" Kit asked.

"Are you always this forward?" The woman seemed almost
nervous. Was it hormonal? Or was she upset that Kit had found her?
If she was following Kit trying to catch her, Kit needed to know.

"Only with beautiful women. Now, will you join me?"

Kit held out her hand and the blonde took it. Kit led her to a bar she'd noticed while making her rounds. She held her hand all the way up to the bar when the woman extricated it from her grasp.

"You're awfully sure of yourself." The woman tried to sound calm, but her voice shook, betraying her.

"I'm sure you're a beautiful woman and I'd like to get to know you better. Now, what can I get you?"

"A dirty martini."

Kit smiled. She was making progress. And she hadn't misjudged the woman. She was clearly interested. Kit ordered a martini for the blonde and a beer for herself. She led the way to a small table in a dark corner in the back of the bar. She set the drinks down.

"I'm Randi," she said.

"Are you?" The woman smiled.

Kit laughed.

"Why yes, yes I am."

"That doesn't surprise me. What's your real name?"

"My real name is Randi."

"I don't believe you, but whatever. I'm Savannah."

"Ah. A beautiful name for a beautiful woman. And, you got me. My real name is Kit," Kit said.

She brought Savannah's knuckles to her lips and brushed a soft kiss over them. Then she pulled out Savannah's chair and waited until she was seated to sit.

"What brings you to Les Ambassadeurs?" Kit asked.

"Same as you I'd imagine. I'm here to gamble."

"Then why were you simply wandering around? Why weren't you at a table?"

"It's only Friday night," Savannah said. "I was just getting the lay of the land. I usually gamble on Saturdays. That's my lucky night."

"Well, this just might prove to be your lucky night." Kit smiled. "So, I've seen you around before. I feel like you're following me."

"Don't be absurd. I don't even know you."

Kit arched an eyebrow.

"Is that right? Okay. Then how is it we happen to end up at all the same casinos?"

"That would be strictly random."

"Would it now? Tell me about yourself, Savannah. What do you do that allows you to travel from casino to casino worldwide?"

"If you must know, I'm a widow. My wife died and left me a small fortune."

"I'm sorry to hear that," Kit said. Though she didn't notice any sadness in Savannah's eyes when she mentioned her dead wife. "You must miss her terribly."

"I do." She wiped an imaginary tear from her eye.

"And now you spend your time jetsetting?"

"For the most part. It keeps me busy and takes my mind off sad things."

"I hope to keep your mind off sad things as well," Kit said. "Where is home? You sound American."

"I am. I live in Maryland. And you?"

"I call California home. Though I'm seldom there."

"And how did you amass your fortune, Kit?"

"I've been very lucky in the stock market. My parents bought stock for me when I was born, and it's done very well."

"Good for you. You're fortunate."

"I am. And the rest of my money came from gambling."

"You're very good at roulette, aren't you?" Savannah said.

Kit grinned.

"Ah. So you do remember me?"

Savannah blushed, obviously embarrassed at outing herself. She took a sip of her drink.

"I suppose I do."

Kit felt the heat inside her belly kick up a notch. This woman would be fun to bed. And she knew she'd be adorned in jewels the next night. Jewels Kit would be more than happy to take off her hands.

"Would you like another drink?" Kit said.

"Thank you, but I should get going."

"Can I buy you dinner first?"

"You are persistent, aren't you?"

"What's the harm? You're a beautiful woman, Savannah. Can you blame me for wanting to know you better?"

"You flatter me, Kit, or whatever your name is. But I really should take my leave. Perhaps I'll see you tomorrow night?"

"Count on it."

"Good night, Kit."

"Good night, Savannah."

Kit sat at the table a long while after Savannah had left. There was something about her. She was dangerous, Kit could sense it. But just how dangerous remained to be seen. Was she after Kit? Was she determined to put her in jail? Or was she really just a widow who enjoyed the finer things in life?

Finally needing to get out of her own head, Kit left the bar and wandered about the casino taking in the lay of the land. Once confident she knew where everything was, she hailed a taxi and went back to her flat.

Alone again with her thoughts, she kept playing over her drink with Savannah. Was that her real name? How had she known Kit was lying about her name? Did she know who Kit was? Did she have a dossier on her somewhere? No. Kit didn't want to believe that. She just wanted to believe that Savannah was another rich, beautiful woman she could rob. Nothing more. Nothing less.

Savannah left the casino as soon as she finished her drink. She didn't want to be there any longer. She'd finally made contact with Kit, if that was her name. She was as charming and sweet as she was good-looking. It was a dangerous combination, and Savannah's whole body hummed every time she thought about her.

She opened her laptop and pulled up the page she had that described Kit. She now had a name to associate with the description. Whether it was her real name or not was left to be seen. But she wrote Kit across the top of the page.

She filled in what little facts she knew of her. Even though she didn't believe her, she jotted down that she'd made her money in the market. She made notes that she was charming, witty, and well spoken. All dangerous traits to unsuspecting older women.

She finally had something on the mysterious woman. Although she was sure it was all fraudulent. At least it was something. She just needed Kit's last name and she'd be able to run a search on her. She could check her real finances as well as a criminal history. So she had a goal. And another reason to spend time with her.

Savannah cautioned herself to be careful. She was playing with fire. Sure, she wanted to catch the thief and yes, she believed Kit was that thief. But she couldn't deny the pure, unadulterated passion that flared whenever she thought of her.

Shaking with desire, she closed her laptop and climbed into bed. She tossed and turned, trying to focus on something, anything but Kit, but she occupied her thoughts. She monopolized them, not allowing her to focus on anything else. And it was more than simply wanting to catch a thief. It was way more than that.

The last time she checked the clock, it was after five in the morning. She awoke at one and took a quick shower before everyone was due in her room for a briefing. The briefing went well, and she finally mentioned Kit to the group.

"She's been at the last three casinos we've been to," Savannah said. "And the last two have had robberies. I'm almost certain she's our culprit."

"But, boss," Li said. "We've been told by several of the women that it's a man who's robbed them."

"And why not?" Savannah said. "If you were a happily married woman who'd been seduced by a cad of a woman who then stole your jewels, would you admit you'd been with a woman?"

There was silence in the room as the others mulled that over.

"You mean these women are cheating on their husbands with another woman?" Li finally said.

"That's exactly what I mean."

He let out a low whistle.

"No offense, boss, but that seems a little farfetched."

"Does it? Think about it."

"So, you want me to put a tail on this woman?" Li asked.

"No, thanks. She's mine. I'll follow her closely. The rest of you keep your eyes peeled. I have a feeling someone is going to get robbed tonight. I just hope we get there in time to catch whoever's been doing these."

Everyone cleared out and Savannah ordered room service. She'd need her strength to make it through another long night. And she knew the night would be long. Dare she hope it would involve sex? Would she be able to seduce Kit and catch her in the act of robbing her? She could only hope. It would almost be disappointing if Kit wasn't the thief. But it would be more disappointing if she didn't end up in bed with her.

She finished her dinner and chided herself to think with the brain in her head and not the throbbing nerve center between her legs. She still had an hour or so before it would be late enough to hit the casino.

Savannah drew herself a hot bath and soaked in it for some time. She dropped some perfume in the water and inhaled deeply of the sensual scent. She felt the warm water lapping at her like a lover and fought to keep her hands on the sides of the tub. She longed to touch herself, to pretend it was Kit's touch on her, and bring herself to an orgasm. But she fought the urge. She would keep her hormones buzzing for Kit. That way she'd be more intent on seducing her.

She dressed in a form fitting dark chocolate dress that really brought out her eyes. She drew her hair up on top of her head and draped her diamonds around her neck. She hung more rocks from her ears and checked herself out one more time in the mirror. She was almost ready. She looked like an unsuspecting rich woman just out for a good time. She slipped her gun and identification in her clutch and headed to the casino.

The whirl of the machines greeted Savannah as she walked inside. Having memorized the floor plan the day before, she went immediately to the roulette table. There was Kit winning big. Savannah surveyed the crowd around her. She didn't see anybody who looked to be with Kit. She made her move.

She cut through the crowd until she was standing only a few people away from her. She kept her gaze on Kit's eyes, hoping she would look up and see her. She did look up. Their gazes met, and Savannah went weak in the knees at the pure lust showing in Kit's eyes. Was it for her? Or her diamonds? She didn't know, but she was dying to find out.

Chapter Six

K it felt Savannah's presence before she saw her. And when she saw her, her heart skipped a beat. She looked gorgeous, absolutely stunning, in a dress that clung to her curves. And the jewels. Diamonds adorned her though her eyes outshone them. Kit had to take a breath and force herself to focus on her gambling. She played a little while more before deciding she'd had enough. She searched the crowd and found Savannah still there, still watching her.

She cut through the throng of people and stood next to her. She looked down and noticed Savannah was wearing flats. Yet she was almost as tall as Kit, who, at five feet eleven inches was used to towering over women.

"You're very good at roulette." Savannah's voice had a deep timbre. It suited her.

"I love to play."

"Are you by yourself?"

"I am for the moment. Can I buy you a drink?"

"Sure."

They found a nearby bar and sat at one of the few empty tables.

"So what do you do for fun in Maryland?" Kit asked.

"A little of everything. I love to garden. I'm a voracious reader. And I paint a little."

Kit was impressed. She was beautiful, smart, and potentially talented. And wearing a mint in diamonds. All things that Kit found irresistible.

"Nice. Sounds like a good life."

"Overall, it is."

"I bet you get lonely sometimes."

"I do," Savannah said. "But then I love to travel and be surrounded by people. And that helps."

"I'm sure it does. When did your wife die, if you don't mind me asking?"

"Five years ago. It still feels like yesterday."

"I bet. And you're not seeing anybody?" Why did she care? Kit couldn't believe she'd even asked it. But there she was, waiting with bated breath for her answer.

"No. I'm not ready."

"I understand."

"And you, Kit? What do you do for fun in California?"

"I play the stock market, as you know. I also surf and hike and do any outdoor activity you can think of."

Savannah laughed. It was an easy, genuine sound.

"I can't imagine surfing. Though I'll admit I've boogie boarded a few times and enjoyed it. I don't think I have the balance for surfing."

"You never know."

"Oh, believe me. I know. When we were kids, we all had skateboards and I was forever skinning my knees and elbows after falling off mine."

"Ouch. Okay, so maybe surfing wouldn't be for you."

"No, definitely not."

"What kind of books do you read?" Kit asked.

"I love a good mystery. Or a thriller. I love reading lesbian fiction. I love reading about women like me, like us."

"Lesbian fiction? I didn't even know there was such a thing."

"There is. And it's wonderful."

"I'll have to give it a try."

"You should."

"I will," Kit said. "Would you like another drink?"

"Sure."

Kit got them two more drinks and settled back into her chair. She was starting to relax more around Savannah, and she didn't know if that was a good thing or not. She was still unconvinced that it was merely coincidental that they kept ending up at the same casinos. She couldn't shake that maybe there was more to Savannah than met the eye.

"What are you thinking?" Savannah asked. "You seem a million miles away."

"Oh, nothing. Just thinking how I'm enjoying talking to you, but the tables are calling to me."

She felt the need to get away from Savannah. On top of everything else, Savannah stirred something deep inside Kit. Something she'd thought long dead. Feelings she didn't want to address or admit to. Feelings dormant since Amanda had dumped her three years earlier.

So she'd finish her drink, thank Savannah for her time, and get as far away from her as possible. On top of everything else, she had a job to do. And she wasn't comfortable targeting Savannah for some reason. She was scared she'd be arrested. She couldn't shake the niggling feeling inside her that Savannah was the law.

Kit finished her beer and set the empty bottle on the table.

"Thank you for another lovely evening," Kit said.

The look on Savannah's face said she wasn't expecting their time together to end so soon.

"What? You're not leaving me, are you?"

"I'm afraid I must. I need to gamble. Call it an affliction."

"I can go with you. I'd love to watch you gamble, Kit."

Kit smiled at her and mulled over the offer. It was tempting. Too tempting. She needed some space.

"Look, Savannah. I like you. I really do. But I'm not in the market for anything serious right now."

"Neither am I. I've told you that. I'm not ready to move on. But companionship is good, isn't it?"

Companionship. Was that code for sex? Maybe Kit could go to bed with Savannah. Maybe she could do it and then take her jewels and be long gone. But she knew deep down it wouldn't be enough for her. And that made her tremble with fear.

"I'm sure our paths will cross again. Maybe tomorrow I can take you on a proper date? Say dinner at nine?"

"I'd like that," Savannah said.

They made arrangements to meet the following night and Kit disappeared into the crowd. She took a deep breath to clear her mind and focus on the task at hand. She needed to score some jewels.

She saw an older woman sitting by herself at one of the slot machines. Kit sat next to her.

"Is this seat taken?"

"Just by you."

Kit smiled her dimpled smile at the woman.

"Thank you. What game is that you're playing?"

"Oh, it's a fun one. There's lots of animation. I keep getting three wilds and watching the penguin's antics. It's a lot of fun."

"Do you think anyone would mind if I just sat here and watched you play?" Kit asked.

"I can't imagine they would."

"My name's Dani," Kit said.

"I'm Adele. It's nice to meet you, Dani."

"Likewise."

Kit watched Adele play and soon grew bored. But Adele was decked out in hundreds of thousands of dollars worth of jewels, so Kit hung out. After a particularly long stretch of watching a penguin do tricks, she made her move.

"Can I buy you a drink, Adele?" she said.

"Are you flirting with me?"

"Maybe."

"Oh, how sweet. I'd love a drink. Let me print my ticket."

Kit glanced around to make sure Savannah wasn't nearby. She didn't see her, so she guided Adele to a bar and had her sit in a corner away from passersby.

"This is romantic," Adele said.

Kit simply smiled at her.

"What can I get you to drink?"

"A glass of Dom Perignon."

"Coming right up."

Kit ordered herself another beer and took the drinks back to the table.

"Tell me about yourself, Adele. Where are you from? Your accent sounds decidedly French."

"Good ear. I'm from Paris."

"And you come to London to play slot machines?"

"My husband is in the baccarat tournament. I have to do something to pass the time."

Husband, huh? That hadn't deterred women in the past and Kit hoped it wouldn't deter Adele either.

Savannah lost Kit after she left the bar. The casino was small, but try as she might, she never saw her again. She was disappointed on multiple levels. She'd blown her chance to bring her in for questioning first and foremost, but there was also an underlying attraction to the rogue, one she couldn't deny no matter how she tried.

It was four in the morning when she gave up and went back to the hotel. It was five-thirty when her phone rang.

"Brown here."

"Li here. The robber struck again. This time the victim was a French woman, Adele Durand."

"Where's she staying?"

"The Four Seasons. Room ten seventeen."

"I'm on my way."

Savannah arrived to find a middle-aged woman in silk pajamas, eyes red from crying.

"What happened?" Savannah asked.

"I was tired, so I decided to leave the casino," Adele said. "A nice young man in a porter's uniform hailed me a taxi and offered to ride with me to see to it I got home safely. We got to my room and when I turned to thank him, he had a gun out and demanded my jewelry."

"Just what you were wearing? Or did he get what was in your safe, as well?"

"Just what I was wearing."

"What did this porter look like?" Savannah asked.

Adele shrugged and wiped her eyes with a tissue.

"He was young. Dark hair. Clean-shaven. I'm sorry. I should have paid more attention."

Savannah turned to Li.

"I want a crew questioning the porters at the casino like yesterday."

"Yes, ma'am."

He stepped out of the room and Savannah turned her attention back to Adele.

"You're sure he worked at the casino?"

"I assumed he did. I don't know."

"I'd like to see if we can sketch the man. Do you think you could help us with that?"

Adele's eyes went wide before she regained a modicum of composure. She shook her head.

"I don't think I could do that. He looked like any other nice young man. I was a fool to think he was kind."

Savannah took in the room, the tussled sheets, the bottle of champagne on the nightstand. Two glasses. This looked more like a seduction gone wrong than an armed robbery. And where was Kit? How did she fit into this?

"I notice you have a bottle of Dom Perignon on your bedside table," she said. "And two glasses." She walked over and looked into them. "Both of which were used. Did you have company earlier, Mrs. Durand?"

Adele started sobbing harder and Savannah went cold. She forced herself to wait, to be patient, until Adele had composed herself.

"I admit. I invited the young man in for a drink. We had one and then he pulled his gun. Please don't tell my husband I invited a strange man into our room. He'll never forgive me."

"And your bed? It looks messed up?"

"I threw myself onto it and cried before I called the police."

Savannah nodded, not believing a word of her story.

"Thank you for your time, Mrs. Durand. We'll let you know if we find the man who robbed you."

"Oh, thank you."

Savannah sent out a group text asking her team to meet her in her suite. Something was fishy about Adele Durand's story. Clearly, she'd had company, but who? Kit? An unfamiliar feeling coursed through Savannah. Was that jealousy? She quickly squashed the feeling. She didn't have time to be petty now. She had an investigation to run.

Once her team had assembled, she set up her white board and began to make bullet points.

"One thing I've noticed about each of the last three scenes," Savannah said. "Sex seems to have played a part."

"You really believe that?" Li said. "I mean, these women seem awfully distraught for someone who's just had sex."

"They've been robbed," Savannah stated the obvious. "Of course they're distraught. But I believe they're being seduced and then robbed."

"So you still think it's the same guy doing them?"

"I do. The same man or woman. I haven't ruled out a woman yet."

"But none of the last three victims have mentioned a woman," Li said.

"No, but that could be because they're too embarrassed. All three have been married women. They've clearly invited someone to their bed they're ashamed of."

"Could just as easily be a man as a woman," Li said.

"It could be. But the level of shame I've seen in these women's eyes indicate to me it's more than just a fling gone awry."

"What about the woman you were tailing? Did you see her near the latest victim?"

Her own shame flooded Savannah. How could she have lost Kit? She could have saved Adele this embarrassment.

"I met up with her early in the night. But then we got separated. I tried to find her again but couldn't. I don't know if she ran into the Durand woman or not. Unfortunately. I truly believe she's our thief though. We just need to catch her in the act.

"And how do you propose we do that?"

"You leave that to me, Li."

"Should we go back to questioning the porters, boss?"

"Yes, please. It's possible one of them saw something even if they didn't rob her. Ask lots of questions. Get to the bottom of this."

CHAPTER SEVEN

K it slept until three the following afternoon. She had made her drop early that morning and smiled to herself as she checked her bank balance. She'd also received a new assignment. Singapore. That should be fun. But she had more than just jewels on her mind at that moment. She was meeting Savannah for dinner in a few hours. Her gut clenched in both fear and excitement.

She was more than simply attracted to Savannah. But could she spend time with her anyway? She'd never let herself fall for one of her targets before. Was Savannah just another target? She had to be. She was either a target or she was a no one. There was no in-between for Kit. She simply didn't have time for emotional entanglements.

She still didn't know why Savannah kept turning up at the same casinos she did. Kit always went where the big tournaments were being held. Yet she'd never seen Savannah gamble. So why would she keep showing up? Unless she wasn't a lonely widow from Maryland. What if she really was trying to catch Kit and she hadn't been paranoid all this time?

Be wary. Keep your guard up. Sleep with her if you can. Just be careful. She went for a walk to clear her head. It was cold and damp in London. She longed for the warmth of the Caribbean again. Maybe she'd go back to St. Thomas before flying to Singapore. She had the time. Or maybe she'd just explore the Orient. That could be fun too. All she knew for sure was that she couldn't wait to get out of London. Sure, it was beautiful and historic, but it was too damned cold.

She wandered back to her flat and took a shower. She dressed in a gray suit with a black shirt. She debated wearing a tie but finally decided not to. She looked nice, dressy but not stuffy. Her palms began to sweat, and her heart raced. She inhaled deeply. She needed to get a grip, needed to stay in control.

Kit took a taxi to the Four Seasons where they'd agreed to meet for dinner. It was convenient for Savannah since that's where she was staying. She arrived at nine on the dot. Savannah was already waiting for her.

"I'm sorry if I'm late," Kit said.

"You're not. I was early. For once in my life." She laughed, music to Kit's ears.

"So you're not the punctual type, huh?"

"Not even close."

Kit stared long and hard at her. She wanted to call bullshit. If Savannah was the agent Kit thought she was then she was probably very disciplined and incredibly punctual. But she kept her mouth shut. She still wasn't sure Savannah was an agent. Almost, but not quite.

She sure didn't look or act like any other stuffy FBI agent. But then it could all be an act. Which was precisely why Kit was determined to keep her guard up.

"Are you ready to get a table?" Kit asked.

"Sure." Savannah stood and Kit almost wolf whistled. She looked amazing in a short red dress that clung to her curves. She was wearing expensive jewelry too. Too expensive for mere dinner. Was she trying to bait Kit? Well, Kit wasn't going to fall for it. Not this time.

She placed her hand on the small of Savannah's back and guided her into the restaurant. She felt the heat radiating from her and grew lightheaded. Why couldn't she keep her cool with this one?

They were seated at a small table near the window. Kit was normally a people watcher and God knew there were plenty walking by. But she kept her focus on Savannah. She longed to trip her up. Almost as much as she longed to bed her. Or more. She shook the thought from her head. There couldn't be more. Wouldn't be more. She had neither the time nor the inclination for that.

"Are you okay?" Savannah said. "You went somewhere far off in your head. Want to talk about it?"

Kit flashed her best smile.

"I'm fine. I'm here with you. Trust me."

"If you say so. How long are you in London?"

"I leave tomorrow. You?"

"Same," Savannah said. "Will you be heading home? Or will you continue to jetset?"

Kit took a sip of wine. How much to tell Savannah?

"I'll continue to globetrot for a while. What about you?"

"Oh yes. There's a pai gow tournament in a week and I really want to be there. You've probably noticed I tend to go where the tournaments are."

"Why is that?"

"What do you mean?"

"It's just that I've never seen you gamble."

Savannah laughed but it sounded forced.

"And you've seen me how many times?"

"True. True. But you're always on the fringe when I do see you. I've never seen you at a table."

"Maybe I'll surprise you sometime."

"Maybe you will."

Kit wanted to press her but decided to hold off. She'd play nice. For now. Eventually, Savannah would out herself and Kit just had to be patient. Easier said than done.

"Tell me, Kit. What's a nice, attractive woman like yourself doing single? Why has nobody snatched you up?"

Ouch. Dare she be honest? Why not. She took a deep breath to steel herself.

"Someone snatched me up several years ago. But it didn't end well."

Savannah sipped her wine.

"What happened?"

"Let's just say she wasn't as into me as I was to her."

"That's vague. But okay. I'm sorry it didn't work out."

"Thanks. And your wife? How did she die if I may ask?"

"She was killed by a hit-and-run driver."

"Did they ever catch the guy?" Kit had to know.

Savannah shook her head. Kit was amazed that she could tell the story with dry eyes. Unless it really was a story; some made-up scenario as her cover.

"What?" Savannah said. "You're looking like you want to kill me."

Kit recovered quickly.

"Not you. The guy who killed your wife."

Savannah fought the chill that threatened. Kit had said that so bluntly. Was she capable of murder? Or did she simply rob unsuspecting women? And who's to say she was the jewel thief after all? She was so friendly. So amicable. So charming. But then, wouldn't those traits help her seduce rich older women?

She was so confused. She took another sip of the wine Kit had ordered. It was really good. Smooth, just like Kit.

"My turn to ask," Kit said. "Where'd you just go? You're lost in thought. What are you thinking about?"

"Oh, lots of things. My wife. You. Wondering why I'm here." She laughed. "My brain's rather jumbled."

"I see."

"Oh, it's not bad," Savannah assured her. "I know you don't want a relationship, yet you could have had a fling last night and you turned me down. And here we are on a date. See? My brain goes a million miles an hour."

"I just want to get to know you better. Is there anything wrong with that?"

"No," she said softly. "Nothing at all."

"Good. Now that that's settled, would you like some more wine?"

"Yes, please."

She studied Kit as she poured the wine. Not only was she charismatic as hell, but she was damned easy on the eyes as well. Savannah chastised herself and reminded herself she was there to catch a thief, not fall for the main suspect.

"What did you do for a living, Savannah? Before you inherited your windfall?"

"I was an accountant many years ago. But as I've said, my wife was very well off, so I was a happy housewife for years."

"Lucky you."

"Oh yes. I've lived a charmed life."

She wondered if she should bring up the thefts. Just to gauge Kit's reaction. She would later. For now, she just wanted to relax and enjoy herself. No. That's not why she was there.

"Have you heard of all the robberies that have been happening at the casinos? Terrible."

She studied Kit's reaction. No noticeable sign of nerves. Her hand was steady as she set down her wine glass.

"I have. Disgusting. Some guy preying on rich women."

Savannah nodded.

"I agree. I hope they catch him." Or her.

"As do I. I admit I could hold my own and I don't wear jewels like you. But I still get nervous at times cashing in my winnings."

"I'm sure."

Maybe she was innocent after all. Maybe Savannah had been dead wrong about her. Part of her wanted that. Part of her wanted that desperately.

"And yet, even with a thief on the loose, you still wear jewels. Aren't you nervous?"

Savannah laughed and hoped it didn't sound forced.

"Oh. You noticed."

"Of course."

She fingered the diamonds at her throat and watched Kit study them. What did she see in her eyes? Lust? Envy? Simple admiration?

"I do worry at times, but I feel naked without my jewelry. Does that make sense?"

"I suppose so. Although I can't really relate." She shrugged. "They look nice. For whatever that's worth."

"Thank you."

Savannah felt the heat rush to her cheeks. Was she blushing? At a compliment from Kit? She needed to reel in her hormones before she forgot her purpose.

Kit sat back in her chair.

"Did your wife buy you all your jewels?"

"Most of them. Yes."

"She had exquisite taste."

Savannah raised her eyebrows.

"So you know jewelry?"

Kit laughed.

"Not really. But I know what I think looks good. And you always look impeccable."

More blushing. This wasn't good. She was losing control.

"Thank you," she murmured.

"You seem more nervous tonight, Savannah. Are you feeling okay?"

"I'm fine. Just tired. It's almost time for me to head back to Maryland and recharge."

Kit simply nodded. Did she believe her? Savannah needed to relax. She had to be flirtatious and try to get Kit into bed. She didn't need to moon over her like a lovesick teenager.

"So where did you learn to play roulette?" Savannah said.

Kit laughed. She seemed so at ease. Why couldn't Savannah share some of that?

"I actually learned at a casino on a reservation near where I live. The game intrigued me, and I soon discovered I had a knack for it and it just kind of took off from there."

"Well, you're obviously very good at it."

"I do okay. Can't complain."

"No. I don't suppose you can."

Dinner was over and they were almost through the second bottle of wine.

"I've really enjoyed myself tonight, Savannah. We should do this again."

Savannah felt the pain start deep inside her. She couldn't say good night. Not yet. She had to take Kit to bed.

"The night is young, Kit. Why don't we go to the casino for a while?"

"I'm hardly dressed for the casino."

"You look fine. Very nice actually. And it'll be slow on a Sunday night. Let's go. You can teach me how to win at roulette."

Kit cocked an eyebrow.

"You're actually going to gamble?"

"Sure. Why not?" She laughed. "I'm no stranger to gambling you know."

Kit smiled at her.

"I suppose not. But I've never seen you place a bet, so I was beginning to wonder."

"If you must know, I prefer slots. They entertain and relax me."

"Fair enough. We'll play some roulette and then we'll hit the slots. You'll have to show me your favorite game."

Shit. Savannah had no clue which slot machines were fun. She hadn't gambled in years. She needed to think fast.

"Oh, I don't really have a favorite. It's pretty much whatever strikes my fancy at the moment."

"Got it. Okay. We'll finish our wine then go play."

"Thank you, Kit. I wasn't ready for the evening to end."

Again, Kit raised an eyebrow. She didn't say anything though. She simply took another sip.

"I'm not going to sleep with you Savannah," she finally said.

"What? I didn't mean to imply…"

"You said what you wanted last night. And I told you, I'm not ready for a commitment." Savannah opened her mouth to protest, but Kit held up her hand. "I like you, Savannah. You're different from most women I interact with. And sleeping with you would only cause more confusion for me. And I don't need to be encumbered by thoughts and memories. So I'll continue to spend time with you, but please don't expect me to sleep with you. Not yet anyway."

"Then is there any point in going to the casino?"

Kit smiled.

"Of course there is. To spend more time together. Who knows? Eventually, you may melt the ice that's grown around my heart."

"I hope so, Kit. I truly hope you'll let me in."

CHAPTER EIGHT

Savannah linked her hand through Kit's elbow, and they walked to the casino. Kit was struggling inside but was determined to play it cool. There was so much about Savannah that she liked, really liked, but she couldn't shake the feeling there was more to her. But really, who cared? Even if she was an FBI agent, she'd never catch Kit. Kit was sure of it.

Of course, everything Savannah had told her could have been a lie. She probably never had a rich wife. Who knew if she even lived in Maryland? Still, she was worming her way into Kit's heart and that was decidedly off limits. So why couldn't Kit stay away? Why hadn't she simply left the restaurant and left Savannah in her rearview mirror?

They arrived at the casino and Savannah looked chilled to the bone.

"Are you okay?" Kit rubbed her hands along Savannah's bare arms.

"It's much warmer in here. I'll be fine, but thank you."

Savannah was looking longingly into Kit's eyes. Kit was so close to her now. She was a mere breadth away from their lips meeting. What harm was there in a kiss? Just one kiss? She lowered her mouth and brushed it against Savannah's. The shock waves that coursed through her body only reinforced how dangerous this little liaison was.

She forced herself to step back.

"I'm much better now," Savannah said. "See? That wasn't so hard."

Kit pulled Savannah to her in a long embrace.

"I'm still not sleeping with you," she whispered in her ear.

"I'll never give up."

Kit stepped away again and laughed.

"You're persistent. I'll give you that much."

"Now, if this public display of affection is over, will you teach me how to win at roulette?"

"I'll do my best." Kit placed her hand on the small of Savannah's back and guided her through the nearly empty casino to the roulette table. They spent several hours there with Kit trying to teach Savannah everything she knew. Savannah seemed to have a grasp of the basics but kept losing. Kit doubled her efforts, and soon Savannah won big. She threw her arms around Kit's neck and kissed her. Right in the middle of the casino. Kit was shocked but was soon kissing her back. She almost regretted it when the kiss ended.

"Do you want to keep playing?" Kit asked.

"What are my options?" Savannah's eyes twinkled.

"Slots, my friend. Roulette or slots."

"Fine. Let's play here a little more."

When Savannah had won several games in a row, she announced it was time to cash in her winnings and try their hands at the slot machines. When they arrived in the area filled with one-armed bandits, Kit wondered just how lucky Savannah was at slots. Or even if she ever played them.

"I love these animated games." She sat in front of a game featuring dragons and knights.

"Fair enough. Show me how it's done."

They played the machines for a couple of hours and each had significant cash-outs when they called it quits.

"Are you sure you don't want to play anymore?" Kit asked.

"I'm sure. It's really late. I think it's time to go to bed. Are you sure you won't join me?"

She looked at Kit as if daring her to say no. Kit's stomach tightened. Her hormones were running amuck. Still, she played it cool.

"Not tonight I'm afraid. Perhaps another time?"

"Who knows when our paths will cross again?"

"We seem to be at the same casinos on nights they have big tournaments. I'm sure we'll see each other again."

"I hope so, Kit. I don't want to scare you off, but I really like you."

"I like you too. Which is why I don't want to fall in bed with you. Like I said, I really want to get to know you better."

"You know everything there is to know about me," Savannah protested.

"Do I?" Kit arched an eyebrow.

"What's that supposed to mean?"

Kit told herself not to give anything away.

"It means you're a wonderful woman, and I'm sure there's so much more to you than I already know. For instance, I don't know your favorite color. Favorite food. Best friend from elementary school."

Savannah laughed out loud.

"I can answer those questions right now for you."

"Those are just examples. Now, come on. Let's take a cab back to your hotel so you don't freeze."

The ride was short, and Kit walked Savannah to her room. Logic and reason warred with desire as they rode the elevator. She wanted Savannah. That was for sure. But she was strong enough to fight that urge. The question was, should she kiss her again? What harm would there be in a simple good night kiss? She'd keep it short and sweet. With a promise for more in the future. She could do that, right?

After they had said good night, Kit rested one hand on the doorjamb and looked into Savannah's eyes. She saw passion there, but something else. What was it? Fear? Confusion?

"I'm going to kiss you good night now," Kit said. "I mean, if that's okay?"

Savannah merely nodded, her gaze focused on Kit's mouth. Kit leaned in and captured Savannah's lips with her own. It was a powerful kiss, and Kit found herself growing dizzy with need. She tried to straighten, but Savannah wrapped her arms around her and held her close. She felt Savannah's tongue on her lips, and her resolve wavered. She opened her mouth and welcomed Savannah in. She leaned into her so their bodies were pressed together. She lost herself in the kiss. Completely lost herself. Her boxers grew damp with need, and she moaned into Savannah's mouth.

The kiss lasted longer than it should have and, when it was over, they were both breathless. Savannah slid her hand into Kit's.

"Come inside with me? Please?"

"I'd love to. I really would. But I can't. Good night, Savannah. Sleep well and sweet dreams."

With every ounce of self-control she had, she turned and walked off down the hall.

Savannah watched Kit walk away then turned and let herself in her room. She latched the door then leaned back against it. What the hell was wrong with her? She was supposed to be trying to arrest Kit. Not falling for her. But she was falling for her. Hard and fast. She needed to get a grip, to get some perspective. She definitely needed time away from her. Sure, there was a major pai gow tournament coming up in Singapore. Maybe, just maybe, Kit wouldn't be there. She could only hope. And maybe no one would be robbed either. Could it be just coincidence that Kit was always where there were robberies? Doubtful, but Savannah could hope. She'd love to catch the thief and then be free to pursue something with Kit. That would be ideal.

She was too keyed up to go to bed. Her hormones were racing through her body at breakneck speed. She poured herself a drink and stripped. She ran a hot bath and made herself close her eyes and try to relax.

But she couldn't relax. The warm water caressed her fevered skin like a lover. Like she wanted Kit to do. Why was this so difficult? Why couldn't Kit be like any other suspect? Why had she wormed her way into the very fabric of Savannah's being? Unable to resist any longer, she slid her hand under the water and found her center wet and throbbing. With her mind on Kit, she fantasized that it was Kit touching her and she took herself to an explosive orgasm.

Still restless, but knowing she needed her sleep, she toweled off and slid between the sheets. She tossed and turned, unable to get Kit out of her mind. Finally, she fell into a fitful sleep and woke the next afternoon feeling anything but rested.

Savannah ordered room service for herself and the team at eight and they discussed strategies on how to finally bring the elusive jewel thief to justice.

"As you no doubt know by now, there's a high stakes pai gow tournament in Singapore coming up. That's our next stop. Any ideas on how to catch this guy?"

Or gal, she thought but didn't say out loud.

"Why don't we post guards at each of the exits up to the rooms?" Li said.

"We would. If we had the manpower. Which we don't."

"How is it that the camera has never caught the victims going to their rooms?"

"That's a really good question. We need to check out the cameras in Singapore before the tournament starts. Make sure they're all working. Li, I want you on that."

"Yes, ma'am."

They spent the next several hours brainstorming and, while she truly believed they were on the right track, she was riddled with doubt that they'd catch the criminal. She believed in her heart of hearts it was Kit and she was afraid she was too good to get caught. Or maybe Savannah simply didn't want to catch her. No. That was ridiculous. She wanted to catch her and put her away for good.

The trip to Singapore was long but uneventful. The team arrived and set up headquarters in Savannah's suite. With whiteboards everywhere detailing the crimes, Savannah knew she wouldn't be able to bring Kit back to her room. Unless she put everything away, which she might the night of the tournament. She was sure Kit was simply biding her time. She knew that her jewels, at least, were irresistible.

Savannah spent the next two days making sure any safeguards they could afford were in place and catching up on her sleep. They worked long hours, but she was sure to be in bed at a reasonable hour. It was almost showtime again and she needed to be on her game.

As the day of the pai gow tournament approached, Savannah was more excited than she cared to admit. She was certain she'd see Kit again and the thought had her heart fluttering in her chest. No matter how she tried to rein it in, her body betrayed her.

"Whatever happened with that woman you were following?" Li asked over dinner Friday night. "Have we crossed her off the list of suspects?"

"Hardly. As a matter of fact, if she shows up here, I want her moved to the top of that list."

"You really think she'll be here?"

"I do. And I think this time she'll slip up and we'll catch her."

"Yes, ma'am. Sounds good. Should we go check out the casino again?"

"We should," Savannah said. "Let me go change. Come to my suite in twenty minutes."

"Will do."

Savannah dressed in a black pantsuit with pearls for jewelry. She looked good. Simple yet stylish. If she saw Kit, she'd feel good about herself anyway. Though she knew Kit wouldn't want her that night. She wasn't showing off enough bling.

She didn't see Kit though. Part of her was bummed, but a huge part of her was relieved. She hadn't known if she'd be able to maintain her composure in front of Li. And she needed to command his respect at all times.

They walked through the casino, gauging easy exits and entrances. They double-checked the security cameras in the hotel. They met with some of the staff and told them to be on the lookout for anything or anyone suspicious. They made sure everyone had their numbers if they needed to reach them. They were ready. Game on.

Saturday night Savannah dressed in a floor-length green sequined gown. She wore diamonds and emeralds. Kit wouldn't be able to resist all those jewels. But would she still be able to resist Savannah? That was the dreaded question.

At ten o'clock, Savannah took the elevator down to the casino. She had butterflies in her stomach. She hoped against all hope that the thief wouldn't strike that night. But she knew the odds weren't in her favor. The chances were great that another unsuspecting older woman would have her jewels stolen from her. If only whoever she was would be honest with Savannah and tell her who really robbed her. She knew these women were messing around with Kit and then too embarrassed to admit it. All she needed was someone to be brave enough to tell the truth.

CHAPTER NINE

K it had thoroughly enjoyed her few free days in Singapore. She'd played tourist and seen the sights of the island. It was a beautiful place and she'd be sorry to leave it. But there would be more jobs. Hopefully not for a while though. She needed to have some down time in California for a bit. She needed to recharge her batteries and commune with nature.

Saturday afternoon rolled around, and she relaxed in her Airbnb. She ate a leisurely lunch and tried to psych herself up for the night's activities. She was feeling less cocky than usual and didn't know why. She assumed it had something to do with Savannah the blond bombshell. On one hand, she really hoped she'd see her that night, but on the other, it could really cramp her style. Plus, if Savannah saw who Kit was with, she could put two and two together and Kit would end up doing time. Lots of it.

She took a long shower and dressed in a tux with red accents. She walked the short distance to the casino at eleven. The area was well lit, and people milled all about. She took a deep breath just outside the ornate doors then walked in.

As usual, the whirl and clang of the machines mixing with the loud chatter made her blood pump. She was in her element. Gone were her earlier nerves, replaced by her normal level of cockiness. She was ready to score some loot.

She sauntered past the roulette table even though she was itching to play. She figured Savannah would look there for her, and she really didn't want to be found. Maybe they'd meet up later. Maybe. Time would tell.

Kit wandered into a bar to check out the offerings. No single women there. She drew in a breath and thought for a moment. Slots. They'd been lucky for her last time.

As she left the bar, she caught movement out of the corner of her eye. She saw a luscious figure in a green sequined dress. She looked up at the face and froze. Savannah. She stepped back into the bar and ordered a drink. She sipped it and waited until she figured enough time had passed then cautiously stepped into the casino. There was no sign of Savannah. Relieved, she made her way to the slot machines.

She made several rounds through the area. The place was packed. She kept her eyes open for an open seat next to an unsuspecting older woman adorned in diamonds. She also kept on the lookout for Savannah. She saw neither until her fifth lap around the slots. A woman who looked to be in her sixties and who was wearing a fortune in diamonds was sitting by herself at a machine. Kit quickly approached her.

"Is this seat taken?"

"Help yourself." Her voice was nasally, and, after closer inspection, she appeared to have just finished crying. Kit paused with a hand on the back of the chair.

"Unless you'd rather be alone?"

The woman gave Kit a tired smile.

"Please. Sit."

"Okay. But I don't need to play. If you need an ear, I've got two good ones."

"I appreciate that. I really do. But you need to play. We can chat and play at the same time."

Kit slid a hundred-dollar bill into her machine. That should keep her busy for a while.

"Sounds good to me," she said. "So what's a beautiful woman like yourself doing sitting alone on this magical night?"

"Magical, huh?" She snorted. "Is that what tonight is?"

"It could be. But first talk time. What's going on?"

"My husband is in the pai gow tournament. I went over to see how he was doing and caught him getting fresh with a waitress."

"Oh, that's how the waitresses make their money. I wouldn't think a thing of it."

"I don't know. I've questioned his fidelity for years," the woman said.

"I'm sorry to hear that. He's a fool if you ask me."

"That's very sweet of you." She patted Kit's leg. "I suppose after forty some years he got tired of the same thing."

"Again. He's a fool."

"But you don't know me. Maybe I'm a bad person."

Kit took her gaze off the machine and looked at the woman.

"I'm a really good judge of character. You're a wonderful woman. I can feel it."

"It's nice that someone thinks so. May I ask you a personal question?"

"Shoot." Kit turned her attention back to her game.

The woman leaned in to Kit's ear and spoke quietly.

"You're one of those lesbians, aren't you?"

Kit almost spit her drink out. She regained her composure.

"Yes. Yes, I am. Does that mean we can't be friends?"

"Oh, no. Nothing like that. I just wonder if maybe that's where I went wrong," she said wistfully.

"How so?"

The woman sighed.

"You see, the night I met my husband? All those years ago? That same night my best girlfriend kissed me. I enjoyed it. Very much. It stirred something inside me. But then I met my husband and did the right thing. I wonder now if I made the wrong choice that night."

"What happened to your friend?"

"I have no idea. We drifted apart over the years."

"Yeah. That happens."

"You're very kind...I'm sorry. I didn't get your name."

"Andi."

"Andi. I'm Cassandra. You can call me Cass."

Kit extended her hand.

"It's very nice to meet you, Cass."

"And you," Cass said.

"Would you allow me the pleasure of buying you a drink?"

"That would be lovely."

Cass linked her hand through Kit's elbow and Kit led them to a dark lounge. She seated Cass at a table in a dark corner.

"What are you drinking?" she asked.

"Captain Morgan and Coke."

"You get comfortable. I'll be right back."

Kit returned with their drinks and handed Cass hers. Their fingers met a moment too long and Kit appreciated the flush on Cass's face. She felt sorry for her. But only to a degree. She quickly compartmentalized her feelings and focused on what was important. Securing those rocks.

"I'm curious." Kit leaned close to Cass. "Have you ever experimented? With women, I mean."

Cass shook her head.

"But I have a feeling that could change tonight. Am I right?"

"That would make me very happy."

Savannah meandered through the casino keeping her eyes peeled for anything or anyone suspicious. Including, and especially, Kit. She had to fight her disappointment when, after her millionth trip by the roulette tables, she'd still seen no sign of her. Maybe she wasn't there. Maybe she'd gone back to California. Maybe their paths would never cross again. The thought made her sadder than she wanted to admit.

But Savannah knew she had to be there. The pai gow tournament was world famous and women had come from all over to participate or root their husbands on. And there was no shortage of jewels on display. She just hoped Kit hadn't found a poor unsuspecting target. Savannah knew only too well how easy it was to fall for Kit's charms.

And she was certain Kit was the jewel thief. She was positive she targeted married women who would be too embarrassed to admit they had fallen prey to a charismatic lesbian. So they made up men who robbed them at gunpoint. Or blamed the robberies on the hotel staff. Anyone that would keep their husbands from knowing their dalliances.

True, it could be a man who was seducing these women. He could be pleasing them then robbing them. They weren't likely to admit to their indiscretions in that case either. But Kit had been everywhere the last few robberies had taken place. Savannah was sure she was guilty.

If only she wasn't everything Savannah looked for in a woman. Strong, independent, confident. And drop-dead gorgeous. Why couldn't she get her out of her mind? Dare she admit even to herself that her feelings for her were more than superficial? And Kit was feeling the same. She'd admitted it openly. No. She was a criminal. Savannah was a potential target. That was all.

She was lost in thought as she walked through the lounges around the gambling areas. She was on autopilot and really didn't see anything. She left the bar by the slot machines and made herself focus. She still had a criminal to find. And Kit. Though they were probably one and the same.

Savannah continued to walk around and remained vigilant. She swung back by the roulette tables. Still no Kit. She couldn't deny the ache inside. But she noted all the women and who they appeared to be paired up with. Just in case.

She walked through the tournament. Everyone seemed so serious and it was so much quieter than the rest of the casino. There were a few bejeweled women there watching, but no one seemed to pay them any unnecessary attention.

She checked her watch. Four o'clock. Maybe, just maybe, there wouldn't be a robbery that night. And Kit wasn't there. Coincidence?

Savannah made one last trip through the roulette tables. There stood Kit, watching but not playing. Their gazes met and Kit smiled and waved. She cut through the crowd to where Savannah stood.

"I was wondering if I'd see you tonight," Kit said.

Savannah's heart soared. Kit was there. And had been looking for her. That combined with the lack of robberies made Savannah happier than she'd been in a very long time.

"I've been here all night. Have you been gambling?"

"A little. Why don't we get out of here? Let's go get breakfast."

"Sounds good. Excuse me while I powder my nose?"

"Sure thing. I'll meet you out front?"

"I'll be right there."

Savannah texted Li that she was going to grab a bite. She also told him to let the rest of the team know they could call it quits for the night. She was walking on air as she made her way out front to meet Kit.

"You look positively radiant tonight." Kit kissed her cheek.

Every nerve in Savannah's body came alive at the feel of Kit's lips. She wrapped her arms around her and pulled her in for a proper kiss.

"Very nice," Kit said. "Save some of that for later."

Savannah's heart raced.

"Later?"

"Sure. When I walk you back to your room. You know I'm going to expect more than that."

Savannah arched an eyebrow.

"How much more?"

"We'll see."

Savannah took Kit's hand and they walked to a restaurant that claimed to be open twenty-four hours. The place was busy, and they had to wait for a table.

"So where were you gambling tonight? I'll admit I cruised the roulette tables more than I care to say," Savannah said.

"I was there. And I even played some slots tonight. Just for a bit of variety."

"Slots, huh?"

"What can I say? I was thinking of you."

Savannah felt herself flush at the compliment. She didn't know why she bothered to fight her feelings. Because Kit was a common criminal. She needed to be arrested. And that was the main reason

Savannah continued to see her. She smiled wanly. She didn't believe that lie. Not even for a minute.

"That's very sweet of you," Savannah said.

"What can I say? It's the truth."

They were finally shown to their table and each had a couple of Bloody Marys and a hearty breakfast. When they were through, Kit looked around nervously.

"Are you staying at the casino then?"

"I am."

She got a text from Li at that moment saying they were waiting for a debriefing in her suite. Shit. Of all the lousy luck.

"Everything okay?" Kit asked.

"Fine. I'm getting pretty sleepy, Kit. Would you mind terribly if I didn't invite you back to my room?"

"Suit yourself." Kit shrugged. "May I at least walk you back to the casino?"

Savannah couldn't fight the smile that spread across her face.

"That would be wonderful."

"Great."

Kit threw some cash on the table and reached for Savannah's hand. She gave it a squeeze. Savannah's heart thudded in her chest. She longed, ached to take Kit back to her room and was almost angry at her team. But she had a job to do and reminded herself of that.

When they arrived back at the casino, Kit pulled her close. Savannah closed her eyes and lost herself in the powerful kiss. Her head grew light and her heart beat an irregular rhythm. She wrapped her arms around Kit to keep from falling over. She never wanted the kiss to end.

When Kit finally came up for air, Savannah struggled to catch her breath. Her lungs didn't seem to want to fully inflate. None of her body was functioning correctly. Except the region between her legs. She was wet and throbbing and needed Kit desperately.

"Will I see you again?" Savannah asked when she finally found her voice.

"Count on it."

"Maybe we should exchange numbers?" She held her breath awaiting the reply.

"That's a good idea. Hand me your phone."

She held her phone out in a shaky hand. Kit took her hand and kissed it before entering her number.

"You going to be okay?" Kit said. Savannah could only nod. "Good. Take care of yourself, Savannah. I'll see you next time."

Savannah watched her walk off and turned on very unsteady legs and walked away.

CHAPTER TEN

Savannah tried to wipe the smile off her face but gave up. She was happy. She'd spent time with Kit, and no one had been robbed. What a great day.

She got to her suite to find the team congregated in the hall outside her door.

"Sorry to keep you waiting," she said.

"It's okay, boss. You deserve to eat sometimes, too."

"Thank you." She was still beaming. "Come on in and let's go over whatever we did right tonight. No thievery this time. I'm so happy."

"I wonder if he was sick or something," Li said.

"Maybe. Or maybe he's been feeling our presence."

"Did you see that woman you thought might be the doer?"

"I did. Obviously, I was wrong. So let's go over what we did differently this time."

Savannah stood at the white board while her team brainstormed. Li's phone rang and he excused himself to take the call. When he came back, Savannah could tell from his face they'd been celebrating prematurely.

"Don't tell me," she said.

He nodded.

"An older woman at a hotel down the street. He got the jewels she was wearing plus took what was in her safe. Bold move."

"Shit. Shit, shit, shit. Okay, team. Let's head over there. Go to your rooms and get your things and meet us...where are we meeting, Li?"

He gave them the name of the hotel and the room number. He and Savannah headed over while everyone got their equipment.

"How could this have happened?" she said. "When did it happen? Did they say?"

"She doesn't know. Apparently, she just woke up and realized they were gone."

"What's the victim's name?"

Li consulted his notebook.

"Cassandra. Cassandra Poulos."

"How old is she?"

"Sixty-seven."

"Dang. And who does she think did it?"

"No idea."

"Great. Just great."

"Husband came back to the hotel and found her asleep. He woke her up to tell her how he'd done in the tournament and that's when she realized her jewels were gone."

"I swear we're dealing with a Lothario here," Savannah said.

"You think?"

"Yep. Love 'em and leave 'em and take their jewels."

"I hope not. That's why you think the victims are lying, right? Too embarrassed to admit they took a thief to bed?"

"That's exactly what I think. And why I suspect a woman."

"As I've said before," Li said, "infidelity with a man would be just as embarrassing."

"Not quite. Embarrassing, yes. As embarrassing? I don't know about that."

They walked the rest of the way in silence. The hotel wasn't far from the casino, and Savannah saw the rest of the team drive by in their vans. That was good. They could get started and she could interview the victim. Cassandra. Such a strong name. Too bad she had fallen such easy prey.

Li knocked on the door when they arrived, and they showed their identification to the older gentleman who opened the door.

"Mr. Poulos?" Savannah said.

"That's me. And you are?"

Savannah handed him her ID.

"I'm Savannah. Savannah Brown."

"Come in. They're with you then?" He motioned to the team dusting for fingerprints.

"Yes, they are. Now, where's Mrs. Poulos?"

"She's in the sitting room. Right this way."

"If it's okay, Mr. Poulos, we'd like to interview her privately for a few minutes."

"Nonsense. Anything she has to say she can say in front of me."

Savannah exchanged a look with Li. The last thing they needed was a stubborn husband trying to strong arm the investigation.

"If you insist," she said.

"I do. My wife has been traumatized enough. She needs me by her side right now."

An attractive woman with dark hair and blue eyes sat sipping a cup of hot tea.

"Mrs. Poulos?" Savannah approached her with her hand outstretched.

"Please," Mrs. Poulos said, "call me Cassandra."

"Cassandra then. Can you tell me what happened please?"

"I don't know. I came back to the room. I went to bed and didn't wake up until Alex got home. That's when I realized I'd been robbed."

Savannah noticed that Cassandra wouldn't meet her eyes. She was glancing up and over Savannah's left shoulder. A pretty sure sign she was lying. She also took in her flushed skin and wondered if she'd been sleeping alone. She had to ask.

"Tell me, Cassandra, were you alone when you came back to the room?"

Cassandra blushed furiously.

"Of course, I was. How dare you!"

"Just wondered if maybe someone walked you back here. I'm assuming it was rather late. I meant nothing untoward," she lied.

Cassandra visibly relaxed.

"I made it by myself just fine."

"You didn't notice anyone shady looking?"

"No. I passed several groups, but no one seemed to pay me any mind. Look, I'm feeling more than a little overwhelmed at the moment. I think I'd like a drink and a bath. I'm sure you don't have any more questions for me?"

"I'll call you if I need you," Savannah said. "In the meantime, if you think of anything, anything at all that might be useful, please take my card."

Cassandra took her card and thanked her.

"I realize you all have jobs to do, but I really must bid you good night."

Savannah nodded to the rest of her team before she walked out, and they all began to pack up. She and Li walked back to her suite together.

"You didn't believe her, did you?" Li said.

"Not for a minute. And you?"

"She was very defensive. Her eyes said she was lying. Why won't people be honest with us?"

"I almost asked her husband if Cassandra always sleeps in the nude."

"Why?"

"Because I'm certain she was naked when he got home. She'd been loved up and left."

"What if your theory is wrong though? What if our perp drugs the women then steals their jewels?"

"If that were the case then he or she would have to half drag the victim. People would notice."

"Shall we ask around to see if anyone saw her this morning?"

"We should."

They approached a group of young men standing in front of a restaurant. But because of the language barrier, all Savannah could do was show them a picture of Cassandra and hope they understood she wanted to know if they'd seen her.

They all shook their heads. Savannah and Li moved on and soon were at the restaurant where Savannah and Kit had had breakfast. They showed the picture to the staff and no one remembered seeing her. But the hostess thought she did.

"I think I saw her walk by," she said. "At least I think it was her."

"Was she alone?"

"No. She was with a younger man."

Savannah saw Li fight not to smile.

"Can you tell me anything else?"

"Not really. Sorry. Like I said, I can't even be sure it was her."

They walked back outside.

"A man, huh?" Li beamed.

"Or a masculine woman."

"We'll see."

"Yes, we will."

Kit wandered through Macau enjoying the sights and sounds. And food. She'd managed to avoid the Cotai Strip where the casinos were. There'd be time for that Saturday night. Her favorite place was old town. The food was amazing as was the architecture on the churches.

She hadn't been inside a church since she was a kid but was drawn to the fancy churches she found there.

She found herself checking her phone several times a day just in case Savannah had texted her. No such luck. It was for the best. She didn't need a woman, even Savannah, interfering with her routine. Much as she'd like to take her to bed and then relieve her of her jewels, she didn't know if she could. Sleeping with the enemy would be dangerous. Besides which, she knew Kit's phone number and real name. Stealing from her would be catastrophic.

But the attraction was there. And it was real. Kit liked Savannah. Really liked her. She often fantasized about what it might be like to give up the jewel thief game and settle down with her. No. She couldn't do that. There'd always be more jobs to do and more money to make. Granted, she didn't need any more money. No. She couldn't think like that. She'd get soft and lose her edge. And she needed it to keep the game going.

Soon it was Thursday and Kit was starting to get excited about the upcoming Saturday night. She had just climbed into bed when her phone buzzed. She didn't recognize the number.

Hey. It's Savannah. Hope I'm not disturbing you.

Kit's heart beat a staccato rhythm.

Kit: *Not at all. What's up?*

Savannah: *I'm in Macau. You?*

Kit: *I'm here, too. Dinner tomorrow night?*

Savannah: *That would be great. Where are you staying?*

Kit: *Near Old Town. You?*

Savannah: *At the casino.*

Kit: *Ah.*

Savannah: *Where shall we have dinner?*

Kit thought for a minute. It would be nice to show Savannah around Old Town. But did she want her that close to her dwelling? What harm could it do?

Kit: *I know a great restaurant if you don't mind coming to Old Town.*

Savannah: *I don't mind at all.*

Kit: *Great. I'll text you the details tomorrow.*

Savannah: *Sounds good. I'm turning in now.*

Kit: *Me, too. See you tomorrow.*

Savannah: *I can't wait.*

And then she was gone. Just like that. Kit felt a mix of emotions. She was happy, ecstatic that Savannah had texted her. But she felt empty now that their conversation was over. And there was a burning in her loins that she needed to keep in check. She didn't need to do anything stupid. She didn't want to sleep with Savannah until she was sure she wasn't an agent. Of course, she was already sure she was.

Kit took her time getting ready for dinner the next day. She took a long, cool shower hoping it would quell her overactive hormones. She dressed in gray linen slacks and a short-sleeved button-down black shirt. She ran some gel through her hair and checked out her reflection. She looked good. She wouldn't embarrass Savannah anyway.

She got to the Portuguese restaurant at six forty-five, a full fifteen minutes early. She couldn't help it. She didn't want to keep Savannah waiting. She sat in the bar and watched out the window. She'd just finished her beer when she saw Savannah walk up. She looked gorgeous in a long denim skirt with a white peasant top. Her skin glowed and her hair, worn down, shone. She was a sight for sore eyes.

Kit walked out to the entrance and got the door for Savannah. She kissed her on the cheek.

"You look amazing," she said.

"Thank you. You said casual."

"And you dressed perfectly. Come on. Our table should be ready."

Kit held Savannah's hand as they followed the hostess to their table.

"What's good here?" Savannah said.

"Everything. I mean it. You won't be disappointed."

Savannah beamed at Kit.

"Thank you for inviting me to dinner."

"Believe me, it's my pleasure."

"Does this mean I won't see you tomorrow?"

Savannah made an ordeal of straightening her napkin in her lap. Kit reached across the table and Savannah placed her hand in Kit's.

"Of course, you will. I just don't know when. Shall we say breakfast at five?"

Savannah visibly perked up.

"Five would be perfect. We should both be through gambling by then. Where do you want to meet?" she said.

They ironed out the details and settled in to a leisurely, but delicious, dinner. After, they walked around Old Town hand in hand. Kit loved being with Savannah. She finally felt like she belonged somewhere. It was a comforting, albeit unfamiliar, sensation. She warned herself not to get too comfortable. Fraternizing with Savannah was indeed like sleeping with the enemy. Still, Kit couldn't get enough of her.

As the night grew darker, Kit knew it was time to get Savannah back to her hotel. She hated to say good night, but she sustained herself with the knowledge that she'd see her the following night.

"I should get you back to your hotel," she said.

"Didn't you say you're staying nearby? Couldn't we go back to your place?"

Kit smiled at her. A for effort. But it wasn't going to happen.

"Not tonight, babe. I'm not ready yet."

Savannah raised an eyebrow.

"Babe?" she said.

"Too soon?" Kit hoped she hadn't blown it.

Savannah smiled.

"Not at all. I like it."

"Good. So do I. I like you, Savannah. More than I should."

"What's your hesitancy, Kit? I don't understand."

"I think you do." Was that too much? Had she just admitted her guilt? She hoped Savannah wouldn't take it that way. "I need to be sure. I don't want you to be just another roll in the hay. I'm sorry for dragging my feet. Sort of. I really like you and want to make sure we can go the distance before I take you to bed."

"What does that look like to you? The distance, I mean."

"It means what it sounds like. Sure, it's fun and exciting here in the land of bright lights and high rolling. But would we be able to maintain the excitement in California? Or Maryland? With no distractions? With just each other for entertainment?"

"You're really thinking that far in the future?" Savannah asked.

"I am. I hope that doesn't scare you off."

Savannah sighed.

"It doesn't. I just hope I don't have to wait long."

"I hope not too. As the song says, the waiting is the hardest part."

CHAPTER ELEVEN

K it slept late the next day. She knew she'd be up until morning and wanted to be sure she could make it. Sleep was not something she needed an abundance of, thankfully. She showered in a leisurely fashion and tried to concentrate on the task before her. But her mind kept drifting back to Savannah. She didn't know how much longer she'd be able to deny her body the pleasures Savannah offered. And, on the flip side, how long would she be able to bed random women when her heart cried out for Savannah?

Disgusted at her lack of concentration, she stepped out of the shower and toweled off. One thing she'd done with her extra days in Macau was have her dry cleaning done. She dressed in her fresh Calvin Klein tux with red accents again since red was considered lucky. Not that she needed luck. She had skill. And plenty of it.

Kit's hired car arrived at eleven and took her to the casino. The tournament should have been in full swing by then and she was sure she could find a nice poker widow to relieve of her jewels. The trick would be avoiding Savannah until after she'd robbed the stranger. That would be hard since her whole body begged her to find Savannah and spend more time with her. Later. She'd see her later. That would have to suffice.

She made her way once around the casino to get the lay of the land. The roulette wheel called to her, but she resisted the pull. That's where Savannah would be looking for her. And she couldn't let her find her. Not yet.

Kit stopped in one of the dark bars and ordered a beer. She leaned against the bar and surveyed the room. She spotted an older woman by herself at a table. Feeling herself slip into jewel thief mode, Kit approached the woman.

"What's a beautiful woman like you doing all alone in a place like this?" Kit knew she sounded corny but didn't care. She hoped it would add to her charm. She stared down at the woman with dark hair in a bun, dark eyes, and plenty of rubies, and waited for an answer.

"That's about the oldest pickup line in the book," the woman said. "But you're a woman, so I doubt you're hitting on me. Or are you?"

"That depends. Would you like to be hit on?"

The woman laughed. It was a high-pitched laugh that grated on Kit's nerves.

"You'd be the first person to hit on me in years. And the first woman ever. Won't you sit down?"

"Thank you. I hope I'm not interrupting your alone time."

"Nonsense," the woman said. "I was just getting a headache so I decided to find someplace dark and quiet for a while."

"How fortunate for me you chose here."

She laughed again.

"Are you always this smooth?"

"Only when I'm trying to impress," Kit said.

"Well, consider me impressed."

"Good. I'm Dani."

"Nice to meet you, Dani. I'm Chen."

They shook hands and Kit was immediately touched by Chen's soft, warm skin.

"What brings you to the casino tonight?" Kit said.

"My husband is playing in the tournament. And you?"

"I'm a bit of a globetrotting gambler. I go where the mood strikes, and this time Macau called to me."

"I'm glad it did. I have to say, it's nice to have someone to talk to. Sometimes playing games by yourself with no one to chat with but the dealer gets old."

"Well, consider me your escort for the night. I'll be by your side to talk about whatever, whenever. Sound good?"

"It sounds wonderful. But I have to tell you, I'm rather tired of gambling. Would you find me awfully boring if I said I'd just like to sit here and visit?"

"Not boring at all," Kit said. "In fact, I'd enjoy that very much. May I get you another drink?"

"I'd love another martini. With Hendrick's, please."

"Coming right up."

When Kit turned away from the bar, she caught movement out of the corner of her eye. Savannah was in the bar. Thankfully, she was at the other side. Kit walked to the table and set the drinks down.

"Please excuse me for a moment," she said.

She hurried into the restroom where she locked herself in a stall for what felt like an eternity. She checked her watch. It had been seven minutes. It was probably safe now. She looked around the bar as she emerged from the restroom. No sign of Savannah. She calmly walked back to the table.

"Is everything okay?" Chen said.

Kit flashed her her best smile.

"Everything is fine. How's your martini?"

"Delicious. Thank you."

"Where are you from, Chen?"

"Hong Kong. And you?"

"The States."

"You're a long way from home."

"That I am. Here's to fellow travelers."

She held up her bottle and Chen clinked her glass against it.

"Why do I get the feeling tonight will be more fun than I could possibly have imagined?" Chen said.

"The sky's the limit. We can have as much fun as you'd like."

Chen looked at Kit questioningly and Kit winked at her. She wanted to rob her now. But knew she had to be patient.

"I like you, Dani. You seem like a lot of fun. Tell me more about yourself. Where in the States do you live?"

"Maryland." It was the first thing that popped into her head. Oh well. Chen didn't need to know the truth.

"It's small, yes?"

Kit laughed.

"Very."

"You have a nice laugh. You should laugh more often."

"Thank you. And I love to laugh."

"Good," Chen said. "Laughter is a good thing."

They had a few more drinks and talked about everything under the sun. Chen wanted to know all sorts of details about Kit, which she fancified for her. After a couple of hours, Kit grew restless, but she needn't have worried.

"Do you drink anything except beer, Dani? I have bourbon in my room. As well as plenty of gin. Why don't we go back there?"

Kit's heart raced.

"Are you sure?"

"Positive. I want to get you alone."

"Sounds excellent to me."

"I'm in a hotel not far from here. You don't mind walking, do you?"

"Not at all."

Kit was surprised when, once they arrived in her room, Chen took Kit's hands in her own.

"I don't usually pick up strangers in a bar," she said.

"I'm not really a stranger anymore am I?"

Chen laughed.

"No. I suppose you're not. Now will you make us some drinks? I need to freshen up."

"I'll be happy to."

While she mixed drinks, Kit looked around the room. Everything was neat and tidy. The safe must be in the sleeping area. Not that she'd need the safe. She'd just take the jewels Chen was wearing. They'd be worth a fortune.

Chen emerged wearing a short red satin robe.

"You look delectable," Kit said.

"I hope I haven't misjudged your intentions?"

"No. Not at all."

"You have me very curious, Dani. And my imagination is running wild. I want to feel everything you can make me feel."

"Now? Or would you like a drink first?" She held up the drinks she'd just mixed.

"One more drink. To steel my nerves."

Kit smiled at her. Chen would be fun. Of that she had no doubt. And, once she was asleep, Kit would take her rubies and let herself out. Easy peasy.

They finished their drinks and Chen led Kit to the bedroom. Chen turned out to be very experimental and Kit thoroughly enjoyed herself. She lay there waiting to hear the soft snores of slumber coming from Chen. She was surprised to hear her voice.

"Make a couple more drinks, Dani? I want to celebrate."

"You got it. Let me use the facilities first."

She washed her face and hands and tried to quell her racing heart. How could Chen possibly not be asleep? Maybe one more drink would send her on her way to dreamland.

But after two more drinks, Chen was wide-awake and chatty. Kit knew the night was a loss.

"I hate to do this, Chen, but I need to get going. It's getting late."

"I understand," she said. "Thank you for one of the best nights of my life."

Kit was glad it had been a good night for Chen since her night hadn't ended how it should have.

"Thank you," she said. "I'll never forget you, Chen."

"Nor I you."

Kit let herself out and hurried down the street. She had five minutes to meet Savannah. She hoped Savannah would be late.

Savannah checked her watch again. It was almost five. Where was Kit? She had her hand on the door and was about to go look inside again when she heard a familiar voice in her ear.

"You're not leaving, are you?"

Savannah turned and smiled at Kit. Kit claimed her mouth in a searing kiss that left Savannah breathless.

"More, please. I need more."

Kit kissed her again before taking her hand and leading her to another hotel down the street.

"How was your night?" Kit asked.

"I don't know. I was really restless. I couldn't stay focused very well."

"What's up with that?"

"Beats me. Maybe I was just passing time until I saw you again."

"Aw, babe. You're very sweet."

"What? You don't believe me?"

"As a matter of fact, I do. I was missing you tonight as well."

"You should have texted me. Maybe we could have met sooner."

"We had plans," Kit said. "I intended to honor those plans."

"We can always meet early. Please know that."

"Sometimes you seem like you're on a mission. I don't like to interrupt your concentration."

On a mission? Was it possible that Kit knew she was with the FBI? No. How could she?

"It's true that sometimes I lose myself in the wonders of the casino." She hoped her voice didn't shake. "But I'll make myself available for you."

Kit just smiled at her. Savannah swore she could see the wheels in her head turning.

"I appreciate that," Kit finally said. "Now how about some breakfast? I'm starving."

They had stopped in front of another casino.

"Breakfast? Here?"

"I understand they have quite a breakfast buffet here. Come on. Let's check it out."

Kit let go of Savannah's hand and held the door for her. Kit was everything Savannah had dreamed of in a woman. She thought again of how handsome, attentive, and chivalrous Kit was. But did

Savannah want to settle down? Or was she ready to admit her job to Kit?

Her job. No. Not until she was sure Kit wasn't behind the string of robberies. And while she hadn't heard of any robberies that night, her stomach was still in knots that they might yet hear from a victim.

"Are you okay?" Kit said. "You look like you're a million miles away."

"Sorry. I'm here. I guess I'm just getting tired. And I know I'm famished."

They found the buffet and Kit paid while Savannah loaded her plate with fruit and eggs and seafood. Everything looked so good and she couldn't remember the last time she'd eaten.

"Look at you go." Kit joined her. "I enjoy a woman with an appetite."

"How could you not load up with all this wonderful food here?"

"I agree. When you're finished, go ahead and find a table. I'll join you."

Savannah found a table not far from the buffet and sat. Her mouth watered in anticipation of all the good food, but she waited for Kit.

"Eat up, babe. Thanks for waiting for me, but it wasn't necessary. Enjoy your food, please."

Savannah dug in. Everything was marvelous.

"How'd you hear about this place?" she asked Kit.

"I asked around. This place was mentioned more than anyplace else."

"Well, thank you for doing your due diligence. This is delicious."

Kit smiled at her. Her dimples were on display and Savannah's heart melted.

"My pleasure," Kit said. "I'm so glad you're enjoying it."

After breakfast, Kit took Savannah's hand and led her back to the other casino. They stopped in front of it.

"Won't you walk me to my door?" Savannah didn't want their time together to end. She hadn't heard from Li and wasn't planning on calling a meeting until Kit was gone. Whenever that may be.

"Sure," Kit said. "Lead the way."

Savannah led Kit through the almost empty casino to the bank of elevators. Kit kissed her while they waited for an elevator and then kissed her with much more ardor when they were in the elevator. Savannah grew weak in the knees as the kiss went on. Kit's tongue was gentle yet insistent and Savannah couldn't help but imagine that tongue all over her body. She moaned into Kit's mouth.

The elevator stopped and Savannah leaned against the wall trying to gather her strength.

"Coming, babe?" Kit held the door open.

"Damn near."

Kit threw her head back and laughed.

"Come on. Let's get you to your room." She extended her hand and Savannah took it. They walked down the hall until Savannah stopped at her room.

"Please tell me you'll come in."

"Tempting though that may be, I'm going to have to decline. Soon I won't have to, my dear."

"Soon? How soon?"

"Very." Kit smiled at her. She kissed her passionately and made Savannah dizzy with need. She squeezed Kit's hand.

"Please?"

"Sorry, babe. Now you get inside and get some sleep. When do you leave?"

"Monday."

"So we'll do Old Town again tomorrow. That is, if you'd like."

"You should know by now I can't say no to you."

Kit flashed her dimples.

"I'm counting on that. Good night, Savannah."

"Good night, Kit."

She closed the door behind herself and leaned against it, breathing hard. Damn. She was actually falling for the rogue. She needed some distance. But distance from Kit was the last thing she wanted.

CHAPTER TWELVE

Savannah's phone buzzed as she pushed herself away from the door. It was Li asking what time their debriefing would be. Savannah knew they should meet right then, but she was tired and still on cloud nine. So she said they'd meet at three that afternoon. That would give everybody time to get some rest.

If you hear of any robberies, call me.

Will do. Sleep well, boss.

Savannah was mentally, physically, and emotionally exhausted. She stripped out of her clothes and climbed into bed. The feel of the cool sheets on her naked body awakened her hormones again. She couldn't wait to be naked with Kit. She needed her with every ounce of her being. More importantly, and scarily, she liked Kit. She was falling for her. It was so hard to remember Kit was a suspect when she was being so suave and debonair. But she was a suspect. Or was she? She was there in Macau and there hadn't been any robberies. That she knew of. Maybe Kit wasn't the thief after all. The idea made her smile. She held on to that thought as she drifted off to sleep.

Savannah woke at one, famished and happy. No one had woken her with reports of any jewels missing. She checked her phone to make sure she hadn't missed anything. There were no missed calls and no texts. Maybe the string of jewel thievery had ended.

She took a quick shower and headed downstairs for a bite to eat. She was back at her suite at two fifty, ready for her three o'clock meeting. Li showed up five minutes later and Savannah was excited to see him.

"No robberies last night?" she said.

"Not a one. Strange, isn't it?"

"Have you checked other casinos around the world? Maybe we were at the wrong one."

"Nothing," Li said. "Nothing reported anyway."

"That's great. Maybe he or she is through."

"I wish. Somehow I don't believe that."

"Must you always be a pessimist?"

"I'm pragmatic. I can't help it."

Savannah laughed but was spared any further discussion by a knock on the door.

The rest of the crew was there. She welcomed them in, and they went over what had gone right the previous night. Everyone seemed in agreement that their diligence had prevented another robbery. Savannah wanted to believe that but couldn't shake the feeling that whoever was behind them had quit. Or retired. Or whatever. She was convinced the string of thefts was over.

"Our next stop is Lisbon." She stopped speaking when her phone buzzed.

Are we still on for this evening?

It was Kit. She fought to keep the smile off her face. She set her phone down. She'd reply later.

"I want everyone there Friday. We'll meet at nine in my suite to set up a plan of action. Enjoy your week off."

One by one her team left. Li hung behind.

"What's up, Li?"

"I feel like we're missing something, boss. Sure, our presence could have been felt, but I feel like there's more to it."

"Whatever the reason, let's thank the powers that be for a quiet night. Now go home and get some rest."

"When do you get into Lisbon?"

"Tuesday."

"I'll be there."

"Li, really, that's not necessary."

"Maybe not. But I'll be there. Maybe I'll do some sightseeing. Maybe I'll sleep until Friday. Who knows?"

"I have friends in Portugal. People I haven't seen in years. I'll be visiting with them. I won't be working all week," Savannah said. "So you should go back to the US and recuperate. We've been traveling for a long time."

"Thanks, boss. I appreciate that. But I'll be in Lisbon."

He left and Savannah shook her head. He was dedicated. That was for sure. She reached for her phone. There was another text.

Kit: *Savannah? You okay?*

Savannah: *Sorry. I was in the shower. Of course we're still on. What time and where?*

Kit: *Seven o'clock. Let's meet in front of the ruins of St. Paul.*

Savannah: *Sounds good. I'll see you then.*

Savannah had just three hours to kill. She soaked in a hot bath with scented oils. She got out of the bath and rinsed off, then dressed in a gray pencil skirt with a baby blue blouse. She brushed her hair until it shone. Satisfied with her appearance, she went down to the street and hailed a taxi to Senado Square.

The place was bustling, and she felt alive. She inhaled deeply of the myriad scents from the selection of restaurants. Her stomach growled. She couldn't wait to meet up with Kit and get some food. But she still had a half an hour to kill.

Savannah revisited some of the shops where she and Kit had window shopped. They weren't open that Sunday evening, but she still enjoyed the sights. Finally, it was five to seven, so she crossed the square to St. Paul.

She spotted Kit as she approached. She looked dapper in her white slacks and periwinkle golf shirt. Savannah's heart raced at the sight of her. Her palms grew damp, as did her panties. Maybe that night they'd finally get together. She was throbbing with unquenched desire. God knew they'd waited long enough in her opinion.

Kit finally saw her and waved. Savannah couldn't help but smile. She was with Kit again. Kit hadn't robbed anybody the night of the tournament. All was right in the world.

"You look like you're in a good mood," Kit said.

"Of course. I'm with you."

"You're so sweet." Kit kissed Savannah's cheek. It burned at the contact. She wanted more. Savannah wanted a real kiss. The kind of kiss that made her toes curl. She knew Kit had it in her. She'd just have to be patient.

Kit took in the sight of Savannah in front of her. Her blouse really made her eyes stand out. Savannah was a looker. Plus, she was intelligent, confident, and seemingly independent. All traits Kit would have looked for. Had she been looking. Which she wasn't. Why then could she not get Savannah out of her head?

"You look lovely this evening," Kit said. "I feel underdressed next to you."

"Nonsense. You look quite handsome yourself."

"Thank you."

Kit's willpower quickly dissolved. She swore to behave and not maul Savannah in public, but she couldn't resist. She leaned in and kissed her. The kiss started out tame enough, but as was the norm, it quickly evolved into an open mouth tongue dance. She came to her senses slowly and remembered where they were.

"Come on," Kit said. "We should get some dinner."

Kit ignored the looks they got as they held hands and strolled through the square. They finally stopped outside a restaurant that smelled amazing.

"We've got to try this place," Savannah said.

"Your wish is my command."

Dinner passed with good food and pleasant conversation.

"Purple, by the way," Savannah said.

"What about it?"

"You said you couldn't sleep with me because you didn't know my favorite color. So I'm telling you."

Kit burst out laughing.

"You're persistent. I'll give you that."

"I can't remember what else you said you needed to know."

"I feel like I've gotten to know you very well," Kit said. "Now I just have to decide if I follow my head or my heart."

"What are they saying?"

"My head is telling me I'm not the settling down type."

"And your heart?" Savannah said.

"It's telling me to give up my globetrotting ways and follow you back to Maryland. To spend the rest of my days relaxing with you as the years melt away."

"That sounds idyllic."

"I admit that it does."

"You know, Kit," Savannah said, "no one's forcing you to make a decision right now."

Kit took Savannah's hand in hers.

"And I appreciate that. I'm glad there's no pressure. But I can't make love to you until that decision has been made once and for all."

She watched Savannah's face fall.

"I'm really leaning toward following my heart, if you must know."

Savannah smiled.

"That makes me very happy."

"But what about you? Could you give up being a world traveler?"

"Why couldn't we travel the world together?"

"I suppose we could, couldn't we?" Kit said.

Dinner was finished and they walked around the Square some more.

"I've really enjoyed my time here," Savannah said.

"As have I." For the most part. "And you're a big part of that."

"Aw. Thank you."

"Where are you off to next?" Kit asked.

"Lisbon. You?"

"Same."

Savannah beamed.

"When do you arrive?"

"I fly there tomorrow."

"Can I see you?"

"Of course, Savannah. I can't stay away from you."

They snuggled together on the cab ride and then Kit walked Savannah to her room. Savannah unlocked the door and held it open.

"Won't you come in?"

"Savannah…I can't."

"Just for a few minutes. I just don't want this night to end."

A battle raged inside Kit. She should go in. She should give in and make love to Savannah. She should enjoy everything her body promised. On the other hand, she should leave. Say good night and go back to the safety of her room. Alone.

"Honest," Savannah said. "Just come in for a nightcap."

"Just a nightcap?"

"I promise."

Kit stepped inside and heard the door close behind her. She hoped she was strong enough to stick to her guns now that she and Savannah were all alone. In total privacy. Out of the view of curious onlookers.

Savannah kept to her word. She was standing by the bar.

"I don't have a wide selection. Or any choice for that matter. How does scotch sound?"

Kit relaxed enough to laugh.

"Scotch sounds wonderful."

Kit took her drink from Savannah. Their fingers met and Kit felt an electric shock start at her fingertips and pulsate its way to her center. Her whole body vibrated, and she barely managed to take a sip without spilling.

"You're shaking," Savannah said. "Are you okay?"

Kit managed a weak smile.

"I'm fine." Savannah glanced over her shoulder one last time before she took her drink to the bedroom. "Where do you think you're going?"

"Oh, calm down. We'll both stay fully dressed. I promise."

Kit knew she was making a huge mistake as she followed Savannah. But she had no choice. She quit thinking and allowed autopilot to take over.

Savannah sat on the bed and Kit sat next to her. She draped her arm across Savannah's shoulders and held her tight. She felt amazing pressed into Kit. And Kit wanted to tear her clothes off and have her way with her. She kissed Savannah. Hard. And Savannah reciprocated. The kiss lasted an eternity, and Kit only came to her senses when Savannah spilled her drink on Kit.

Kit jumped then laughed.

"Sorry," Savannah said. "I guess I kind of lost myself in that kiss."

"It's all good. I'll get a towel."

She dried her pant leg to the best of her ability and walked back out to find Savannah pouring another drink.

"I should go." Kit was all too aware she almost lost control of the situation. "We both have a lot of traveling ahead of us tomorrow."

"At least finish your drink."

Kit downed her scotch in one swallow. She kissed Savannah good night. It started out innocently enough, but Kit soon felt Savannah's tongue along her lips. Her determination wavered but only briefly. She ended the kiss and stepped back.

"Safe travels tomorrow. Text me when you land."

"I miss you already," Savannah said.

"We'll get together soon. I promise."

Kit walked out into the crowded street and hailed a cab. The ride to her place was uneventful and that was unfortunate. It gave her time, too much time, to reflect on her evening. Savannah had definitely wormed her way into Kit's heart. She didn't know how much longer she'd be able to deny them both what they so obviously wanted.

But to give in to the pleasures that awaited her meant giving up the thrill of her lifestyle. Yes, she'd struck out in Macau and it hadn't killed her. But it left her feeling empty. Only until she'd seen Savannah and then the emptiness was gone. Savannah filled her up. In a way nothing or no one ever had.

So why was she dragging her feet? What made her so hesitant? She realized that if she got out of the game, she'd have a hell of a time getting back into it. There was that to consider. So she had to be sure she and Savannah could go the distance. She'd have to make love to her eventually to know they were compatible that way. So why not give in and taste her wares? Why not indeed?

CHAPTER THIRTEEN

As soon as her plane touched down in Lisbon, Savannah texted Kit to let her know she'd arrived and see when they might meet up. She was exhausted from her trip but would force herself to power through if Kit was available.

She received no answer and figured Kit must still be in the air. She got to her hotel where she ordered room service, took a bath, and climbed into bed. But sleep didn't come right away. She couldn't stop thinking about the lack of a theft in Macau. Did it really mean the thief was through? Kit had been there. Did it mean she was innocent? The questions tumbled over each other in her mind. It was after noon by the time she finally fell asleep.

She slept until nine o'clock that night and woke up famished. She wanted dinner and she wanted Kit. Not necessarily in that order.

Savannah remembered Li saying he'd be in Lisbon early. She checked her phone for messages from him. There wasn't one from him but there was a text from Kit.

Dinner tomorrow?

Tomorrow would be great. But I'm hungry now. Have you eaten?

She waited impatiently for the reply.

I haven't. Shall we get together?

I'd like that.

Let's meet at Alma in a half hour. Dress somewhat nicely.

Will do. See you then.

Savannah took a quick shower and dressed in a black cocktail dress. She put on some pearls mostly to look pretty, but also to tempt Kit, just in case.

She packed her clutch and was on her way out the door when her phone rang. Assuming it was Kit, she answered without looking.

"Hello?"

"Hey, boss. It's me. Want to get together and strategize for a few?"

"Hi, Li. I'd love to but I'm meeting a friend for dinner. Can we plan to meet tomorrow? Say two o'clock?"

"That'll be great. I'll see you then. Enjoy your dinner."

Savannah disconnected the call and hurried to the street to catch a cab. She arrived at Alma five minutes late. Kit greeted her at the door wearing a gray suit with a purple shirt and a lavender tie. She looked absolutely devourable.

Kit kissed her cheek and Savannah went weak in the knees. She couldn't get over the effect Kit had on her. She needed so much more than Kit was willing to give. She needed her completely.

"You look positively radiant," Kit said.

"And you're looking more handsome than ever."

"I hope you're as hungry as you claim to be. I understand the food here is to die for."

"I could eat a horse right now."

Kit laughed, and the sound sent shivers through Savannah's body. Kit's laugh was deep and sensual, just like her voice. She could listen to her all night. But she'd rather do other things with Kit all night. Even if Kit robbed her. It would be worth it.

They were seated at their table and Kit took Savannah's hands in hers. Savannah melted at the touch. She grew warm all over and felt a rush of wetness between her legs. She was more than ready for Kit. Why wouldn't she just give in already?

"You doing okay?" Kit said.

"Fine. Why?"

"You look a little flushed."

Savannah withdrew her hands and sat back against her chair.

"That's not surprising is it? You were touching me, you know."

Kit laughed again.

"Fair enough. I do appreciate your honesty."

"Speaking of honesty," Savannah said. "Are you just going to toy with me forever?"

Kit tilted her head and stared at Savannah.

"What do you mean?"

Savannah lowered her voice.

"You know what I mean. Are you ever going to take me to bed?"

"That's really important to you, isn't it?" Savannah nodded. "What's wrong with taking things slow? Or is that too old-fashioned for you?"

"I don't mind taking things slow, but I feel like we've been doing that long enough. I need to know if I'm wasting my time." There. She'd said it.

"Wasting your time? Is that how you really feel? Just because I like and respect you too much to just jump in bed with you?"

"Is that how you really feel?"

"What?"

"You know, you like and respect me?"

"That, my dear, is exactly how I feel."

"Then I apologize for acting like a teen with overactive hormones."

Kit smiled at her.

"No apology necessary. Truth is, it's nice to be wanted."

Savannah scoffed.

"I'm sure there's a whole line of women who want you, who wish they could be me."

"I don't know about all that."

"I do."

"Well, I do love your perception of me."

Savannah damn near swooned. She loved that Kit was articulate as well as drop-dead gorgeous. It was a killer combination.

They finished dinner and sat talking until the restaurant was closing.

"We should get going," Savannah said.

"Oh, yeah. I suppose we should."

They wandered down the street and came to a nightclub. It was fairly tame since it was Tuesday night. They enjoyed a few drinks and chatted some more. Savannah's phone buzzed, and when she checked it she saw it was three o'clock in the morning.

Her text was from Li.

Had a great idea. Text me when you wake up.

"Anything important? Who's texting you at this hour?" Kit said.

"A friend from the States. And it's not the middle of the night there."

"What did she want?"

Savannah hated lying to Kit and wondered if she'd ever be able to be completely honest with her.

"She's just checking in. No biggie."

"Go ahead and reply," Kit said.

"It's not important. I'd rather focus on you."

Kit appeared relieved and draped her arm across Savannah's shoulders. She pulled Savannah to her and kissed the top of her head.

"Good answer," she said. "Very good answer. I understand concerned friends and all, but I really don't like to share."

"You're very sweet. And don't worry. When we're together I'm all about you."

Kit relaxed at the feel of Savannah against her. She wondered who had really texted her but tried to block the fear that washed over her. Was Kit just a target for Savannah? Was she toying with Kit in order to catch a jewel thief? Surely Kit must be a suspect. She'd been at the scene of all of the robberies.

Kit exhaled heavily. She shouldn't have allowed herself to fall for Savannah. If this was a trap, and it very well could be, she was setting herself up for major heartache. Maybe she should make love to Savannah. She certainly wouldn't steal from her. Maybe that would convince Savannah of her innocence and remove her from the list of suspects. Then she'd find out for sure if Savannah really liked her or not.

She seemed to be interested. She flushed and blushed at Kit's attention. Her lips and tongue certainly implied that she wanted Kit. Only time would tell. Kit just wasn't sure how long she could hold out. She really wanted Savannah. All of her. In every way possible.

Kit leaned forward and whispered in Savannah's ear, "Would you like to dance?"

Savannah shook her head. She leaned back into Kit, causing electrical currents to course through Kit's body.

"I'd rather stay here with you," Savannah said.

Fair enough. Kit was enjoying her closeness. She didn't need to dance. She sat holding Savannah close and mentally planned out the rest of their week together. She knew she'd enjoy spending extra time with Savannah, but she also knew she had to stay focused. She had a job to do. And she'd failed in Macau. She couldn't fail in Lisbon.

She was disappointed when she heard that it was last call but figured four o'clock was late enough. She needed to get Savannah back to her hotel and then get some shuteye. She kissed Savannah on the cheek.

"Come on. Let's call it a night."

"Do we have to?" Savannah said.

Kit laughed.

"Yes. We really should."

On the street Kit hailed a cab and they rode back to Savannah's hotel. It was right by the casino. Kit rode up to Savannah's room with her.

"Stay with me?" Savannah said.

"Not a good idea. You and I both know what would happen if I stayed with you and we both need some rest."

"Please? I promise to behave. No hanky-panky."

"I don't know if I'm that strong, babe. So I'll kiss you good night now."

They kissed for long moments, Kit knowing she needed to leave but not wanting to. Would she be strong enough to only sleep with Savannah? To share her bed and not claim her as her own? Her resolve weakened.

"Let's get inside," she murmured against Savannah's lips.

Savannah fumbled in her purse, finally found her key, and opened the door. Kit pressed her against the door as soon as it closed behind them and kissed her soundly.

"You sure you only want to sleep?" Savannah said.

Kit straightened up and put some distance between them.

"Positive. Now come on. Let's get some shuteye."

"Kit, if you sleep with me, I'll still respect you in the morning."

Kit laughed loudly.

"You crack me up. The question is, would I respect myself? Seriously though. I'm about asleep on my feet. Show me where I can snooze."

"You'll ruin your suit if you sleep in it."

"I'll be in my boxers and undershirt. You'll be in my shirt." She took Savannah's hand. "I mean it. Come on. It's time to call it a night."

Kit stripped down to her underwear and handed her dress shirt to Savannah. She held it to her nose.

"It smells like you," Savannah said. "Kind of woodsy."

Kit couldn't help but smile.

"I'm sure it does. Now, if you're not adverse to that smell, please go to the bathroom and slip into the shirt."

"Yes, ma'am."

She watched Savannah disappear and questioned her own sanity. Was she really strong enough to simply sleep with Savannah? Could she keep her hands to herself? She'd have to. She didn't have a choice. Not yet.

Savannah came out looking adorable in Kit's shirt. Kit's heart raced, and her palms sweat. She questioned again the intelligence of attempting to simply spend the night with Savannah in her arms.

"Come on then. Let's get some sleep." Savannah climbed under the covers facing Kit. "Oh no, you don't. Roll over. No more kissing tonight."

Savannah did as she was asked, and Kit wrapped her arm around her. She was exhausted and needed her sleep. But sleep eluded her. Her hormones raced, and she looked around the room without moving, to try to find something to focus on. Anything but Savannah.

Her gaze landed on the pearls Savannah had been wearing. They lay temptingly on the dresser. Kit could take them and walk away and never see Savannah again. No. She needed Savannah in her life in a way she hadn't needed anyone in years. She wasn't going to mess it up.

She closed her eyes and welcomed sleep as it washed over her. She didn't sleep well though. She had nightmares about Savannah arresting her. The look of disappointment and disgust in her eyes forced Kit awake before she was ready.

The bed next to her was empty. She reached for her phone and checked the time. Eleven thirty. Too early. She needed more sleep. But first, she needed to find Savannah. She found her in the sitting room reading something on her phone.

"What are you doing out here?" Kit said.

Savannah looked up at her and smiled.

"I was awake and didn't want to disturb you. Although you didn't seem to be sleeping well at all. Anyway, I started the coffee. It should be ready any minute now."

"Excellent. I need coffee. How about some breakfast?"

"You don't have anything to wear. Not that I would complain if you wore what you're wearing now."

"True. I guess I'll get dressed and hit the road then. After coffee."

"Yes. After coffee. Will I see you later?"

"I thought we'd grab a dinner cruise tonight. How does that sound?"

"Extremely romantic."

"Good," Kit said. "Then that's settled. I'll meet you at the dock at seven?"

"Sure thing. But first, get dressed and have some coffee."

"Anything to prolong my time with you, babe. Anything at all."

CHAPTER FOURTEEN

Savannah had been shocked to wake up and find both Kit and Savannah's pearls still in place. She had worried that Kit would take the pearls and disappear from her life. Maybe she wasn't the jewel thief after all. Or maybe the pearls weren't rich enough for her. Savannah made a mental note to wear as many diamonds as she could get away with Saturday night at the casino.

When Kit appeared in the sitting area in just her boxers and undershirt with her nipples on full display, it took every ounce of self-control not to take her back to bed. She looked so cute with her hair mussed and her eyes full of sleep.

But she worried about her. Kit had obviously been having nightmares when Savannah woke up. It was her moaning and groaning that had awakened Savannah.

"How did you sleep?" Savannah asked while she poured the coffee.

"Okay. Not great. I need to get home to California soon to get a good night's sleep. Hotels don't lend themselves to solid sleep. Or so I've found."

"I'm sorry to hear that. You seemed to be having a bad dream this morning. Do you remember it?"

Something flashed in Kit's eyes, but Savannah couldn't be sure what it was.

"Nope. I don't ever remember my dreams."

They sipped their coffee and Kit finally announced it was time to go. Savannah went into the bathroom and reluctantly removed Kit's shirt. She dressed in a robe and handed Kit her shirt.

"Here you go. You can get dressed now."

"Thanks. I will."

Kit disappeared into the bedroom and came out looking as dapper as she could in a slept in shirt.

"So I'll see you at seven?" Savannah hated to see Kit leaving. But she had to get ready for her meeting with Li.

"I can't wait." Kit kissed her good-bye and was gone.

Savannah took a long, hot shower and ordered breakfast from room service. When she had finished her breakfast, which included another pot of coffee, she dressed and checked the clock. Li should be there any minute.

She heard a knock on the door. She opened it to find Li looking much fresher than she felt.

"Come on in, Li. What's on your mind?"

"Did you get my text last night?"

"I did."

"Sorry to text you in the middle of the night, but I had a most excellent idea."

"And what might that be?" Savannah said.

"You know how you've been spending time with that one woman you suspect?"

Savannah hoped he didn't notice her blush.

"Of course."

"I think you should seduce her," Li said.

"You think I should what?"

"Hear me out. I think you should take her to bed. Leave your jewels out when you do. Then, when she takes them, we'll be waiting right outside your door and we can nab her."

Little did Li know she'd been trying to seduce Kit for several weeks now. She couldn't admit that to him. And she didn't like the pain in the pit of her stomach as she thought of Kit caught in a sting of her doing. But it was a good idea. She'd had the same thought. Only she hadn't considered an audience while making love to Kit.

"I don't know, Li." He opened his mouth to speak, but she held up her hand. "I want to catch this thief as much as the rest of you, but I don't know that I'm willing to sacrifice myself in that way."

"I think it's going to be the only way we can truly find out if she's behind these robberies. And if she's not, it's no loss really."

"There are thousands of people at these casinos," Savannah said. "And yes, I consider this woman a prime suspect. But I don't like the idea of the whole team waiting outside my door when there could be another thief at work."

"Fine. Not the whole team then. Just a couple of us. Myself included. Come on, boss. At least think about it. Don't just dismiss it out of hand."

"I'll think about it. Now, shall we work on other strategies? In case she's not the culprit?"

"Sure. Although I think we're doing everything we can," Li said. "And I think the fact that there was no robbery in Macau had a lot to do with our presence."

"I think that's a possibility. Of course, our thief might have just had an off night. Or maybe he or she wasn't even in Macau."

"Why wouldn't they be? They've been at every major tournament for the last month or so."

"True," Savannah said. "Very true."

"I'm perplexed about it. I think it was a one off. I'm sure they'll strike here in Lisbon and we need to be ready. I think you should think seriously about seducing that woman. If she's our suspect, what better way to catch her?"

"I tell you what. I'll consider it. But I make no promises."

"Fair enough." Li stood. "I think it's time for me to explore Lisbon. See what this city has to offer. When are we meeting as a team?"

"Friday. At four in my suite. I'll see you then?"

"If not before."

After Li left, Savannah went back to bed. She was exhausted. Even though she'd slept hard in Kit's arms. She'd felt safe and secure. Which was dangerous. Because if Kit robbed her, she'd be devastated. She didn't know how she'd allowed her heart to become involved with the rogue, but it had. In a big way.

She woke at five and climbed into a hot bath. It was soothing and relaxing, though the water felt like a lover's caress. And she wanted to feel that in reality so desperately. She hoped against all hope that tonight would be the night that Kit finally gave in and made love to her.

Savannah got out and rinsed off then slipped the fluffy white robe on again. She got on her laptop to check the dress requirements for an evening cruise. As she expected, she needed to dress nicely. Not a problem. She'd had all her dresses dry-cleaned in Macau.

She chose a red, form fitting cocktail dress. She wore ruby earrings and a diamond choker. She checked herself out in the mirror. Was it too much? Was it obvious she was trying to tempt Kit? She didn't know. She exhaled heavily. Savannah grabbed her purse and headed to the street to hail a taxi.

Kit greeted Savannah at the boat slip with a low wolf whistle.

"I swear you're more beautiful every time I see you," she said.

"You're too kind."

"I only speak the truth. Are you ready for that romantic evening we discussed?"

"I'm more than ready."

Kit smiled at her and took her hand.

"Great. Let's do this."

Dinner was delicious and the soft music playing in the background had Kit ready for more than just having Savannah sleep in her arms. She was keyed up. Her hormones were raging. Try as she might to convince herself to wait, it was a losing battle. She knew she had to stay strong, but her heart and other body parts were overruling her brain.

"What are you thinking about?" Savannah said.

"Nothing. Everything. I don't know. Why?"

"You look upset. Is there anything I can help with?"

"You can dance with me."

"I'd love that."

They danced several songs until the closeness of Savannah and the press of the other bodies on the dance floor caused Kit to overheat.

"Let's go on the deck," she said. "I could use some fresh air."

It was windy topside, and Savannah turned her head to keep her hair from blowing in her face. It was a natural move, but so seductive at the same time. Kit couldn't resist. She leaned in and nibbled on Savannah's exposed neck. Savannah shivered.

"What was that for?" Savannah said.

"Does a boi need a reason to nibble her girl's neck?" Savannah leveled a stare at Kit. "What?"

"Am I your girl then?" Savannah said.

"I'd like to think so. That is, unless I'm not the only person you're seeing right now?"

"Oh no. There's no one but you."

"Will you be my girl, Savannah? Or is it too soon for you to move on? Either way, I'll understand."

"I'd like to be your girl, Kit. I need to move on. It's time. And there's no one I'd rather move on with than you."

Kit kissed her then. Under the full moon with several onlookers close by. She didn't care. She was falling hard for Savannah and wanted Savannah to know.

"I really like you, Savannah," Kit said. "Like really."

"I like you, too. As I'm sure I've made perfectly plain by now."

"That you have."

Savannah pulled Kit close and whispered in her ear, "Let it be tonight, Kit. Show me how much I mean to you. Claim me. Make me yours."

Kit's knees went weak. The feel of Savannah's soft breath on her ear, as well as the words she said, made Kit's resolve weaken tremendously. She made up her mind. She'd throw caution to the wind. That night would indeed be the night.

Kit led Savannah to the bow of the boat, and they watched as it was tied to the dock.

"What shall we do now?" Kit said. "The night is still young."

"Let's go back to my suite. Please?"

"Sure, Savannah. We'll go back to your place."

They debarked, caught a taxi, and made out like a couple of teenagers the whole way back to Savannah's hotel. By the time the driver announced they were at their destination, Kit was throbbing with need. Savannah was such a wonderful kisser and her tongue promised talent that Kit couldn't wait to experience.

They kissed some more in the elevator and Kit forced herself not to molest Savannah as she followed her on shaky legs to her rooms. Savannah opened her door and Kit walked in. It was really going to happen. She was going to give in and give herself to Savannah. Savannah would be hers without a doubt after tonight. Kit's gut clenched. Was she really ready? Could she trust Savannah implicitly?

Savannah took Kit's hand and led her to the bedroom. She loosened Kit's tie and pulled her close for another round of kissing that left Kit breathless. When she stepped back to look at Savannah, she saw a flushed face, large pupils, and eyelids that fell to cover half her eyes. She knew that Savannah wanted her. Her response was physical. That was obvious.

Kit stood there shifting her weight from foot to foot. She was as nervous as if this was her first time. God only knew how many women she'd been with, but this was different. This meant something. And she wasn't used to that.

Savannah unclasped the diamonds from her neck and lay them on the dresser. She placed her earrings next to them.

"Shouldn't you put those in the safe?" Kit said.

"Why? You're not going to take them, are you?" She smiled.

Was it a test after all? Was Savannah trying to get her to steal from her? Did she care about Kit at all? The questions crashed through Kit's haze of arousal and suddenly she was aware yet again of why she needed to wait. She needed to find out for sure if Savannah worked for the FBI. She'd asked around, but no one could confirm or deny that for her. Who knew if Savannah was even her real name?

"I need to go," Kit said abruptly.

"Why? Because I won't lock up my jewelry? What's going on, Kit? I don't understand."

"It has nothing to do with the jewelry," Kit lied. "It's just… well…I'm not ready. I thought I was, but I'm not. I'm really sorry."

She turned and made a beeline to the door. Savannah caught up and grabbed her arm.

"Kit, please. What's going on? Talk to me. Tonight you said I was your girl. Treat me like it. Make love to me. What did I do wrong?"

"You didn't do anything wrong, babe. I just need to be certain it's the right thing. And I'm not certain yet."

"When will I see you again?"

"Let's have breakfast around five Sunday morning. After a night at the casino."

"So I won't see you tomorrow?"

"I don't think so," Kit said. "I think I need to do some serious thinking."

"I hope you won't run away, Kit. I really want to be your one and only."

"I want that, too, babe. I really do. Let me get my head on straight, okay?"

"Okay. I'll see you Saturday night then."

CHAPTER FIFTEEN

Savannah latched the door behind Kit and fought tears. Why had Kit run off like that? Was the temptation of the jewels too much for her? Was she in fact the infamous jewel thief after all? The thought was too much for Savannah and the tears spilled. She wiped her cheeks and eyes, but they kept coming. She couldn't stand the thought that she might have to arrest Kit, but reality was reality. She had a job to do. It was just a damned shame her heart had decided to get involved.

She undressed and slid into bed, missing Kit with every fiber of her being. She'd thought the ache would finally be relieved that night. She'd thought Kit was finally ready to seal the deal. And yet, there she was. Alone again. She was tired of being by herself. She longed for someone to share her life with. And she wanted that person to be Kit. Thief or not, she wanted Kit for a life partner.

Savannah woke at noon. She was still feeling morose and not in a mood to deal with anybody. Least of all her team. She didn't want to plant traps to catch the thief. She wanted to forget about the thief, about jewels, about everything. She wanted to go back to Maryland and stay there. And she wanted to take Kit with her.

Her team showed up and she forced herself to focus. They discussed strategies then walked over to the casino to check out the lay of the land. They discussed who needed to be where when and then she dismissed them. She was confident they were ready, and she didn't have the strength to deal with anything else. She just wanted to be alone.

Li walked with her to her hotel.

"Have you given any more thought to what we talked about the other day?" he said.

Savannah's gut churned. She had to make a tough decision. Her job or her personal life? It sucked. It was a no-win situation.

"I'll tell you what," she said. "I'll try to get her to bed tomorrow night. You can wait outside my room for four hours. If she's not out by then, she's not our thief."

"Fair enough, boss. I think you're doing the right thing."

"I hope so." And, if it was the right thing, why did it feel so wrong?

She ordered room service and sat feeling more alone than she'd ever felt. She was just finishing dinner when her phone buzzed. Her heart leaped. It was Kit.

Kit: *I miss you.*

Savannah: *I miss you, too.*

Kit: *I'm sorry about last night. Cold feet and all.*

Savannah: *Just don't let it happen again. LOL.*

Kit: *I won't. I'm scared, Savannah. I haven't felt this way in a very long time.*

Savannah: *I'm right there with you. It's terrifying. Yet, at the same time, so right.*

Kit: *Yeah. Hopefully, I'll be able to go through with it tomorrow night.*

Savannah: *I hope so, Kit. I'm miserable without you.*

Kit: *I hear you. I'll let you go now. See you tomorrow.*

And she was gone. Savannah's hands shook as she set the phone down. Damn Kit for having this effect on her. Damn her for worming her way into her thoughts. And especially damn her for finding her way to Savannah's heart.

She'd torn down the carefully placed wall that had been there for years. A wall that had been built out of self-preservation. A wall that had protected her well. And now it was gone. It was down, and Savannah was exposed. And tomorrow night Savannah had set up a sting to catch Kit in the act of robbing her. She'd never been more miserable.

Savannah forced herself to stay up late watching movies, but finally, at three, she could no longer keep her eyes open. She undressed and climbed into bed. She slept long and hard and woke at two the following afternoon.

Fifteen hours. Only fifteen hours until she saw Kit again. She couldn't wait. She told herself to get it together. She needed to focus on the task at hand first. She needed to try to catch the thief before he or she got away with more jewels.

At eight o'clock, she showered and dressed in a blue gown. She wore diamond and sapphire earrings and a diamond necklace that was worth a small fortune. If she succeeded in seducing Kit that night, her jewels would be far too great a temptation for a thief. She'd know for sure one way or the other. It was only a matter of time.

Savannah slid her gun, key card, badge, and a wad of money into her clutch and took the elevator down. It was time to get to the casino. It was showtime.

She wandered through the casino as nonchalantly as possible, noting where her team was and making sure no one was out of place. Satisfied that everyone was where they were supposed to be, Savannah began making her rounds. She kept her eyes open and was on the lookout for Kit every moment. She finally caught herself. She took a deep breath and began the circuit anew, this time looking for anything or anyone suspicious.

There were older women everywhere decked out in millions of dollars of jewels. She paid close attention to any younger men or women who showed them too much attention. She saw one such young man and approached him.

"Are you enjoying playing blackjack?" Savannah said.

"I am."

"Ma'am. Is this gentleman bothering you?"

"Nonsense," the older woman said, "he's my son."

"Sorry to have bothered you then."

She wandered off, adrenaline coursing through her. She'd been sure she'd been on the right track. Oh, well. There were plenty of other people milling about. It would be up to her to detect the thief in the crowd.

❖

Kit watched Savannah make her way through the casino. She seemed to be on a mission. She followed her from a distance and saw her speak to a woman who was with a younger man at the blackjack table. She wondered what that was about. Did she think the young man might be preying on the older woman?

If so, that could certainly indicate that Savannah was an FBI agent. But it would also seem to indicate that she hadn't made up her mind that Kit was the thief. That was a good thing. Could Kit actually settle down with a law enforcement officer? That went against everything she believed in. But settling down was exactly what she had in mind. She also had it in mind to make love to Savannah that night. She'd do that, not steal from her, and remove herself from the list of suspects. That would help things out tremendously.

But first, before that could happen, Kit needed to find a target. Which meant she'd have to quit following Savannah around like a lost puppy. She wandered through the casino on her own and kept her eyes peeled for any bejeweled woman sitting alone. She'd seduce her, rob her, and then head off to meet Savannah. She smiled to herself. It was going to be a good night.

She spotted a likely mark seemingly by herself watching a craps game.

"Are you going to try your hand?" Kit sidled up and asked.

The woman looked at Kit, glanced back to the table, and then back to Kit.

"Oh, I wouldn't know where to start." She laughed.

"I'd be happy to tutor you," Kit said.

"I'm too fond of my money to throw it away. But thank you."

"Are you here by yourself?"

"No. That's my husband throwing the dice right now."

"He's a fool to be concentrating on that instead of you," Kit said.

"Aren't you a charmer?"

Kit flashed her best smile.

"I just don't think beautiful women should be ignored."

"He'll be playing for hours. I'll keep myself entertained. I'm used to it. But, thank you."

"Well, if you don't think he'll notice if you disappear, may I buy you a drink?"

The woman looked Kit up and down.

"What's your angle?" she asked.

"No angle. I just enjoy spending time with lovely women. And I meant that I hate to see you ignored. Let me show you a good time."

The woman, most likely in her late sixties, with short gray hair and sparkling brown eyes, simply stared at Kit. Kit kept her eyes focused on the woman's eyes and refused to drool over the diamonds she was sporting.

"I don't know," the woman said.

"Aw, come on. He'll never notice and all I'm offering is a drink. Don't deny me. Please?"

The woman laughed and seemed to relax.

"Fine. One drink."

"That's all I'm asking for." Kit smiled again before placing her hand on the small of the woman's back. "I think I saw a bar over this way."

She guided the woman through the crowd and, once they emerged, looked around for any sign of Savannah. Not seeing her, she steered the woman to a bar and led her to a dark table in the back.

"Now, what can I get you to drink?" Kit said.

"Dom Perignon."

Kit arched an eyebrow.

"Impeccable taste. I'll get a bottle."

She was back at the table and poured them each a glass.

"I said one drink."

"One drink. One bottle. Same difference."

"Are you going to try to get me drunk?" But the woman's eyes smiled.

"I just thought we could have a few laughs. No harm, no foul."

"You really are smooth. And so handsome to boot. I bet you seduce a lot of women, don't you?"

Kit shrugged, unwilling to admit the truth.

"I just enjoy the company of attractive women. Is there anything wrong with that?"

"And just what makes me attractive?"

"Your eyes for starters. They're the color of milk chocolate and they glisten when you smile."

"Oh, my. Don't stop. Tell me more."

Kit laughed. She was still unsure whether or not this woman would be up for seduction, but it was certainly worth a shot.

"Your hair shines. It looks soft and silky."

The woman ran her hand over her hair.

"This old mop?"

Kit laughed again.

"That's not a mop. That's a well-cared for head of hair."

"Okay, okay. I won't pester you anymore. You're very sweet and very kind. And you shower me with compliments like I haven't heard since I was a much younger woman."

"Your husband doesn't tell you every day how beautiful you are?"

"Hardly."

"He's a fool."

The woman placed her hand over Kit's.

"You're too kind."

She pulled her hand back but not before Kit ran her thumb along it.

"Tell me about yourself," Kit said. "Where are you from? I detect an accent, but I can't place it."

"I'm from Missouri, if you must know. In the States."

"Ah. A Midwest accent. Got it. I'm from the States, as well."

"I figured. And where are you from?"

"Maryland."

"You don't have an accent. I would have pegged you for West Coast."

"Really? Nope."

"So, what are you doing here? You're not in the tournament. You're not gambling. What brings you to this casino on this night?"

"It's early still. I'll gamble a little later. I love roulette."

"I'd love to watch you play."

"What? And take my attention away from you? That's not going to happen."

"You really are sweet. I'm enjoying you very much. I get the feeling you're dangerous though."

"Dangerous?" Kit said. "How so?"

"Like I'd better stay on my toes with you."

Kit extended her hands, palms up.

"I'm not nefarious in the least. I'm just looking to pass the time, same as you."

"Okay. If you say so. Though I'm not sure I believe you."

"What could I possibly do that would make me dangerous?"

"I don't know. It's just a feeling I get."

"Well, relax. I'll go get another bottle of champagne."

"Another one?" the woman said.

"Sure. Why not? What else would you be doing if not sipping Dom Perignon with me?"

Chapter Sixteen

K it thoroughly enjoyed the woman's company and almost felt bad about planning to rob her. Almost, but not quite. Maybe she was getting soft. Maybe it was time to get out of the game after all. She'd certainly have to give it some serious thought.

"If you were a man, I'd think you were trying to seduce me," the woman said as they finished their second bottle of champagne.

Kit decided it was time to make her move.

"I'd love to seduce you," she said. "I'd love to show you how a beautiful woman should be treated."

"Buy me another bottle of Dom Perignon and I just might let you."

Kit grinned at her.

"You've got yourself a deal."

She purchased another bottle and returned to the table.

"Bring your chair around and sit next to me," the woman said.

Kit faltered. She didn't want to sit with her back to the entrance.

"You come over here. We'll people watch together."

"You're the only person I want to watch. But I'll come join you."

They got situated and Kit placed her arm around the woman's shoulders.

"Isn't this nice?" Kit said.

"Very." She snuggled closer.

Kit was feeling good about things. One more bottle of champagne and the jewels would be hers. Then she'd be free and clear to meet up with Savannah.

"You know, I've never done this before," the woman said.

"What's that? Been with a woman?"

"Cheated on my husband."

"Oh, you mustn't think of it that way," Kit said. "We're just a couple of women having a good time. No more, no less. And after tonight, I'll be out of your life which you can go on living guilt free."

"I like the way you think."

"Thanks. Now, relax and enjoy your champagne."

They finished the bottle and Kit escorted the woman back to her hotel.

"Should we have told your husband we were leaving?" Kit said.

"No. I often leave earlier than he does. It's fine."

Kit pleased the woman in the manner she knew she'd never experienced and lay next to her until she heard the soft snores indicating the woman was asleep. She dressed quietly, pocketed the jewels, and let herself out. Another successful night.

She hailed a taxi and made it back to her place. She stashed the jewels, took a shower, and rode back to the casino. She still had time to play some roulette before she and Savannah were meeting.

Kit was winning. She felt unstoppable. It seemed she could do no wrong that night. She only hoped the next few hours panned out as she planned, as well.

She was just about to place one more bet when she sensed a presence behind her. She turned to see Savannah standing there. Savannah beamed at her and Kit smiled back. She gathered her winnings and left the table.

"Hey there. You look ravishing," Kit said.

"Thank you. I hope I didn't disturb you. You still have time to play some more."

"Nonsense. Let's get out of here."

"Let me powder my nose first. I'll meet you out front."

Kit waited in the cool early morning air. It was crisp and made her feel alive. Her whole night had made her feel more alive than she had in a long time. The robberies were fun, but not that challenging. She had to admit she'd been a little leery about that night's target. She was thinking she might have missed the mark. But then she had turned on the charm, kicked everything up a notch, and ended up with a beautiful haul. She turned when she heard the casino door open and her heart soared at the sight of Savannah.

"All ready," Savannah said.

"Great. Let's get some food. I'm famished."

They wandered into a restaurant that was open twenty-four hours and found a table.

"You look radiant tonight," Savannah said.

"Thanks. I had a really good night."

"Did you win a lot?"

"Babe, I scored big time." She couldn't fight the smile that she felt spread across her face.

"That's great. Winning looks good on you."

"Thank you. And how was your night?"

"I enjoyed myself immensely. I watched the tournament a lot. Poker players fascinate me. I don't have a poker face myself, so I could never play. But I do love to watch."

"Good. Did you play anything yourself?"

"I did. I tried my hand at roulette. And, remembering everything you taught me, I managed to win a little."

"Good for you. That makes me so happy."

"It made me pretty happy, too."

When breakfast was over, Kit took Savannah's hand and they walked back to her hotel.

"What a glorious night," Kit said.

"And a beautiful sunrise."

Kit followed Savannah's gaze and saw the sky highlighted with pink and orange hues. It looked like a painting. It matched her mood, glowing bright. She was with a woman she adored and was about to spend her morning making love to that woman. Life couldn't possibly get any better.

They kissed in the elevator, and Kit knew her hair was a mess from Savannah running her hands through it. She didn't care. She was about to get naked with Savannah. She couldn't care less how she looked at the moment. Savannah wanted her and that was all that mattered.

Kit wondered anew about life on the gambling circuit. They passed several people on the way to Savannah's room and Kit thought about how elsewhere in the world, people, normal people, would be asleep at that hour.

When Savannah's door closed behind them, Kit took her in her arms and held her tight. She felt the swell of Savannah's breasts pressed into her and felt them rise and fall as Kit nibbled her neck, earlobe, then lips.

Savannah's response was visceral. She needed Kit more than ever. And Kit didn't seem to be in any hurry to leave. Could this be the night? Finally?

And then she remembered the diamonds she was wearing. Is that what had Kit so worked up? Would they make love finally only to have Kit steal from her when she dozed? It had all come down to this. It was the moment of truth.

Kit broke the kiss and stood looking into Savannah's eyes. Her deep blue eyes showed her desire and Savannah had to look away.

"Is everything okay?" Kit said.

"Of course. Better than okay." She hoped she sounded more convincing than she felt. She was scared. That was the truth of the matter. In a few hours, Kit could be arrested and taken from her life forever. That's what happened when you fell for a criminal. She had to stop that train of thought and focus only on Kit.

Maybe she wasn't the thief. Maybe she and Savannah could make mad, passionate love then start a calm, restful life together. It was possible, wasn't it?

Her phone buzzed in her purse.

"Who's texting you at this hour?" Kit asked.

"I don't know. Let me check."

She pulled her phone out and walked to the window to read it in privacy.

We're on our way to your suite. There's been another robbery.

Give me a minute.

We're on our way.

"Shit," Savannah said.

"What's up?"

"Bad news. Would you mind if I take a rain check? I need to deal with some stuff."

"I'm sorry. I'll leave. I'll see you soon?"

"Definitely."

She opened the door and kissed Kit good-bye, then dressed in street clothes to go interview the victim. Li and the rest of the team showed up minutes later. They might have even passed Kit. How would that look?

Ugh. She hated the cat and mouse game she and Kit were playing. She wanted to be completely honest with Kit, but was Kit being completely honest with her? She had no way of knowing. The only way to find out would be to sleep with her. With an agent waiting outside the door. Great.

"You ready, boss?" Li said.

"I am. Where are we going?"

"The hotel is only two down from here. The victim is pretty shaken up. She says it was a woman, boss. You may be on to something."

Savannah thought she would be sick. How she wanted to be wrong about Kit. How desperately she wanted her to be innocent. Maybe the woman wasn't Kit. Maybe she'd learn something else when they got there. But she knew better.

They arrived at the room to find the fingerprint team working away. An older woman sat on the bed, dressed in a blue silk robe. Her eyes were red rimmed from crying and her cheeks were splotchy and swollen.

"Hello, Miss...?"

"Mrs. Mrs. Miller. And you are?"

"I'm Agent Brown. I'm the lead on the team. Can you tell me exactly what happened?"

"She was raped." Savannah heard the shout before she saw the large, bald man enter the room with a glass of water. "Some freak took advantage of her and raped her and robbed her."

"Is this true?" Savannah said.

"I wasn't raped," Mrs. Miller said quietly.

"You don't know that. You were passed out. Who knows what that freak of nature did to you while you were asleep?" the man continued to rant.

"Mr. Miller?" Savannah said.

"I am. This is my wife. She's clearly been taken advantage of."

"Okay," Savannah said. "Now, I really need to hear the story in your wife's own words. Would you mind waiting in the other room for a few?"

"Fine. But then I'll tell you what really happened."

"That would be great. Officer Nguyen here will take your statement."

Li shot her a look but dutifully followed Mr. Miller to the sitting area. When they were out of earshot, Savannah turned her attention back to Mrs. Miller.

"I wasn't raped," she said again. "Nothing happened. Not like that."

"Okay. So what did happen?"

"A nice woman walked me back to my room. I must have passed out and when my husband got home, we discovered that my diamonds were missing."

"Your diamonds are insured, aren't they?"

"Of course. But they were a family heirloom so they're irreplaceable."

"I'm sorry. Now, can you describe this woman to me?"

Mrs. Miller shook her head.

"Not really. I'd already had a few drinks when she approached me. She offered to buy me a drink. Several bottles of champagne later, we came back here."

"Several bottles? That must have taken some time to consume. So you must have noticed something about her. What color hair did she have? What was she wearing?"

"She had dark hair."

"Short or long?"

Mrs. Miller shook her head.

"I want to say short, but I can't be sure."

"And her attire?" Savannah probed.

"I'm pretty sure she was wearing a black suit."

"Like a tux?"

"I can't remember."

Savannah exhaled.

"Mrs. Miller, we really want to catch whoever is behind this. So I need you to think as hard as you can and tell me anything you remember."

"Her eyes," Mrs. Miller said.

"What about them?"

"They were blue. Bright blue. And so expressive."

Savannah's stomach roiled. She knew one person who had the bluest eyes she'd ever seen. Fighting overwhelming nausea, she stood and handed Mrs. Miller her card.

"If you can think of anything else that might help, please don't hesitate to call."

"Please catch her. I want my diamonds back."

Savannah didn't have the heart to tell her they'd probably already been fenced by then.

"We'll do our best."

Li walked into the room.

"All through here?" he said.

"Yes. Did you get any information from the husband?"

"Quite an earful."

"Okay. Let's head back to my suite and compare notes."

They arrived at Savannah's suite at eight thirty. She was exhausted and frustrated and sick to her stomach. But she was working a case. That was the single most important thing in her life at the moment. She needed to get her priorities straight once and for all.

CHAPTER SEVENTEEN

"What did you learn?" Li asked. "Was it the woman you've suspected all along?"

Savannah took a deep breath before she spoke.

"It could be. It could very well be. Mrs. Miller couldn't describe her very well. She couldn't say how long her hair was or what she was wearing. The woman I suspect was wearing a tux last night. I'd think Mrs. Miller would remember that. But she didn't. The only thing concrete we have to go on is that the suspect has blue eyes."

"And the woman you're after? Does she have blue eyes?"

"She does indeed."

"This is great. This is awesome. Let's bring your suspect in for questioning. Like now."

"Because she has blue eyes? That's hardly reasonable. I'll continue to work on her. Now, what did the husband say?"

"Something about a deviant who took advantage of his wife's naiveté. You heard his theory. He's sticking by it. Do you think that woman took advantage of Mrs. Miller?"

Savannah didn't want to think about it. The concept of Kit sharing the bed of another woman didn't sit well with her.

"I don't know," she said. "I think it's another case of a rich woman being seduced by a young charmer. I do believe they slept together. And then she robbed Mrs. Miller. I, however, believe the sex was consensual. There's something about this woman that makes older women unable to say no. She's dangerous. She's a menace. And we have to catch her."

She fought the tears that threatened. She didn't like describing Kit that way. She was so sure it was her again and she hated that the woman she was falling for was a cold, manipulative criminal.

"So are you going to seduce her?" Li said.

This made the other team members sit up straighter. They were focused on her. She had their undivided attention.

"That's the plan. I'll keep you all posted. Now go get some sleep. I'll see you all Friday."

They left, and Savannah stripped and climbed into bed. She checked her phone before falling asleep and there was a text from Kit. Shit. Why did her heart skip a beat when she saw it? She needed to be cool.

Worried about you. Everything okay?

Fine. I just had some stuff to deal with.

She waited but there was no answer. Kit was probably sawing logs. Something Savannah needed to do. She closed the drapes and fell sound asleep.

It was three o'clock in the afternoon when Savannah finally awoke. She stretched, kicked off the covers, and reached for her phone. There was another text from Kit.

I'm glad you're okay. Lunch?

Savannah checked the time on the text. Two hours before. Damn. She wondered if Kit would be up for dinner.

Savannah: *Sorry. Just woke up. How about an early dinner?*

Kit: *Sounds great. I'll pick you up at five?*

Savannah: *Excellent. See you then.*

Kit: *I can't wait.*

Savannah: *Me, either.*

And as she typed it, she realized it was true. She missed Kit. She couldn't wait to see her again. Who cared if she happened to have blue eyes? That didn't make her the guilty party. Or did it?

Savannah let the tears wash over her face. She was so torn. Her heart was fully vested in Kit. But her mind and soul were one hundred percent into catching the thief. She could only hope against hope they weren't one and the same.

She got out of bed and took a long shower. She dressed in a long gray skirt and a pink blouse. She looked dressy enough to go somewhere nice and casual enough to go anywhere. Happy, she slipped on her shoes and waited. Kit should be there soon.

Savannah was reviewing her notes when she heard the knock on her door. She quickly tossed the notes in the safe, closed and locked it, and answered the door.

Kit looked adorable in charcoal slacks and a long-sleeved black shirt. She smelled heavenly and Savannah thought about skipping dinner and having Kit for dessert.

"Hey, babe," Kit said. "Invite me in?"

"Sure. Come on in."

Kit kissed her. Hard, passionately, with a sense of desperation. Savannah kissed her back tenfold. She needed Kit. Wanted to have her completely. And to be had by her. In every meaning of the word.

The kiss ended and Kit exhaled heavily.

"Come on," she said. "If we don't leave now, we just may end up skipping dinner."

"I wouldn't complain."

Kit's stomach growled loudly.

"Ah, but I would. I skipped lunch today. And you haven't eaten in like twelve hours. You've got to be starving."

"I am. We could order room service."

"And waste an opportunity to show off how good you look? Not a chance. Let's go. I saw a restaurant up the street I'd like to try. It's a steakhouse. And I'm jonesin' for a steak."

"Fine." Savannah had to laugh at how cute Kit was. "We'll go have dinner."

Since it was early on a Sunday evening, they didn't have to wait long to be seated. They perused their menus, placed their orders, and sat back gazing into each other's eyes. Kit shook her head.

"What?"

"I don't know. I don't know how you've melted the ice I keep in place around me."

"Is that a bad thing?"

"The jury's still out on that."

Savannah felt her face fall.

"Why?"

"Because I'm not sure about you yet. I want to be. God, how I want to be. But what if you're not the perfect woman I've built you up to be?"

"Nobody's perfect, Kit."

"You know what I mean. Besides, you're damned close."

"And what about you?" Savannah said. "How do I know you don't have some deep, dark secret you're keeping from me."

Kit glanced out the window for a long minute. Then looked back at Savannah.

"You'll just have to trust me."

Alarm bells rang in Savannah's head. Would she ever know the truth behind Kit? Did Kit have secrets? Was seducing and robbing women one of them?

"Trust you? I suppose I have no choice."

Kit felt horrible. She hated deceiving Savannah. But she had to. Especially if Savannah was the agent Kit believed she was.

"So where to next?" Kit said.

"South Africa. You?"

"Klerksdorp?"

"That's the place. Will I see you there?"

"You will indeed. There's a huge tournament going on there. We'll have to plan on spending some time together. If you'd like."

Savannah beamed at her.

"I'd like nothing more."

"Great. So that's settled. When do you arrive?"

"Tomorrow. Late. What about you?"

"Same. So shall we plan on lunch Tuesday?" Kit was hopeful Savannah didn't feel smothered. But she couldn't get enough of her. She wanted to spend every waking hour with her. And, hopefully, some sleeping hours, as well.

"That would be wonderful."

"Excellent. I was planning on hitting the animal sanctuary Wednesday if you'd like to join me."

"That sounds like a lot of fun. Let's do it."

"Consider it done. I'll make all the arrangements."

"Thank you."

By the time they finished dinner, every nerve ending in Kit's body tingled with anticipation. She wished she could make love to Savannah that night but knew it wouldn't happen. Maybe Tuesday night? Or Wednesday? Hell, why not both? She smiled.

"What are you thinking?" Savannah asked. "What's that shit eating grin for?"

"Just thinking of all the fun we'll have in Klerksdorp."

"We will have a good time, won't we, Kit?"

"I promise you. And now, I should get you back to your hotel."

"What's the hurry?"

"We both need to pack and we both have long days ahead of us tomorrow. Flying takes a lot out of you. So I'll walk you home, say good night. And then we'll spend all Tuesday afternoon and evening together."

"And night?" Savannah looked hopeful.

Kit smiled at her.

"One never knows. You may be tired of me by then."

"I don't think I could ever be tired of you, Kit."

Kit stopped where she stood and turned to look at Savannah.

"Do you mean that? I mean, honestly?"

"I do."

"You've just made me the happiest woman on earth."

"Good. Now we just need for you to do the same for me." She grinned lasciviously.

"I plan to, Savannah. Believe me. It's on my agenda."

"That's good to hear."

They got off the elevator and started walking to Savannah's room.

"Hey. I meant to ask you. Was there some kind of commotion on your floor last night or I guess early this morning?"

"Not that I know of. Why?"

"I saw a bunch of suits get off the elevator. They looked like government types. They were in a hurry. They all seemed awfully serious. I just wondered what was up."

Savannah shrugged.

"Beats me."

They'd arrived at Savannah's door. Kit said nothing more about the agents she'd seen. She knew FBI when she saw them. It didn't occur to her until she was on the ground floor that she should have watched to see if they went to Savannah's room. That would have been the smart thing to do. But she was sure they had.

Why had she let Savannah get so close? What did she want from Kit? Did she really want forever? Or was that an empty promise? Well, the woman in her may have caught Kit's heart, but there was no way the agent would catch Kit. No way in hell.

"You want to come in for a night cap?" Savannah said. "It's so early."

"It is early. And I'd love a drink. Thanks."

Savannah poured them each a drink.

"You know," Savannah said, "we could make love for a few hours and still get plenty of rest for our flights."

"Ah. Nice try. But we need to pack. And I'm not going to make love to you tonight, Savannah. I'm still working things out."

"When then? In Klerksdorp?"

"I hope so."

"What are you working out? I'm crazy about you and you seem to feel the same. Unless it's all an act?"

"No, babe. Definitely not an act. You get the real deal. The side of me most people never see. I just get nervous thinking about the enormity of making love to you."

"I'm just a woman, Kit. Don't you dare put me on a pedestal."

Kit laughed, mostly to relieve the tension.

"I can't help it. I do hold you to higher standards because I really care about you."

"Well, if you put me too high, I'm bound to crumble. I'm only human."

"I won't put you too high. Just high enough for me to strive for."

"That's fair. Now, if you're not going to stay the night, kiss me good night and I'll see you in South Africa."

Kit was happy to oblige. They kissed and kissed and kissed some more. Savannah wrapped her leg around Kit and pulled her closer. Kit came to her senses. If she didn't leave then, she'd never leave.

She ended the kiss and leaned her forehead on Savannah's.

"Okay. Okay. I'm leaving. Travel safe, babe. I'll text you when I land. You do the same."

"I will. Good night, Kit."

Kit planted one more kiss on Savannah's swollen lips and let herself out. She heard Savannah latch the door behind her. She was restless, keyed up. Her hormones were racing through her body at breakneck speed.

When she got back to where she was staying, she went for a walk. It was in a quiet residential neighborhood and it was still early enough for her to feel safe. After a couple of hours, she let herself back into the house she was renting. She began the tedious process of picking up her messes and packing. She'd definitely need a dry cleaner in Klerksdorp. That would be the first order of business. After seeing Savannah again.

Savannah. Don't put her on a pedestal? Too late. Sort of. She adored her. Admired her. Craved her. But she also knew Savannah's main goal in life was to throw Kit in prison. For a very long time. Still, she couldn't stay away. She sent her a text.

Kit: *Thinking of you.*

Savannah: *You're so sweet. I'm thinking of you, too. Why don't you come over?*

Kit : *LOL. Very funny. Get some sleep, my dear. I'll connect with you tomorrow.*

Savannah: *Can't blame a girl for trying. Sleep well, Kit.*

Kit: *Good night, babe.*

Savannah: *Good night.*

Kit smiled to herself as she finished packing. South Africa was next on her agenda. South Africa with Savannah. She couldn't wait.

CHAPTER EIGHTEEN

Savannah landed in Klerksdorp at eight the next evening. She was tired and hungry. Hungry for food and hungry for Kit. Her hunger for the latter was a deep, throbbing ache. One only Kit could soothe. She knew she'd wait until Kit was ready though. She'd be worth it. Savannah was sure. And then there was that nasty business of the jewel thief they were out to catch. She'd have to stick close to Kit until Kit robbed her or they solved the crimes.

She'd worked herself into a foul mood by the time she exited the plane. She went to baggage claim, picked up her bags, and hailed a taxi.

It was chilly there. It was the wrong season to be in the Southern Hemisphere. Yet there she was. She pulled her coat tighter around her as she slid into the cab and told the driver she was staying at the casino.

She sat back and watched the city speed by. Her phone rang. She glanced at it. It was her boss. Shit. This wouldn't be good.

"Hello?"

"Nguyen tells me you have a suspect you haven't interviewed."

"That's not entirely true, sir," Savannah said.

"You mean you still have no suspects? What do you think your job is? A paid vacation?"

Savannah rolled her eyes.

"No, sir. There's one woman who may, and I emphasize may, be a suspect. All we know at this point is she has the same color eyes as the person we're looking for. I'm tailing her closely and plan to catch her in the act soon."

"You better, Brown. Or I'll have you stateside so fast it'll make your head spin."

"Yes, sir. I understand."

The line went dead. Shit. The last thing she wanted was to turn over the investigation to someone else. She needed to catch Kit in the act. That was all there was to it.

She moved to slide her phone back into her coat pocket when it buzzed.

Kit: *Hey, babe. You on the ground yet? How about dinner?*

Savannah: *Just got in a cab. I'll be ready for dinner in an hour.*

Kit: *Are you at the casino?*

Savannah: *Yes. I'll text you my room number as soon as I know it.*

Kit: *I'll be waiting. See you in an hour.*

Savannah forgot all about the conversation with her boss. She'd be seeing Kit soon, so all was right in her world. She got out of the taxi and went inside the elaborate casino. The bellman took her bags and placed them on his cart. He followed her to the registration desk and waited patiently while she got her key.

She led him to her room and tipped him generously. She needed to unpack, and the bed looked awfully inviting, but she had more important things on her mind. She grabbed her toiletries and took a long, hot shower. She lathered the rich oil all over her body and was acutely aware of each drop of water that cascaded over her needy nipples as she rinsed.

She dressed in a long black leather skirt and a black sweater. She slid her feet into warm black boots and was ready for Kit. She texted Kit her room number and poured herself a glass of wine while she waited.

Kit was there ten minutes later and as soon as Savannah saw her, she pulled her in for a kiss. It was soul searing and Savannah's heart raced at an irregular pace.

"I've missed you," she said.

"So I see. Don't get me wrong. I'm not complaining. Show me again how much you've missed me."

"Save room for dessert," Savannah said. "There'll be plenty of time for more of that after dinner."

"Promise?" Kit moved in for another kiss. Savannah placed her hands on Kit's chest.

"I promise. Now, let's get some food."

"Fine. If you insist. Do you like sushi?"

"I adore it."

"Then, have I found a restaurant for you."

Kit wrapped her arm around Savannah, and they walked out to the elevator. Savannah was very proud of herself. She'd wanted to let Kit take her right then. It had been so tempting. But she'd stayed strong. And now she was walking on rubbery legs alongside Kit.

Dinner. Who the hell cared about dinner? Damn. Would tonight be the night that Kit finally caved? God, how she hoped it would be.

They arrived at the bright, clean restaurant and read over the menus. Though Savannah could hardly concentrate. Kit's legs were extended under the table and their ankles were rubbing. The sensation made Savannah's head spin. She slid her ankles back under her chair and pretended not to notice when Kit lowered her menu to look at her.

They ordered then sat back with their Saki. Savannah just knew she was in for a treat. At least for dinner. And she held her breath for afterward.

After dinner, they took a nighttime tour of the city, which was romantic but cold. They took a taxi back to Savannah's suite and Savannah sat on the heater as soon as they got there.

"What are you doing?" Kit said.

"I'm freezing. Aren't you?"

"I'm chilly. I thought maybe we could warm each other up."

"I do like the sound of that. Come over here and warm me up."

Kit grinned that boyish grin and Savannah's heart melted. She was so damned cute. It wasn't fair.

"You don't have to ask me twice." Kit crossed the room and pulled Savannah up. "I believe someone promised me more after dinner."

Her voice was husky, and Savannah squeezed her legs together. She was swollen and wet and ready for Kit in a way she'd never been ready for another woman. Not even the love of her life who she'd lost in such a horrific fashion. No one. Not a single woman had ever taken her where she knew Kit could. And would. Hopefully soon.

Kit kissed her and Savannah's toes curled. She felt that kiss in every atom of her being. Damn but she needed Kit. She made up her mind to not take no for an answer.

"Come to bed with me, Kit. Please. I'm begging you."

"Lead the way."

Had Savannah heard correctly?

"Are you sure?" she said.

"Are you trying to give me time to change my mind?"

"No. Hell, no. Come on."

She took Kit's hand and led her to the bedroom. They lay on the bed and kissed some more until Savannah thought she would explode from pure desire. Kit was the perfect kisser and she knew she'd be the perfect lover, as well.

"I need you. Like, now."

Kit laughed softly.

"Impatient, huh?"

"We've kissed enough. Time for the good stuff."

"Yes, ma'am."

Savannah lay back and let Kit undress her. Kit kissed, nibbled, and sucked every inch of skin as she exposed it. Soon Savannah was shivering all over. Her excitement was greater than it had ever been.

Once Kit had Savannah naked, she stripped and lay next to her again. Savannah wrapped her legs around Kit as they kissed. She reveled in the feel of Kit's naked body against hers. She was ready to give herself to Kit. Willingly and completely.

Kit kissed down Savannah's neck and chest. The ache between Savannah's legs was almost unbearable. And then, from somewhere, she had a thought. This might be the last time she saw Kit. If Kit took the diamonds lying on the dresser and left, Savannah would never see her again. It made her sad and distracted from all she was feeling. She pushed the thoughts from her mind and lost herself in the sensations Kit was creating. If she had to say good-bye to Kit, this was how she'd want to do it.

Kit couldn't get enough of Savannah. Her skin was soft and sweet. She tasted delicious and felt amazing. She was enjoying the anticipation of claiming her completely. Soon. But first, she'd explore.

And explore she did. She kissed and sucked every inch of her, committing her to memory. She wanted to remember each groan, each shiver, each goose bump forever. There would never be another first time with Savannah and Kit wanted it to be perfect.

Kit claimed every speck of Savannah's skin with her lips and tongue. She voraciously loved on her nipples which took Savannah to an early orgasm.

"That's never happened before. I'm kind of embarrassed," Savannah said.

"Don't be. I think it's wonderful that you can come from nipple play."

"But it means I was overexcited. And I came too soon."

"Does that mean you don't have any more in you?"

Savannah laughed, a breathy sound that spurred Kit's hormones onward.

"Hell, no. There's plenty more where that came from."

Kit didn't answer. She went back to savoring the hardened points of Savannah's breasts until her own need urged her downward. She sucked on Savannah's inner thighs, leaving marks that no one else would see. They were mementos for Savannah and Savannah alone. And maybe Kit? Did she dare to dream she and Savannah might sleep together again? She had no idea, so planned to make the most of her opportunity.

When she could hold out no longer, Kit gave in and tasted Savannah. She was delicious, sweet and musky. Just as Kit had known she would be. Kit cherished Savannah's flavor as she swirled her tongue in her and over her. She licked as deep as she could get, coating her tongue with Savannah's essence.

Savannah's nerve center was swollen and slick and Kit finally turned her attention to it. She expertly licked and sucked on it until

Savannah arched off the bed, froze, and cried out. Kit lapped up the remnants of her orgasm then kissed her way up Savannah's body until she took her in her arms.

"That was amazing." Savannah sounded half asleep.

"Good, baby. You sleep now." She kissed the top of her head.

"Mm."

Kit lay there listening to Savannah's soft breathing. She was filled with satisfaction and pride at having been able to please Savannah so soundly. But there was something else she was feeling. Could it be? She pushed the feelings down deep inside of her.

Savannah was beautiful, exquisite, and easy to please. But she was also an FBI agent. That thought came crashing into Kit's mind, unbidden. It was like a cold shower after their euphoric lovemaking. She wanted to pull her arm out from under Savannah, get dressed, and get out of there. But she couldn't make herself do that. She had fallen too hard to let go now. She'd just have to see how everything played out.

Kit finally dozed, but it wasn't a restful sleep. She dreamed that she'd been arrested by Savannah. It was a horrible, sickening dream, and she woke up drenched in a cold sweat.

"Are you okay?" Savannah's voice was soft, filled with concern and sleep.

"Sorry. Just a bad dream. Go back to sleep, babe."

"Do you want to talk about it?"

God, no!

"No, thanks. I'll be fine. Snuggle in close against me and I'll go back to sleep."

Kit finally fell back asleep after watching the clock on the nightstand pass four thirty. She wasn't disturbed by her dreams then. She dreamed she had a harem and was taking her turn pleasing the women. She woke with a painful need to take Savannah again.

She found Savannah awake and watching her.

"What?" Kit said.

"You're cute when you sleep."

Kit was glad she didn't blush, or she was sure she would have been beet red.

"Thanks?"

Savannah chuckled.

"Yes. It was a compliment."

Kit ended the conversation with a powerful kiss. They kissed forever, until Kit thought she would lose her mind. Desire coursed through her, threatening to short circuit her brain. She slid her hand between Savannah's legs and found her ready for more.

She entered Savannah, slowly and tenderly. Savannah arched off the bed, demanding Kit go deeper. She was happy to oblige. Savannah was so soft and silky, and Kit wanted to keep her fingers inside forever.

Savannah clamped down hard around her fingers as she let out a tortured scream, which grew louder then settled to a whimper as she found her release.

Chapter Nineteen

Savannah lay basking in the afterglow of Kit's lovemaking. She'd never felt more complete, never imagined she could be this happy. There was more to her happiness than the orgasms Kit coaxed from her.

There was the fact that Kit was still there in the morning. As were Savannah's diamonds. She could finally cross Kit off her list of suspects. She was flooded with relief. She couldn't wipe the smile off her face. Maybe it was time to seriously consider a future with Kit. Maybe it was time to tell her about her job and everything else she'd been keeping secret. Something told her to hold off though. It wasn't time. Not yet. Hopefully soon.

"You have the most beautiful smile." Kit was looking down at her. "I could wake up to that smile every day."

"You could, huh?"

"Does that scare you?"

"Not at all."

"Good."

Kit took Savannah again and left her breathless and satiated. Savannah could wake up to Kit's lovemaking every day. She was in heaven. Maybe this was what all that soul mate talk was about. Kit really did seem to be the perfect match.

"We should go downstairs for breakfast," Savannah said. "I'm famished and I know you've worked up an appetite."

"That I have." Kit grinned. "But my clothes are a wrinkled mess. I need to go home and shower and change. I'll meet you back here in an hour or so?"

"Don't be silly. We'll shower here then I'll run down to one of the shops and pick you up some slacks and a sweater. See? Problem solved."

"I'll have to insist you take my credit card," Kit said.

"Don't be ridiculous. Now, let's get in the shower so we can get this ball rolling."

The shower had plenty of room for both of them though they were pressed together much of the time. They kissed then kissed some more. Kit dropped to her knees and buried her face in Savannah, taking her to new heights yet again.

Kit was by far the best lover Savannah had ever been with. Not that she'd been with very many women. Barely a handful. But Kit stood head and shoulders above the rest.

Once they were dry, Savannah dressed, kissed Kit, and left her sitting there in her boxers and undershirt. Savannah promised to hurry back as she was starving and couldn't wait to get some food in her system.

But once she was in the shop, she forgot about food. She had so much fun shopping for Kit. She bought a couple pairs of slacks, one black and one charcoal. She found a pair of 501's, two sweaters, and a hoodie. She spent over seven hundred dollars, but it was worth it. She checked her watch as she walked out of the store. She'd been gone over an hour. Kit was probably worried about her.

Savannah hurried back to the room to find Kit pacing.

"I thought you'd run away," Kit said. "Didn't you get my texts?"

"Sorry," Savannah said sheepishly. "I didn't check my phone. And I lost track of time. Forgive me?"

"You're back now so of course I forgive you." Kit kissed Savannah and soon she couldn't stand any longer. Her legs were weak, and her center throbbed. Kit took her back to bed and alleviated the ache as only she could.

"So what's in all the bags?" Kit asked when they were both breathing regularly.

"Just some stuff for you."

Kit arched an eyebrow.

"I thought you were getting me something to wear to breakfast. Which has morphed into lunch by the way."

"Sorry. And I did. But I found more and more things to buy you. I couldn't resist. You're going to look so handsome."

Kit laughed.

"If you say so. Okay. Fine. Let's see what you bought."

Savannah laid her purchases out on the bed.

"Damn. Your taste is impeccable," Kit said.

"Thank you."

"What shall I wear to lunch?"

"The jeans and the hoodie. I think you're going to look stunning."

"If you say so."

Kit pulled on the Levi's and slipped the eggplant colored hoodie over her head. Savannah whistled at her.

"That hoodie really brings out those eyes of yours," she said.

"Thank you." Kit kissed her. "Now let's go get food before I waste away to nothing."

After lunch, during which they'd each had two Bloody Marys they climbed back into bed and took a booze snooze. Savannah awoke to Kit licking her inner thighs and felt her center clench with need.

Once again, Kit expertly made love to her, coaxing two more orgasms out of her. She passed out again and woke an hour later in an empty bed.

She sat straight up and looked at her dresser. The diamonds were still there. That was a relief.

"Kit?" she called. "Where are you?"

Kit came in from the sitting room, dressed and looking adorable.

"I'm right here, babe. I was just watching TV. Are you okay? You look like you've seen a ghost."

Savannah lay back down.

"I'm fine. I just thought you were gone."

"Nope. I'm not going anywhere. At least not at the moment."

"Good. You really like me, don't you, Kit?"

"Very much. Why?"

"I was thinking. Maybe we should stay together on our trips. There's really no reason for us each to have a place. Wouldn't you agree?"

"Let me think on that, okay? What you say makes good sense. But I need to ponder it."

"Of course," Savannah said. "You weigh the pros and cons. I'm fine either way. I just thought it made more sense."

It did make sense. Logically. But Kit couldn't stay with Savannah. She needed a place to stash the jewels after a job. And she wanted to be free during nights when there was a tournament so she could find women and steal from them. Of course, if she agreed to it, how would Savannah explain needing to do her own thing at the casino. Would she admit she was an FBI agent? Would she tell Kit about the jewel thief she was after?

Kit decided she'd rather not hear it. She needed her own place for her own reasons. She changed the subject.

"Would you like to go see an animal sanctuary?" she said.

"I'd love to. When?"

"Oh. I suppose it's too late to go now."

"I think so."

"Okay. So, tomorrow?"

"That sounds great. We'll get an early start and make a day of it."

"Right. So, what shall we do now?"

Savannah looked from Kit to the empty space next to her. Kit certainly couldn't say no. She made short order of her clothes and lay next to Savannah.

She made love to her for the next couple of hours. She teased her, drawing Savannah close before backing off again. She kept at it until Savannah begged. Kit took her to a climax that left Savannah shuddering in its wake.

They dozed again and when Kit woke up, she heard the shower. She got up and joined Savannah for the second time that day. She pleased Savannah again, then showered and helped Savannah get dry.

While Savannah did her hair and put on her face, Kit dressed in new charcoal slacks and a thick black sweater. She felt good and was ready for a night on the town with her girl.

"So, what's on the agenda for tonight?" Savannah emerged looking breathtaking.

"I thought dinner and dancing."

"Sounds good. Then maybe we can come back here and gamble before bed?"

Kit took Savannah's hands in hers.

"Would that make you happy?"

"Yes. I believe it would."

"Then that's what we shall do."

She kissed her then and felt her world tilt off its axis. Savannah was such a good kisser. The fact was, she was good at everything. And now she owned Kit's heart. Not that Kit was ready to admit that to Savannah. No. It would be her little secret.

They went to dinner, then found a disco and danced the night away. Savannah was a hell of a dancer. She could really move on the floor. Kit enjoyed watching her, but it was when Savannah was in her arms during the slow songs that Kit felt all was right in the world.

When four o'clock rolled around, Kit and Savannah left the disco and took a cab back to the casino. There they played roulette with Kit raking in the winnings and Savannah trying to choose numbers different from Kit and not doing well at all.

They laughed, played, and drank until Kit could no longer keep her hands off of Savannah.

"I need you. Now," she whispered in Savannah's ear.

"Ready when you are."

"Let's get back to the room."

Kit made love to Savannah in a hurried, rushed fashion. There was no time for teasing and flirting. Her need to have Savannah was complete and she dove right in and took Savannah over the edge.

With the edge taken off, she pulled Savannah into her arms and held her. That night, Kit slept like a baby. She was relaxed, at ease, with nothing weighing on her mind. She'd started stressing about the job coming up but tamped her fears down. She'd be able to pull it off. She was sure of it.

Kit woke later that morning. She was alone in bed. She dressed in her jeans and hoodie again and went looking for Savannah. She found her asleep on the couch. Her neck was at a funny angle, so Kit woke her gently.

"Babe?"

"Hm?"

"Babe, why are you sleeping on the couch?"

Savannah looked around, clearly disoriented.

"Oh yeah," she said. "I thought I was awake and didn't want to disturb you, so I came out here to watch TV. I must have dozed."

"Okay. Well if you're awake now, get dressed and we'll go get some food then check out the sanctuary."

Savannah's eyes lit up.

"Oh. Okay. Sure. I'll get a move on."

While Savannah got ready, Kit researched sanctuaries in the area.

"What would you like to see?" Kit leaned against the counter where Savannah was applying her makeup.

"What are my choices? You know what? Never mind. You decide."

"If you don't mind, I'd like to see the elephants and monkeys."

"Oh, yay. Monkeys are my favorites."

"Mine, too. Excellent. I'm glad that's settled."

They started with the elephants. They walked with them and pet them. Kit was astounded at how huge they really were. One of them knocked Savannah over and Kit's heart skipped a beat. The workers got her up and settled. It had scared the shit out of Kit though.

"Maybe we should go back to the hotel," she said.

"I'm fine. Really. But I think I'm ready to see the monkeys."

The monkeys were a hoot and they got up close and personal with them as they walked through the forests on the elevated wooden walkways.

Kit held tightly to Savannah's hand and made sure nothing bad happened to her again. They spent several hours with the monkeys then headed back to the hotel.

"Did you want to get some dinner?" Kit said.

"I think I'd like to relax first. I'm still a little shaken."

"I'm sure."

They got back to the room and Kit settled on the couch.

"What are you doing?" Savannah asked.

"I thought I'd let you have a lie down for a bit."

"I was hoping you'd join me."

"Really? Okay. But no hanky-panky."

"Are you serious?"

"I think you need your rest."

"In that case, I'm going to soak in a hot bath."

Kit stood.

"I'll come wash your back."

"Easy there, turbo. Let me soak for a bit. I'll call you when I'm ready for you."

Kit sat back down and cooled her jets for the next half hour until Savannah finally called her in.

"Are you a prune now?" Kit said.

Savannah laughed.

"No, but I'm much more relaxed."

Kit scrubbed Savannah's back and then her front. She was all worked up and barely gave Savannah time to dry before she took her to bed once again.

CHAPTER TWENTY

Kit was disoriented when she awoke Saturday afternoon. It took her a moment to remember that Savannah was not next to her and she was in her Airbnb and not in Savannah's suite. She felt alone, so very alone, but only for a moment. Then she remembered why she was actually in Klerksdorp. She had a job to do. People were waiting for the jewels and she could always use more money.

Not that she wasn't already filthy rich. She could easily retire and live out her life in comfort. But is that what she wanted? She thought of waking up every morning in Maryland or California with Savannah. She would start her day making love to her then they'd spend the rest of the day doing whatever they pleased. If they were in California, she could teach Savannah to surf. If they were in Maryland, Kit could finally have a garden. Or maybe two. She'd plant vegetables in one and flowers in another. She smiled to herself. Yes. She thought she just might be ready to do that.

But that was in the future. Her relationship with Savannah was still so new. But Kit knew what she wanted from it. She wanted forever.

She got out of bed, pulled on some sweats, and walked down the street to a deli. She bought lunch and took it back to her place. She sent Savannah a text.

Kit: *Hated waking up without you.*

Savannah: *You didn't have to.*

Kit: *I know. But this way we're both rested for our big night.*

Savannah: *I suppose. Can't believe I won't see you until five am.*
Kit: *I'll make it worth your while.*
Savannah: *I'm going to hold you to that.*
Kit: *LOL. Please do. I'll see you then.*
Savannah: *Have fun tonight.*
Kit: *You, too.*

Kit almost added not to work too hard, but Savannah still hadn't fessed up to being an FBI agent and Kit didn't want to let her know she suspected her. So she let the conversation end and set out for a longer walk after lunch.

She loved the sights and sounds of South Africa. Klerksdorp had a very comfortable feel to it. When she returned from her walk, she hit the shower then dressed for her night at the casino. She slipped into her Hugo Boss tuxedo with a black shirt. Silver dice worked as both cuff links and tie clip. She added a gray tie and pocket square and was ready to go.

Kit rode to the casino in a hired car. It was how she preferred to get around, finding them more elegant than taxis. Plus, she wanted to make an entrance. Who knew? Her victim might see her pull up. She had to consider that.

There was quite a crowd milling about as she pulled up. She got out of the car and surveyed the area for any sign of Savannah or a single older woman. Seeing neither, she strutted to the door and let herself in.

The place was teeming with people. She knew it was the fifth largest casino in the world, but that still hadn't prepared her for the sheer number of people. They were all dressed to the nines, with men in tuxes and women wearing hundreds of thousands of dollars of jewels.

Her palms itched. The game was on. Kit made a pass past the roulette tables. She spotted Savannah in a floor length sea foam gown. The sight of her took Kit's breath away. She was stunning. And she was sporting enough diamonds to make Kit drool.

Kit managed to tear herself away from the vision lest she be seen. She pushed through the crowds and covered every inch of the casino looking for a likely target. But there were people everywhere and no one seemed to be alone. So it would be a challenge. And Kit loved a challenge.

On her second trip through the slots, a man got up just as Kit walked by. She took his vacated chair and slipped a hundred-dollar bill into the machine. She glanced to her left. A woman who looked to be in her mid-thirties sat there focused on her game. To her right sat a cigar smoking bald man. Great. Oh well. The night was young, so she'd just get comfortable and play for a while. She was nothing if not patient.

"These machines are thieves," the young woman said.

Kit laughed.

"That they are. Just relax and have fun."

"Easy for you to say. You're winning."

She cashed out and walked off. Kit was still grinning when she heard a sexy South African accent.

"Is this seat taken?"

She turned to see a statuesque dark woman with cornrows pulled into a bun on the top of her head. Her hair had some gray in it and there were lines around her eyes but, damn, she was gorgeous.

"Please, have a seat." Kit stood while the woman sat.

"Do tell if you please. What exactly are we playing here?"

"It's about ants on a picnic. The bonus rounds are fairly entertaining."

The stranger folded her arms across her chest.

"Hm. I'm not sure I'm interested."

"Just try it, okay? On me?"

Kit slid a twenty into the woman's machine. The woman stared flatly at her.

"I can afford my own slot money," she said.

Kit took in the thick gold chains strewn with chocolate diamonds the woman wore draped around her neck. She didn't doubt the woman had money. She just wanted her to stay longer. She smiled her best smile at her.

"I'm sure you can. I certainly didn't mean to offend. I'll be honest. You intrigue me. And I didn't want to see you walk off."

The woman arched one carefully shaped eyebrow at Kit.

"Is that right?" She didn't smile.

Kit fought the urge to look away. She wouldn't back down. She wanted this woman to be her target. She wanted that necklace. She didn't trust her voice so she simply nodded slowly.

"Well, you've already put the money in. I might as well play for a while."

"Great," Kit said. "Enjoy."

She turned back to her own game and was watching the ants scurry all over the screen when she heard the bells chime on the machine next to her. The woman had hit it big. On Kit's cash. Good for her. She smiled at the woman who was talking to casino officials.

"These winnings are rightfully yours," the woman said a little while later.

"Not really. You won them fair and square."

"At least let me buy you a drink to celebrate."

"If you insist."

"I do." The woman smiled showing rows of straight white teeth. She was a knockout. Not that that mattered to Kit. She was only in it for the jewels.

Kit stood and followed the woman to a lounge. She looked around then motioned to a table at the back. She sat facing the entrance, so she'd know if Savannah walked in.

The woman sat across from Kit. Her movements were graceful, effortless.

"What's your story?" She said.

Kit shrugged.

"No story."

"You always bribe women to sit next to you?"

Kit smiled.

"Is that what I did?"

"Yes. Now I'm going to get a bottle of Armand de Brignac. Will you join me? Or do you not drink champagne?"

"I'd love to join you."

Kit forced herself not to sit there with her mouth hanging open. Armand de Brignac was high dollar champagne. So high dollar she'd only had it once before. And it was delicious.

The woman was back empty-handed. The bartender followed behind her with the champagne and two flutes. He poured for them then backed away. The woman picked up her glass and held it to Kit.

"To new friends," she said.

"I'll drink to that."

Kit took a sip of the liquid gold and almost moaned. It was delicious.

"Do you have a name?" the woman said.

"Andi. And you?"

"My name is Zoya."

"That suits you."

Zoya cocked her head and looked at Kit.

"Thank you," she said. "What brings a Yankee to my corner of the world?"

"I'm just here to gamble. It's what I live for."

"Slot machines?"

Kit laughed.

"No. I was just escaping the crowd for a bit."

"Ah. I see. And I intrigued you? How?"

Kit shrugged again.

"I don't know. Your accent. The way you carried yourself. I wanted to know your story."

"What would you like to know, Andi?"

"What will you tell me?"

Zoya threw her head back and laughed. It was loud and soft at the same time.

"So much. I have so much to tell."

Kit was at once intrigued and growing bored. She was sure Zoya had stories to tell, but Kit was growing restless. She wanted to steal the jewels and be on her way. She tried not to think about what would come before the theft. Would she be unfaithful to Savannah? No. That was pleasure. Zoya was strictly business. She had no reason to feel guilty. Why wasn't she convinced?

Zoya told Kit stories of her childhood in poverty, how she met her husband, and her life now. It was interesting, really, but Kit had a hard time focusing. She smiled and laughed and nodded, but her heart wasn't in it.

By the end of their second bottle of champagne, Kit had lightened up considerably. She was relaxed and enjoying Zoya's tales immensely.

"Now you tell me, Andi. What's a young, nice looking, seemingly available woman doing passing the time with an older woman like myself?"

"I'm just enjoying myself. That's all."

"Have you ever been with a man? I'm curious."

The question shocked Kit. She shook her head.

"Why do you ask?"

"We are like night and day, you and I. I have never been with a woman."

"Have you ever considered it?"

Zoya leveled a stare at Kit.

"Not before tonight."

Kit fought not to let her surprise and relief show.

"So you're contemplating it now, huh?"

"That I am. I am a woman of diverse needs. Perhaps you can meet those that have gone unmet."

"I'd like that."

"Then meet me at my room in ten minutes."

Zoya gave Kit her room number and left. Kit slowly sipped the rest of her champagne. She checked her watch. She had four minutes. She sauntered out of the bar as casually as she could manage. She didn't want to be late.

She was under complete control until she walked down the hall and realized Zoya's room was just down the hall from Savannah's. She got a knot in her stomach and began to feel guilty. Nonsense. She was doing a job. Nothing more.

Once in Zoya's room, Kit found herself unable to follow through. She couldn't get Savannah out of her head or her heart. And she didn't want to. She had a few drinks with Zoya, but when push came to shove, she couldn't seduce her.

She did, however, pocket Zoya's necklace when she took it off to slip into something more comfortable. Kit knew she'd disappointed Zoya by not making love to her, but she knew she'd disappoint herself more if she had.

She bid Zoya good night and hurried past Savannah's suite and, as she turned the corner to the elevators, crashed right in to a medium height dark haired man in a dark suit and tie. Shit. He looked like FBI. She quickly pushed past him and waited for the elevator. She needed to get away. He was probably on his way to Savannah's. Damn. That had been close. How good of a look had he gotten at her? Would he be able to describe her? Shit. Shit, shit, shit.

Kit got back to her rental and hid the jewelry. She took a shower then dressed again to meet Savannah. Who knew what that man had said to Savannah? She might not want to see Kit now. Her mind was whirling as she rode back to the casino.

She arrived at four forty-five. She had fifteen minutes to kill. She played roulette and was on a roll when she felt her phone buzz. A text from Savannah.

Can we make it seven instead of now? Something's come up.

Shit. So they knew about Zoya. What would she say? Things could be over between Kit and Savannah.

Sure, babe. I'll see you at seven.

All she could do was wait.

CHAPTER TWENTY-ONE

I'm telling you," Mrs. Pillay said. "I have no idea who robbed me."

Savannah exhaled slowly. They'd been at it for half an hour and the victim, one Zoya Pillay was not being very helpful.

"Tell me about coming back to your room after you left the casino," Savannah said.

"I told you. I came back to my room alone."

"And no one followed you? You didn't give your room number to anyone?"

It was Mrs. Pillay's turn to let her breath out slowly. She glanced at her husband and then back to Savannah.

"If you must know, I invited a woman back to my room with me."

Savannah's stomach tightened.

"And what did this woman look like?"

"That's inconsequential. She didn't rob me."

"And you're certain of that?"

"Yes. We had some drinks, shared some laughs, and then she left. When I went to bed my necklace and rings were still on the dresser."

Frustrated, Savannah closed her notebook. She handed Mrs. Pillay her card.

"If you think of anything, anything at all, please call me."

Savannah stood. Li joined her. The rest of the crew were wrapping up their duties.

"I don't know what you think I'll think of, but thank you," Mrs. Pillay said. She walked everyone to the door.

Savannah led her team back to her suite. She looked at the whiteboard and cringed, knowing they didn't have anything to add.

"You don't believe her do you, boss? Li said.

"No. I think she slept with that woman and then was robbed and is too embarrassed to admit it."

Savannah hated, despised, abhorred the thought of Kit sleeping with random women. Savannah thought of herself and Kit as an item. Was she fooling herself?

"Oh, shit," Li said.

"What?"

"I totally forgot. I literally bumped into someone on my way here earlier."

"Who? When? A man or a woman?" Savannah peppered him with questions.

"Right before I got here for our briefing. I don't know if it was a man or a woman. They were taller than me, but that doesn't mean anything."

"Li! You need to be more alert! Did they act suspicious?"

"I'm sorry. And not really. We just bumped into each other, then they sidestepped to let me go by and they presumably took the elevator."

"That might have been our thief," Savannah said. "Think. Really try to remember. Man or woman?"

Li simply shrugged.

"I don't know. First impression would be a man."

"Or a masculine woman?"

"Maybe. I'm sorry, boss. I honestly don't know. I wish I'd paid more attention."

"So do I. Well, since we didn't learn anything there...I'm guessing there were no fingerprints?" Her fingerprint specialist shook her head. "Okay then. You're all free to go. I'll see you Friday."

Everyone left but Li.

"I really am sorry, boss."

Savannah refrained from ripping him a new one, tempting though it was since they were alone.

"Just be more attentive next time. Every encounter could be vital."

"Yes, ma'am."

They left her room together and took the elevator down. He got off at his floor.

"Good night, boss."

"See you in a few days, Li."

Savannah took a deep breath. She was on her way to see Kit. Had Kit just had sex with another woman? And robbed her? The thought made Savannah's stomach sour. She needed to not think like that. Kit had had several opportunities to rob Savannah and hadn't. Surely, she would have if she was a thief? She wouldn't be able to help herself, would she? And Kit had been in Macau when there hadn't been a robbery. She wasn't the thief. The woman in Savannah knew it. If only the agent in her would get on board.

It was seven o'clock when she stepped off the elevator and was assaulted with the sights and sounds of the casino. She wasn't in the mood for bright lights and loud noise. She slipped into a dark lounge and texted Kit.

I'm in the casino. Where are you?

"I'm right here," Kit said.

Savannah looked up to see Kit and felt herself break into a wide smile. She was dog tired, but seeing Kit rejuvenated her and gave her a thrill. Kit leaned down and kissed her and Savannah felt her worries and suspicions fade away.

"It's so good to see you," Savannah said. "How'd you do tonight?"

"I won. Big. How about you?"

"I broke even. So I won't complain. Are you ready for breakfast? And do you mind if we find someplace away from the casino? I could do with some peace and quiet."

Kit whipped out her phone and in no time was ready to go.

"I found a place that looks great. Nice and quiet with rave reviews. Come on, sweetheart. Let's get out of here.

Savannah swooned at the term of endearment. She wondered if Kit even realized she'd said it. It didn't matter. She wouldn't read too much into it. She'd just enjoy Kit. That was easy enough.

Kit hailed a cab and they slid into the back seat. The ride to the restaurant was short. Too short for Savannah who was enjoying Kit's arm around her holding her close. She needed to be close to Kit, to lose herself in this woman who was working her way into Savannah's heart.

They ate their breakfast and rode back to the hotel. It was nine o'clock and Savannah was dead on her feet. Still, she invited Kit into her room.

"Thank you, babe," Kit said. "But we both need our sleep. I trust you'll be traveling again tomorrow?"

Savannah nodded.

"You, too?"

Kit laughed.

"But of course. Where are you headed?"

"Vegas, baby."

"Me, too. The MGM?"

"That's where I'll be."

"So that's a day long flight," Kit said. "What time do you leave tomorrow?"

"Around eight in the morning."

"Okay. Get some rest and I'll see you there. I fly out tonight."

"Can I plan on dinner Tuesday night?"

"But of course."

"Excellent. I'll see you then. Travel safely, Kit."

"You do the same."

Kit kissed Savannah good-bye and, even though she could see Savannah was dead on her feet, temptation reared its head deep inside her. How she wished she could make love to Savannah right then. But that wouldn't be fair. So she kissed her one more time and regretfully turned and left.

Returning to the States made Kit homesick. Not that she wanted to see her family and she only had a few friends left to see. But she missed the place. She missed San Luis Obispo and surrounding areas. She longed to go wine tasting in Paso Robles. She'd kill to surf at Pismo Beach. Not this trip though. She should have taken a few days to visit but she didn't want to miss a moment with Savannah.

And Savannah hadn't seemed strange around her, so she assumed Zoya didn't admit to spending time with her. And robbing her. That was a huge relief on so many levels. Kit knew she wouldn't be able to take any more strangers to bed. It didn't feel right. In fact, it felt damned wrong. Even if it was part of the job. She craved the day she and Savannah could quit their respective jobs and live peacefully somewhere. But would Savannah ever give up the FBI life? God, Kit hoped so.

She went back to her house and packed for her next adventure. She forced herself to stay awake so she could sleep on the plane. She settled in with a scotch and waited for her car to pick her up.

Kit was fairly well rested when she climbed into her car in Las Vegas. It was hot, stiflingly so. But the car was air-conditioned and she knew her room would be, too. For once, she wasn't renting a place. She had a room at the Four Queens on Fremont Street. She loved the old part of town and, while it would be crowded, it would be nothing compared to the hustle and bustle of the strip.

She unpacked and put on shorts and a golf shirt and walked around Fremont, taking in the sights. It was a casual atmosphere and she even stopped in at the Golden Gate to play some roulette. She won big then went back to her hotel. She ate some dinner then jet lag caught up with her. She climbed into bed knowing she'd see Savannah the next day.

She woke around noon and checked her phone. There was a text from Savannah.

Just landed. Exhausted. See you tonight?

Kit smiled. She was crazy about Savannah.

We are still on for tonight. I hope you're sleeping now.

There was no answer, so Kit knew Savannah was indeed asleep. She sent her another text.

When you wake up, text me your room number and I'll pick you up at nine.

With nothing in particular she had to do, Kit took a leisurely shower then wandered Fremont Street again. She stopped for a light lunch, did a little gambling, and was back in her room at seven. She ordered a car for later, took another shower and dressed in a gray linen suit with a light blue shirt open at the collar. Satisfied her appearance would meet with Savannah's approval, she poured a drink and vegged for a while.

When it was time to go, she went downstairs and found her car waiting for her. She rode to the MGM in a state of nerves. Her stomach was filled with butterflies and she couldn't shake the feeling of unease that crept over her. Maybe Zoya had been a mistake. Maybe Savannah was biding her time, waiting to arrest Kit. All negative thoughts rushed through her mind threatening to consume her.

She fought them off and was in a reasonable mood when she was dropped off at the MGM. She was excited to see Savannah. Extremely so. If only she didn't have to worry so damned much. But it was her life that was at stake. In so many ways.

Savannah looked breathtaking when she opened her door. She was wearing a light green sundress that accentuated her curves and made her eyes shine. All Kit's worries disappeared the minute she laid eyes on Savannah. She kissed her cheek and knew she was where she belonged. Everything else would work itself out. It had to, right?

"You look divine." Kit stepped into Savannah's suite and took her in her arms. "I've missed you."

"I've missed you, too. I wish we could take the same flights when we have those long travel days. It would be nice to spend that time together."

"True statement."

"Are you ever going to kiss me?"

Kit laughed.

"I was thinking about it."

Savannah wrapped her arms around Kit.

"Enough thinking. Kiss me already."

Kit was happy to oblige. She brushed her lips over Savannah's. It was soft, tender, and quick. And not enough. She kissed her harder and Savannah pressed against her in response. Kit held on to Savannah for dear life. She could feel the earth giving way and needed Savannah to anchor her.

They came up for air and Kit stood there, staring into Savannah's eyes. They were dark with passion and Kit longed to take her to bed.

"What are you thinking?" Savannah asked.

"How hungry are you?"

"Famished."

"Then we should get dinner. Come on, m'lady."

She took Savannah's hand and they took the elevator to the main floor. They found a restaurant that appealed to both of them and went inside. There was a long wait, so they waited in the bar.

"What can I get you to drink?" Kit asked.

"I'll have a martini, please."

"Coming right up."

When she was back with their drinks, Kit found herself thinking too much again. She wondered if she should press Savannah then figured why not? She was curious what she'd say.

"So, babe?" Kit began.

"Yes?"

"Why did you delay breakfast the other day?"

"Hm? When?"

"Our last day in Klerksdorp. You pushed our breakfast back two hours."

"I don't remember now. Why do you ask?"

Kit hoped her smile looked genuine.

"No reason. Just making conversation."

She told herself to relax but she couldn't stop the niggling in her brain that said Savannah was close to catching her. She needed to seriously consider her options. Quit robbing or quit Savannah. Neither would be easy.

CHAPTER TWENTY-TWO

Savannah fought to keep the panic from her voice when she answered Kit. Should she just admit to Kit that she was an FBI agent? What harm could it do? If she truly believed Kit was innocent, why hide that fact from her? Maybe she still wasn't convinced Kit was innocent. No maybes about it. Every single victim, every single time, Savannah held her breath hoping they wouldn't describe Kit to her. They hadn't yet, but why couldn't Savannah shake the feeling that Kit was their main suspect?

She smiled back at Kit, determined to get out of her own head.

"Do you have any plans while you're in Vegas?" she said. "Will you be spending any time in California this trip?"

"No California this trip. As for plans, I thought we'd take a helicopter over the Grand Canyon. How does that sound?"

Savannah thought that sounded fantastic. It would get her out of Vegas and away from her thoughts and her job for a day.

"That sounds great. When shall we do that?"

"I took the liberty of making reservations for tomorrow. It's about a four-hour gig so I figured we'd have breakfast then take off at eleven. Sound good?"

"Sounds wonderful. Thank you for making the plans."

"My pleasure, babe. My pleasure."

They finished dinner and Savannah relaxed in Kit's presence. Everything was right in the world as Kit held her hand and guided her through the hotel. They gambled a little but mostly people watched. It physically hurt when Kit said it was time to call it a night.

"Will you be staying with me?" Savannah asked.

"Not tonight, my dear. Tomorrow though. I promise."

"I'm going to hold you to that."

"Please do."

Kit kissed Savannah in the hallway outside her door. The kiss lasted forever, and Savannah never wanted it to end. She held her tight and refused to let her go. When the kiss finally ended, she kept her arms around Kit's neck.

"I don't want this night to end."

"I understand. But we have a big day tomorrow. I'll be here at nine to take you to breakfast."

Kit kissed Savannah again then disentangled herself. The cold Savannah felt was from more than just the air conditioning. She hated space between herself and Kit. She longed to feel her lithe body pressed against her, pleasing her like no other. She took a deep breath.

"Until tomorrow then," Savannah said.

"Sleep well."

"You, too."

Savannah tossed and turned while sleep escaped her. Every time she'd start to doze, she was assaulted with nightmares of Kit with other women and stealing jewels. She'd wake up covered in sweat and struggle to fall back asleep. It was a long night and she was glad when six o'clock rolled around.

She got out of bed, took a long shower, and dressed for a day with Kit. That would end in a night with Kit. Her whole body quivered imagining the pleasures that lay in store for her. Kit was extremely talented. Of that there was no doubt. Savannah pushed her nightmares to the back of her mind and focused on the day ahead.

When she was dressed, she checked her phone. She had two texts from Kit.

Breakfast in a half hour?

Babe? You there? Can I come get you?

Savannah quickly answered.

Sorry. Was in the shower. Ready now though.

Great. I'm on my way.

Kit arrived looking adorable in khaki cargo shorts and a black golf shirt. She smelled clean and fresh and Savannah didn't want to leave her room.

"Maybe we should skip breakfast." She draped her arms across Kit's broad shoulders.

"Very funny. Come on. We have a big day ahead of us. I promise to make it up to you tonight."

Savannah tried to pout but ended up laughing instead.

"Okay. But I don't know how I'll be able to concentrate today with all this pent-up frustration."

"I'm sure you'll be fine." Kit laughed with her.

They made their way out into the Vegas heat and walked along the strip until they came to a cheap looking diner.

"I'm famished," Kit said. "I think I'll have one of everything."

"How do you stay so trim?"

"I could ask you the same thing. Metabolism has been good to me."

They settled on their orders and held hands across the table.

Kit could barely sit still.

"Are you okay?" Savannah said. "You seem restless."

"Just excited, sweetheart. I've never taken a helicopter to the Grand Canyon before."

"Neither have I. And I'm excited too, but at least I can sit still." She laughed.

"I love your laugh. It's magical and it warms my cockles."

"Your cockles, huh?" Savannah arched an eyebrow.

"Sure. My cockles. Why not?"

"If you say so."

They finished breakfast and arrived back at the hotel just as the van arrived to take them to Boulder City. It was a half hour drive and Savannah snuggled against Kit for the duration. She loved the feel of Kit's arm around her and lost herself in Kit's hard body pressed into her. She was almost sad when they arrived at their destination.

They climbed aboard the helicopter and soon Savannah had all but forgotten her disappointment at not being against Kit. The views of Hoover Dam and Lake Meade were simply breathtaking. And when they flew into the Grand Canyon, she was in awe of the natural beauty that surrounded her.

They landed at the bottom and Kit and Savannah got out and took hundreds of photos of the surrounding beauty as well as selfies of themselves with the majestic background.

Their guide came over and got them when it was time to go, and Savannah snapped a few more pictures to remember her day by. They flew back to Boulder City and Savannah was still quaking from the experience. They climbed into the van and drove back to the hotel.

"Did you enjoy it?" Kit said.

"Oh, Kit. It was magnificent. Thank you so much."

Kit's chest swelled with pride. She loved pleasing Savannah in every meaning of the word.

"Had you seen the Grand Canyon before?"

"Never. It's always been on my bucket list."

Savannah positively glowed and Kit was proud to have given her the reason to. It thrilled Kit how much fun it was to make Savannah happy. She hoped to be able to do that for many years to come.

And then the doubt came back. Reality reared its ugly head. Savannah was trying to throw Kit in prison. For a long time. What would happen then? Was this all a plot on Savannah's part?

No. She mustn't think like that. She needed to simply enjoy her time with Savannah and take each minute as it came.

They were back at the hotel and Kit's stomach growled loudly. Savannah laughed and rubbed Kit's belly.

"Is that right?" she said.

"Sorry. That was embarrassing."

"Not at all. I could eat, too. Let's find a good burger."

Kit pulled up burger places near them on her phone. Savannah's wish was her command. She found one and they walked to it. It was ungodly hot, and Kit rued wearing a black shirt. She was sweating by the time they arrived at the burger joint.

"Are you okay?" Savannah said.

"Fine. Just hot. Let's eat."

After lunch they walked back to the MGM.

"Would you like to gamble?" Savannah said.

Kit leered at her hoping to make her intentions known.

"I'd like to take a shower and then take you if you don't object."

Savannah smiled brightly.

"No objections from me. I'll race you to the room."

Kit burst out laughing.

"I don't think so, babe. No need to make a scene. We'll be there soon enough."

"It can't be soon enough."

"You're so sweet."

Kit kissed her as they waited for the elevator. She was crazy about Savannah. She tried to warn herself to protect her heart but knew it was too late. She kissed her harder and was disappointed when the elevator arrived.

"Care to join me in the shower?" Kit said when they reached Savannah's suite.

"I thought you'd never ask."

Kit kissed her again and carefully disrobed her, tenderly caressing each patch of skin she exposed.

"Your skin is so soft," Kit murmured against Savannah's lips.

"Mm."

Kit opened her mouth and Savannah's tongue wrapped around hers. Gooseflesh covered her body. She was aroused beyond measure. She had to have Savannah, to claim her as her own. She quickly undressed and took Savannah's hand.

In the shower, Kit pleased Savannah with her fingers and tongue and Savannah soon begged her to stop.

"I'm going to fall over. Please, Kit. Save some for the bed."

They barely took the time to dry each other off before they fell into bed together. Kit devoured every inch of Savannah, leaving nothing unkissed. Savannah squirmed and writhed and screamed out Kit's name. Kit grinned to herself, loving how easy Savannah was to please.

They slept after and Kit woke to find Savannah watching her.

"What's up?" she said groggily.

"I'm always so surprised to find you still in my bed when I wake up."

"Why's that?"

"It's like, wow. That really did happen. And you really are here with me. It wasn't a dream."

Kit smiled at her.

"Nope. No dream. It's reality, baby." She thought carefully before she said her next words. "I'd like it to become more real, Savannah. Have you ever considered just heading home and settling down?"

Something flashed quickly in Savannah's eyes. It was gone as soon as it appeared leaving Kit no time to analyze what it might have been.

"Are you serious?"

"Very. Wouldn't it be nice?"

"It would," Savannah said. "But would you really be able to give up your globetrotting ways?"

"I think so. I think I'd like to live in a house with a white picket fence and grow old with you, Savannah. I hope that doesn't scare you."

Savannah was silent and Kit feared she'd said too much. She didn't want to scare Savannah off but couldn't help but be honest. She needed to know if they were on the same page. Or if Kit was living in a fantasy world.

"Say something, Savannah."

She noticed the moisture pooling in Savannah's eyes and braced herself for the worst.

"That sounds wonderful," Savannah said

"But?"

"But are you ready? Really ready? You've been traveling the world, seeing its most exotic locations, gambling at its finest casinos. Are you truly ready to give that up? Wouldn't you get bored with just me to hang out with?"

"I'd never get bored with you, Savannah. I could easily make you my life."

"If you're serious, Kit. I mean, really serious, then let's talk about this some more. When would you want to settle down? How much time? And where would we settle? California? Or Maryland?"

"I don't care. Don't you see? Being with you is all that matters. We could set up base in Maryland and I could keep my place in California. We could use it as a winter home. Wouldn't that be nice? To escape from the cold? I'm telling you, Savannah, we could make this work."

"When?" Savannah asked again. "When would you like to do this?"

"After the tournament this weekend."

Savannah laughed softly. It wasn't a mean laugh, but Kit didn't like the sound of it anyway.

"That might be a little soon," Savannah said. "But I definitely think it's something we can work toward. Maybe in a month or so? We're still so new. Let's make sure we're solid, okay? I'd hate for you to do something you'll regret."

"I'd never regret being with you, Savannah. But if we need to wait so I can prove it to you, then we wait. But now, I can't wait any longer. Let's go get dinner."

They took another shower together. It was a long, leisurely shower filled with lovemaking. They dried, dressed, and headed down to the casino floor to find a place to eat.

Chapter Twenty-three

Saturday afternoon found Kit snoozing in bed with Savannah. She woke up, stretched, and gazed longingly at Savannah's shapely curves lying next to her. She knew she should have spent the night in her own room but wasn't able to tear herself away from Savannah. Not even for a few hours. She'd be without her that night and that would be hard enough.

She thought about the night ahead of her. She knew she was supposed to be bedding some stranger and stealing the poor unsuspecting woman's jewels. She was excited for the challenge but felt guilty about the act. She needed to talk herself out of the guilt. She needed to push it away and remember she was simply doing what she was paid to do. How much longer could she keep doing it? She supposed she could stop. And then Savannah could quit trying to catch her. And then they could retire together to the States. Maybe that's what she'd do after tonight. Maybe.

"What's with the furrowed brow?" Savannah was awake.

"Hm? Oh nothing. Just thinking how much I'll miss you tonight."

"You're so sweet. Show me now how much I mean to you."

And Kit did. She took Savannah to the precipice and sent her reeling over the edge time and again. Savannah lay there flushed and satisfied and Kit was sad but knew she had to get going.

"Okay, babe. It's time for me to head out. I'll see you around five?"

"I hate being away from you for that long. But I understand your need to gamble. You do your thing and I'll see you in the morning."

Kit kissed Savannah and left. Her stomach hurt and the guilt was back. She forced it away. Who knew? Maybe that night she wouldn't even find a willing target. Then there'd be nothing to feel guilty about. But she knew she'd try her damnedest to find one. She needed the thrill of the chase. The excitement of the robbery. The financial rewards that came with it all. She was addicted. But she could quit. If Savannah gave the green light, Kit would walk away forever. And never look back.

She had a casual, cheap dinner at a hot dog stop then headed up to her room to get ready. She pushed all thoughts of Savannah out of her head and got into her jewel thief persona. She took a long, hot shower. She dressed in her favorite tux and slipped into her polished shoes. She sprayed on a bit of cologne and she was ready.

It was ten o'clock when she slid into her hired car and rode the short distance to the MGM. People were milling about in front of the casino dressed in everything from formal attire to tourist shorts and T-shirts. She supposed she hadn't needed a tux, but she felt good. She entered the casino and made her rounds.

People were everywhere. The noise was deafening between the whirling and buzzing of machines and ringing bells and chatter of people enjoying themselves. She didn't see anybody who looked like an easy target.

She did see Savannah talking to the man Kit had bumped into in Klerksdorp. She quickly about-faced and headed in the other direction. No reason to be seen by either of them. She made her way to the craps tables. She found a group of young women there, all dressed to the nines wearing jewels that were probably family heirlooms. She pondered approaching one, but then thought better of it.

Kit cruised through the blackjack area and sat and played a few hands. She lost so got up to leave. As she did, she literally bumped into one of the young women from the craps tables.

"Sorry," she mumbled.

"Don't be," the woman said.

She was a plump young woman with a cherubic face and cupid bow lips. Her skin was olive, her eyes brown, her teeth gleaming white.

"Excuse me?" Kit said.

"I'm here for my bridal shower," the woman said.

"Oh, well, congratulations."

"I have a favor to ask of you."

"What's that?" Kit said.

"I saw you checking us out at the craps tables. I find you very attractive."

"Thank you?"

The woman laughed. It was soft and sensual.

"I don't mean to be so forward, but I have to ask, are you a lesbian?"

"Why yes. Yes, I am." She looked around for the rest of the women, but they had vanished.

"Can I buy you a drink?" the woman said.

"Sure." Kit was curious what the woman wanted from her. She would have a drink with her, then send her on her way. Kit had business to attend to. And, while the woman was cute enough, and was adorned in diamonds that Kit would love to have, she wasn't exactly her target type.

"So what's up?" Kit asked when they were seated with a bottle of champagne.

"My name is Tiffany. I'm from New York. And we're here for my bachelorette weekend."

"That's great. What has that got to do with me?"

Tiffany took a deep breath, held it, and exhaled slowly.

"I'm getting married in a few weeks."

"Right."

"To a wonderful man."

"Again, I offer my congratulations."

"Well, here's the deal. I've never been with a woman. I've always been curious. No one knows about my curiosity. Not even my closest friends. And certainly not my fiancé. I was wondering, would you kiss me?"

"Just a kiss?" Kit said.

"Well, we'll start with a kiss and see where it leads."

Kit smiled at her.

"That's an interesting proposition. Let's relax and enjoy our champagne. Maybe after getting to know me you won't want me to kiss you."

"Oh, I doubt that. I find you drop-dead gorgeous."

"Thank you for that. I find you adorable, but that doesn't mean a kiss is in order. We have to jive, you know?"

Tiffany seemed to relax as she sat back in her chair.

"I suppose you're right. So, tell me about yourself. What's your name? Where are you from?"

Kit laughed.

"You forgot to ask me what's my sign."

"What?"

"Never mind. You're too young. My name is Ronnie. And I'm from Maryland. Are you from the state or the city?"

"The city. Manhattan to be specific. Upper East Side."

Kit raised her eyebrows. Tiffany obviously came from money. The night just got more interesting.

"Nice. And your fiancé? Where's he from?"

"I'd rather not talk about him. Let's talk more about you."

Kit chuckled.

"Okay. What do you want to know?"

"Are you originally from Maryland? You don't sound Eastern to me. And you seem very cultured. Are you from wealth, as well?"

"I'm originally from California. I did not grow up with wealth. I made some smart investments and tend to be very lucky at gambling. Money isn't something I lack."

"Very interesting. Tell me, Ronnie. What's your favorite color?"

"Honestly? Black. And yours?"

"Black isn't really a color," Tiffany said. "But, okay. Pink for me. I love pink."

Kit smiled at her. She could have guessed that.

"What?" Tiffany said. "Are you laughing at me?"

"Not at all. You seem like a pink girl."

"Oh, very much. I guess I'm a femme, huh?"

Kit almost spit champagne out her nose.

"I suppose so."

"So it makes sense I'm attracted to a butch like yourself."

"Yes. It makes perfect sense."

"You're very easy to talk to, Ronnie. I find my nerves are settling down."

"Were you nervous when you approached me? You didn't seem like it."

"I was terrified." She laughed.

"Are you used to getting what you want, Tiffany?"

"For the most part. Does that make me a bad person?"

"Not at all."

"Would you like to go back to my room? I have champagne there."

"Are you in this hotel?" Kit worried about running into Savannah.

"No. I'm at Treasure Island."

"Let's get a cab."

"Lead the way."

"Oh, no," Kit said. "After you."

Kit got to Tiffany's room and once again got cold feet. She wanted her jewels, there was no doubt about that. But she couldn't take her to bed. It just didn't feel right. It was wrong and she knew it. But the boss would love those diamonds and she'd make a pretty penny.

She plied Tiffany with glass after glass of champagne. Soon her eyelids were drooping and she was slurring her words.

"I feel terrible, but I can't keep my eyes open. Stay with me and make love to me when I wake up?"

"That'll be fine."

"Will you be here when I wake up?"

"I promise," Kit lied.

"Thank you, Ronnie. You'll make my dreams come true."

Before Kit could answer, Tiffany was snoring. Kit shoved Tiffany's diamonds in her pocket. She hailed a cab and locked the jewels away in the safe in her room. She took a quick shower and dressed again then texted Savannah.

Kit: *Can we meet a little early? Or are you busy?*

Savannah: *I'd love to meet early. Like when?*

Kit: *In about fifteen?*

Savannah: *I'll be by the roulette tables.*

Kit: *Excellent. See you soon.*

Savannah sought out Li to tell him she was going to get food.

"I think we can call this a night. Hopefully, we won't hear of any robberies later."

"I wish I could be as optimistic as you, boss."

Savannah smiled at him.

"I just want it to end. It has to sometime."

"Not until we catch whoever's behind this."

"Or until they quit."

"But I want to catch him. Or her. I want them locked up."

Savannah thought of Kit behind bars and forced herself to smile.

"So do I, Li. So do I. For now, get some sleep or do whatever you need to. I'm off to get breakfast."

She saw Kit milling around the roulette table and walked up behind her. She wrapped her arms around her and nibbled on her ear.

"Hey, gorgeous. Come here often?"

Kit spun around and kissed Savannah.

"Hey, baby. So good to see you."

"I'm glad we're meeting earlier. I was missing you."

"Come on. Let's hit a buffet."

"Where are we going?"

"To the Bellagio. I love their buffet. Let's go outside and catch a shuttle."

They enjoyed the buffet and almost ate their money's worth. It was a pricey meal, but Kit didn't care. She loved it. She was with Savannah and she was as happy as she could remember being.

"Where are you traveling to next?" Kit asked.

"Connecticut. And you?"

"Same. I don't really like that casino, but I thought I'd check it out next weekend."

"Great. I'm sure we'll find something to do to pass the week."
Savannah wiggled her eyebrows suggestively. Kit smiled at
her. Her dimples showed and Savannah's heart skipped a beat.

"I'm sure we will. While we're on the east coast, do you think
you'll stop by home?" Kit asked.

"No. Not this trip. Soon though. I'm getting a little homesick."

"Will you take me home with you then? When you're ready?
At least for a visit?"

"We'll see."

They walked back to the MGM and made out in the elevator on
the way up to Savannah's room. Savannah couldn't get enough of
Kit. She couldn't wait to feel Kit on her and inside her again.

Kit didn't disappoint. She made love to Savannah until the sun
was up. Savannah dozed in her arms, content and satiated. She was
startled awake by the shrill sound of her telephone.

"Hello?"

"It's Li. There's been a robbery."

"What? Where?"

"Treasure Island."

"Okay. Give me a few."

"What's going on?" Kit asked.

"You need to go. I'm sorry. But something's come up that I
need to deal with."

"What is it? Can I help?"

"Sorry. Not this time. I'll text you later."

She watched Kit dress and tried to be present while she kissed
her good-bye. But her mind was already working. Another robbery.
Another woman victim. What would she learn? Was Kit behind it?
Would the woman admit to it?

Savannah dressed in black slacks and jacket with a white shirt
underneath. She grabbed her bag and headed to Treasure Island.

CHAPTER TWENTY-FOUR

The victim was a young woman. She couldn't have been thirty years old. Definitely different from previous victims. Was Kit behind this? Did she seduce this young woman? The woman, a Tiffany Weems, was very cute. Is that why Kit targeted her? Had she enjoyed herself with this one?

Savannah knew her line of thinking wasn't healthy, but she couldn't stop it. She wanted to cry. She felt like her heart was breaking. But she had to get it together. She didn't know Kit was behind it. So why did she feel like she'd just lost her best friend?

She took a deep breath and approached the young woman wearing a fluffy pink robe.

"Ms. Weems?" Savannah reached out her hand. "I'm Agent Brown, but you can call me Savannah."

Ms. Weems smiled at her.

"Thank you, Savannah. And I insist you call me Tiffany."

"Will do. Now, please tell me what happened."

"I wish I could remember. I had a little too much champagne and was beginning to feel ill. So I came back to my room. That's all I remember."

"Who did you bring back to your room with you?" Savannah probed.

Tiffany sat up straight, looking indignant.

"I resent what you're implying, Savannah. I'm a respectable woman. And I'm engaged to be married." She held up her gaudy engagement ring as if to prove her point.

"I don't mean to imply anything, Tiffany. I simply noticed that the champagne was open and there are two glasses by the bottle. Both appear to have been used."

Tiffany opened her mouth in a shocked expression.

"I don't have an answer for that," she said.

"Look, Tiffany, I'm going to be frank with you. You're not the first woman to be robbed in a casino. We believe the thief is a middle-aged man or masculine woman. Now I need to know, were you here at Treasure Island all night?"

Tiffany seemed to weigh her answer.

"Yes."

Shit. Savannah had assumed Kit was at the MGM all night. But she couldn't prove that. Could Kit?

Savannah stood and handed Tiffany her card.

"Please call me if you remember anything that might help us."

"I will. Believe me."

"Team, meet me at my suite in fifteen minutes."

She walked back to her rooms. She was tired and disgusted. They needed a break. Desperately. So why couldn't they catch one?

The team showed up and Savannah began her meeting with a question.

"Does anybody notice anything different about this case?"

"She was young," Li said.

"Yes. Yes, she was. What else?"

"She didn't meet her robber at the main casino."

"Also true. Do you believe her?"

"Why not? Why lie about that?"

"I wish I knew. But I don't. I don't have any more answers than I had when this investigation started. Did you guys find any fingerprints?"

The team shook their heads.

"Damn. Did we learn anything?"

"Sorry, boss," Li said. "There were so many people at the casino last night. I have no idea if I saw Tiffany there or not."

"Me, either," Savannah said. "Okay, well, this meeting is going nowhere fast. We need to put our thinking caps on and come up with a way to catch this person. I feel like we might get lucky at Foxwoods. We need to tweak our strategy though. I want each of you in my suite Thursday afternoon. Three o'clock. And come with ideas."

She dismissed them and watched them all file out. All but Li.

"You wanna brainstorm now, boss?"

"Not now. I need a break. Go see your family. I'll see you Thursday."

She closed the door behind Li and collapsed on her bed. The tears that had been threatening overflowed and she sobbed thinking of Kit with Tiffany. Had Kit been gambling at Treasure Island? Is that where she met Tiffany? Savannah needed to know. She pulled her phone out of her bag. She had texts from Kit.

Hey, babe. How're things? Are you okay?

Babe, I'm worried about you.

Savannah. Please text me back. I'm freakin' out here. Is everything okay?

And one final text.

I didn't like leaving you this morning. Please text me so I'll know you're okay.

What did she really want? To know if Tiffany had fingered her? Or was she really worried? Savannah had no way of knowing. She began composing a text in her mind when her phone rang. Director Bremer. Double shit.

"Hello?" she said.

"Another robbery? And no suspects? What the hell kind of investigation are you running, Brown? Do you even care to catch this guy?"

"We're trying. This last one didn't even happen at the casino we were at. We can't be everywhere at once."

"Save it, Brown. I'm tired of your excuses."

"I really believe we'll catch him in Foxwoods. I can feel it."

"You know what I feel?" Bremer said. "I feel you're not giving this your all. I don't know why but I wish you'd tell me what's going on."

Savannah felt like she'd been punched in the gut.

"Sir—"

"Yes?"

"There's nothing to tell. We're trying. We're all trying."

"Not hard enough. You're off the case. I'm putting Nguyen in charge. I want you to come home. Take some R and R. Get your head on straight."

"But sir—" She couldn't believe her ears. She was being pulled from the case.

"I want you in my office Tuesday morning. Eight o'clock sharp. Do I make myself clear?"

"Yes, sir."

The line went dead. Savannah threw her phone on the bed and cried again. What would her next case be? Would it be as exciting? She doubted it. And when would she see Kit again? Kit! She grabbed her phone and sent her a text.

Sorry. Life got out of hand. I'm fine now. Want to come over?

I'm on my way.

What could she tell Kit about having to go home? She needed to think of something. Maybe a sick aunt. That was always a standard excuse.

She took a shower and dressed in linen shorts with a short-sleeved button-down shirt. She was drying her hair when Kit knocked on the door. Savannah was about to answer when she realized the whiteboard was still up.

"Just a minute," she called.

She quickly cleaned up the sitting room and let Kit in.

Kit was relieved when Savannah opened the door and didn't greet her with handcuffs. She pulled Savannah into her arms and hugged her tightly.

"Are you really okay?" She searched Savannah's eyes. "You look like you've been crying."

"I'm fine. I do have some bad news though. Come. Sit on the couch with me."

Kit pulled Savannah close with one arm and held her hand on the couch. Shit. Was she about to be told Savannah knew about her? Kit's stomach was in knots. And yet Savannah didn't speak. The longer she drew it out the more nervous Kit became.

"Babe?" Kit finally said. "Talk to me."

Savannah took a deep breath.

"I have an aunt who's not doing well. I have to fly home and help my cousin take care of things."

Kit's heart soared in relief. It had nothing to do with her. Thank God.

"Would you like me to come with you?" She asked.

Savannah kissed her cheek.

"That's very kind of you, but no thanks. This is something I need to do alone. I can't have any distractions."

"Okay. I understand. How long will you be home? When will I see you again?"

"I don't know, Kit. It may be a long, slow process."

"What are you saying? That we'll have to do a long distance thing? That's not ideal, but I'm willing if that's what needs to happen."

"I think it may be best if we don't see each other anymore. I really need to focus."

"Savannah. Babe. I can't accept that. You can't be dumping me."

"Please, Kit. Don't make this harder than it has to be. If things resolve themselves sooner rather than later, I'll get in touch with you. But until then, we need to cool it."

Kit stood up and paced the sitting room. She couldn't believe her ears.

"Has this been some sort of game to you?" she demanded. "Was I just a fling?"

"No, Kit. You mustn't think that. I care for you. So very much. But I can't leave you in limbo."

"I'm willing to wait in limbo. For forever if need be."

"I appreciate that. I really do. But I can't ask that of you."

"When do you fly home? Can we still have tonight?"

"I'm sorry, Kit. I think it would be best if you leave now."

Kit stopped and stared at Savannah. She felt like she'd been punched in the gut.

"So your mind's made up?"

"I'm afraid so."

Kit walked to the door. With her hand on the knob, she turned to face Savannah.

"I'll never forget you, Savannah."

"Nor I you. Take care of yourself, Kit. And be careful out there."

Kit turned the knob and walked away. She was devastated. Crushed. Her heart ached. How could Savannah have written her off so easily? She'd never get over her. Ever. And she'd never give her heart again. Of that she was certain.

She wandered through the casino seeing nothing. She found herself at the roulette table and gambled for a while. She won big but didn't feel any better. She cashed in and caught a taxi back to Fremont Street. She had to pack and get ready for Connecticut. Like it or not, life would go on. The pain in her chest intensified as she picked up her rooms and loaded her suitcases. She didn't want to go to Foxwoods. She wanted to go to Maryland. That's where she belonged.

What had really happened to take Savannah home? Had she been pulled from the case? Was there really a sick aunt? Kit would never know. She fought the tears that threatened. She wasn't a crier, but damn it, she hurt.

That night she hardly slept at all and finally got up at three to walk up and down Fremont Street. Even at that hour in the morning the street was teeming with tourists. Kit wandered in and out of casinos stopping here and there to play cards or roulette.

She couldn't believe it was ten o'clock when her stomach growled and reminded her to eat. She got brunch then called a car to take her to the airport.

This time there'd be no Savannah waiting for her. Would Savannah really someday reach back out to Kit? Kit felt like those had simply been kind words meant to soften the blow. But she wanted so desperately to believe them. She couldn't imagine a life without Savannah.

Kit's car was waiting for her at the airport in Connecticut. She asked the driver to turn off the music. She wanted silence. Deafening silence to be alone with her thoughts.

Her Airbnb was quaint and comfortable. She barely noticed. She sank into a chair and stared at the wall. Her whole world was shattered. She knew she had to pick up the pieces and move on but had no desire to do so. She just wanted to wallow in her misery.

She got out her phone and searched for the closest liquor store. There was one on the corner two blocks from her. She walked down, bought a bottle of whiskey and walked home. She poured herself a glass and downed it. That's what she needed. Something to numb the pain.

Kit woke the next morning, alone and with a pounding head. She walked to the kitchen to make some coffee and saw the whiskey bottle now half empty. Hair of the dog. She took a long swig straight from the bottle. It tasted vile in her hungover state, but she didn't care. She took another drink then set the bottle down and started making her coffee.

When her coffee was ready, she poured a cup and took it out to the wraparound porch. She sipped it as she watched people drive by. Everyone was going about their day as if the world hadn't ended. She knew better.

CHAPTER TWENTY-FIVE

Savannah sat in the apartment she kept in the city for occasions such as these. She had to meet with Director Bremer in the morning, so she hadn't bothered going home yet. Hampstead, where she lived and escaped to, was close to Baltimore. It was an hour and a half from DC, but that was an hour and a half she didn't feel like driving. She'd go there tomorrow to regroup. For the moment, she needed to clear her mind.

Easier said than done. She missed Kit with every fiber of her being. How else could she have handled it though? She couldn't very well have told Kit she was an FBI agent who needed to fly home because she hadn't caught an international jewel thief. Who may or may not be Kit. Probably was. But not necessarily. But maybe. Stop. She had more important things to worry about.

What did this demotion mean? Would she still be a lead agent on another case? Would she be confined to desk duty? Would she even have a job? Too many questions and she wouldn't have any answers until morning.

She ordered some dinner, but then couldn't eat. Her stomach was in knots. Her nerves were running rampant. And she missed Kit. Life, which had been so exciting on so many levels, was now a dull gray. There was no brightness. No sunshine. It was dismal indeed.

She went to bed missing Kit and tossed and turned all night, thoughts alternating between Kit and her meeting. She gave up at four and made coffee. She wondered what Kit was doing. Was she truly in Connecticut? Or had she gone home? Not that it should matter to Savannah. She'd made her bed and now she'd have to lie in it. Only lying in bed without Kit was nowhere near as fun.

Savannah showered and dressed in a black pencil skirt with matching blazer. She wore a white blouse, slipped on black flats, gathered her notes and things from the investigation, and headed to headquarters.

She arrived fifteen minutes early and sat in the director's waiting room. His assistant offered her coffee and doughnuts, but Savannah was too ill to partake. She hated the unknown and wasn't crazy about change, so she sat in a state of nausea waiting to be called in.

Director Bremer was always so punctual. He must be really pissed to leave her stewing in her own juices for so long. It was an hour later, at eight forty five, that he finally opened his door.

"Brown. Come in."

His tone was icy, and Savannah forced herself not to pull her jacket closer around herself. She felt the chill to her bones. This was not going to go well.

Bremer closed the door behind her and walked behind his desk. He motioned to one of the chairs across from him and Savannah sat.

"I take it all this is associated with your quote unquote investigation?"

He motioned at her briefcase and whiteboard.

"Yes, sir."

"You really disappointed me on this one, Brown. I don't mind saying so."

"Sir, this thief is really good. He leaves no evidence behind and everyone he steals from tells a different story."

He held up his hand to silence her.

"I understand there was a woman. Who might have been a prime suspect. Was she ever interviewed?"

"No, sir. But I investigated her myself. Turns out she was clean."

God how she wished those words were true. She wished she was positive Kit was innocent. Damn how she wished that.

"So in all that time you only had one suspect who you supposedly investigated. How many other suspects did you investigate?"

"We didn't have any suspects. I'm telling you, if you listened to the victims, it was a different suspect at every scene."

"Spare me. You blew it. You traveled around the world living in the lap of luxury. You weren't interested in catching the criminal. You were too busy enjoying the good life."

"That's not fair."

"Hand over everything associated with the case. I'm putting Nguyen in charge. I want you to take two weeks while I decide what's next for you."

"What are you leaning toward?"

"Honestly? I haven't decided. But I'll meet with some people, try to calm down, and make my decision. Meantime, I don't want to see you or hear from you for two weeks. Think about how badly you messed up on this case and what you'd be able to do next time to improve. Now go. Get out of here."

Savannah stood, legs quaking. She managed to keep it together until she was on the Metro. Tears escaped and trickled down her cheeks. She struggled to keep the rest in check. She finally arrived at her stop. Savannah hurried to her apartment, slammed the door behind her, and threw herself on the couch. She pounded it with her fists as the tears flowed freely. She was gagging she was sobbing so hard. And yet the tears kept coming.

She couldn't abide the thought of being taken off the case. How dare Bremer think he could discard her like yesterday's trash? She had proven herself a great agent. The jewel thieves were unsolvable. Li wouldn't have any better luck than she had.

Or maybe he would. He wouldn't lose his objectivity. He wouldn't be seduced by her charm and intelligence. He wouldn't let his heart become involved. Yes, he could do so much better than she had.

Feeling marginally better, Savannah loaded her car and drove to Hampstead. The farther she got from DC the calmer she felt. When she drove down picturesque Main Street, she breathed a sigh of relief. She was home. And she'd be fine if she never had to leave again.

❖

Kit dressed for her big night, but her heart wasn't in it. She still ached for Savannah and knew taking some strange woman to bed would only deepen her grief. She questioned yet again how much longer she could do this. She didn't need the money. And the thrill of the chase was gone.

She rode to Foxwoods and the site of the big tournament. Let It Ride was the game of choice that night and Kit noticed many tournament widows as she passed through the slots area. Lots of women seemingly alone adorned in copious amounts of diamonds. She needed to find her groove. But she just wasn't feeling it. She walked into a bar and ordered a drink.

"Hey good-lookin'," a soft voice said in her ear. "Come here often?"

Her stomach tightened. Had one of her victims found her? She slowly turned toward the voice and saw an attractive woman just a few years older than herself standing there. She smiled. An easy target. How nice.

"Have we met?" Kit said.

"Only in my dreams."

How cliché. But again, she'd be an easy target and Kit could use that.

"I'm Andi," Kit said.

"Madeline. And it's such a pleasure to meet you. You'll have to forgive me for coming on so strong, but you're like my ideal woman. Right down to the dimples."

Kit smiled more broadly.

"Wow. Thank you. I thank you and my ego thanks you."

"I see I'm too late to buy you a drink."

"Yes." Kit raised her glass of whiskey. "But perhaps I can buy you one?"

"I have a drink at the table. Join us? We're just a group of lonely old lesbians and we'd love it if you'd join us."

Kit thought for a minute. Group? That meant witnesses. That wasn't going to happen.

"Thank you, but no. I'm just going to finish my drink and be on my way."

Madeline looked crestfallen.

"I'm sorry to hear that. Can we meet up later?"

"I'll keep my eyes peeled for you."

"You're such a doll. It was a pleasure meeting you."

"And you."

Madeline walked back to her table and Kit turned back to the bar. Her mood, which had elevated oh so slightly was back in the basement. She didn't need to be here. She didn't need to steal. Sure, she'd get in trouble for not scoring, but she didn't care. She had to get out of there. The noise from the machines, the perfumes, the chatter all combined to make her nauseous. She stepped out into the evening air and called for a car. She was through.

She felt lower still as she rode back to her house. She had nothing to live for. No Savannah. And now, no career. She'd never felt more lost. The ride back to her house was uneventful. She arrived, packed her things, and pulled out her phone. She looked for flights. How she wished she knew how to find Savannah. But all she knew was that she lived in Maryland. She didn't even know which city. Annapolis? Baltimore? Somewhere in between? And what was her last name? Could it be Savannah never told her? It was possible. Damn.

She booked a flight that left in three hours. She'd be home soon. Home. California's Central Coast. It would be nicer there. So beautiful. And lonely. She could barely face the thought of being alone on her acreage. Sure, the horses probably missed her, and her dogs probably wouldn't remember her. Carlos, her friend who stayed at her place with his boyfriend, had probably given up on her ever coming back.

Kit sent him a text saying she'd be home that night but not to worry. She'd stay in the guest house that night. He could move back in the following day. She climbed into her hired car and headed for the airport.

As she sat in the terminal wondering what she would do with her life, she grew lonelier and lonelier. And her thoughts kept returning to Savannah and how right everything had seemed. Had Savannah really been toying with Kit the whole time? Was Kit just another suspect to Savannah? She didn't want to believe it. She refused to. She sent her a text.

I miss you.

She waited and waited and, when she finally turned her phone off on the plane, she still hadn't gotten a response. She ordered a double whiskey and Coke and settled in for the flight home.

It was a long flight with a dreaded layover. It was four in the morning when she landed at the tiny municipal airport. She climbed into the waiting car and closed her eyes for the drive to her ranch. She let herself into the guesthouse, stripped, and climbed into bed. She was home. She opened the bedroom window and smelled the sweet smell of the apple trees. She let the cool breeze wash over her.

Kit woke up at two the following afternoon. She was hungry, lonely, and wanted nothing more than to sleep some more. She made herself get out of bed and lug her baggage to the main house. She found Carlos sitting in the living room watching TV. He jumped up when he saw her come in.

"Hey there, world traveler. Welcome home."

Her two beagles, Scout and Buddy, bounded over to greet her. She gave them lots of love as she spoke to Carlos.

"It's good to be home. I suppose."

"You suppose? What gives? And what's with the abrupt arrival? I didn't expect you home for months. I figured you'd be out breaking hearts all over the world, loverboi."

She quit petting the dogs and looked at Carlos.

"That's exactly what I was doing. For a while. Then I met somebody. Long story short, she broke my heart."

"Oh, Kit." He pulled her into a bear hug. "I'm so sorry to hear that. I thought you were doing a fine job of protecting that organ."

Kit sighed heavily.

"Yeah. I was. But she worked her way in then dumped me out of the blue. I'm crushed."

"Oh, honey. What can I do to help?"

"Let's go to the beach. I need some salt water therapy."

"Are we going surfing?"

"No. Let's just go to Avila. We'll get lunch and watch the waves. You up for that?"

"I'm up for whatever you need, Kit. Anything for you."

Chapter Twenty-six

Savannah stared at her phone in between weeding her flower beds. The yard women had done a fine job of upkeep while she was gone, but she spotted a few weeds and, loving to work in the yard and needing something to do, she decided to have a go at the weeds. But the more she pulled, the more she thought. And the more she thought, the more she wanted to cry. She missed Kit so very much. And as her late night text informed her, Kit missed her, too.

Should she respond? What would she say? It was a big mistake and I'm flying out to find you? I miss you too so please come visit? Neither of those was practical. There was nothing she could do for at least two weeks. And then? Well, if she got a new assignment, she'd be too busy to worry about Kit. God, she hoped that was how it would play out. And if she was dismissed? She didn't want to think about that. How the hell would she survive without her career? Yes, she had plenty of money thanks to everything Lucinda left her. But her career was her life. She'd be lost without it.

She was hot and sweaty so went inside to cool off. She took a cool shower and poured herself some of the lemonade Mrs. Dennis had made that morning. She loved the elderly woman who took care of her and her house. At least Savannah had had someone to talk to that morning. Though it wasn't the same. And for a few hours, Savannah hadn't been alone.

"And, young lady?" Mrs. Dennis said as she left. "If you decide you want to talk about her, I'll be back tomorrow."

Was Savannah that transparent? She didn't like the concept that she was moping around, simply going through the motions. But that's exactly what she was doing. She needed to find something that interested her. Something to keep her busy and get her mind off Kit. But what?

She had a strange, painful feeling in her stomach and realized she was hungry. She hadn't eaten all day. Maybe she should go down to Main Street and have some dinner. She could interact with neighbors. While that seemed like a lot of work, it also sounded like something to keep her busy. She went upstairs in the old Victorian house and took another shower.

Savannah dressed in a long blue denim skirt with a pale green blouse. She slipped on some sandals, grabbed her purse, and walked the half mile to Main. She stepped into her favorite restaurant and let the familiarity wash over her. It was early yet, but there were a decent number of patrons there. One by one, the women of the tables approached her, hugged her, and asked how she was doing. She smiled and told everyone she was fine. She had several offers to join her neighbors for dinner, which she graciously declined. While it was good to see everyone and wonderful to feel included, she didn't think she'd be good company for a full meal.

So she took a table by herself and enjoyed the breadsticks while she waited for her crab cakes. Dinner was tasty which surprised her. She hadn't tasted anything, really tasted anything, in several days. Not since she'd told Kit good-bye. The thought caused a lump in her belly and she was glad she'd finished dinner.

Her next-door neighbors appeared at her table. The Goldens. They invited her to join them at the bar for some after dinner drinks. She wanted to decline, was just about to when Nadine Golden spoke.

"You've been gone for months. We must get caught up and we won't take no for an answer."

Savannah managed a weak smile.

"Of course. Maybe just one."

"At least," Frank said.

This made Savannah chuckle for real. Nadine and Frank were such good people. She couldn't ask for better neighbors. Sure, they were older and both retired, but they weren't too old to keep an eye on her place while she was gone.

"My treat," Savannah said as they settled on their barstools. "I want to pay you back for watching my place while I was on assignment."

"Our pleasure," Nadine said. "And now that you're home, can you tell us where the assignment was?"

Savannah smiled at her.

"It was actually all over the world. I traveled everywhere from the Caribbean to China, from South Africa to Portugal. And various other places. I really got around."

"I hit some of those spots when I was in the Air Force," Frank said. "I bet you had more fun."

Fun? Is that what she'd call it? It had been hard work. Except for the time with Kit. Her lower lip trembled, and she took a deep breath. Not trusting her voice, she simply nodded.

"Are you okay, dear?" Nadine patted Savannah's hand.

Savannah nodded again. She took a calming sip of her wine. "I'll be fine."

"Let me guess," Frank said. "You left a girl in one of those stops?"

"Something like that."

"Don't think about her," Nadine said. "Tell us what kind of assignment took you to all those fabulous places?"

"I was after an international jewel thief."

"Did you catch him?" Frank said.

"No." She could have elaborated but didn't feel like it.

"That's okay, dear. I'm sure you did everything you could."

Savannah took another sip of wine and looked at Nadine.

"That's not what the director thinks. Which is why I'm home for a couple of weeks."

"A rest will do you good," Frank said.

"I hope so. I really do. I just hope that wasn't my last assignment."

"You mean it could be?" Nadine looked concerned.

"Indeed, it could."

"Then what would you do?"

Savannah thought of Kit and how wonderful it would be to spend the rest of her life with her.

"I don't know, Nadine," she said. "I honestly have no idea."

Kit zipped up her wetsuit and braced herself for the chilled morning air. She loaded her surfboard into her truck and waited for Carlos. He came out a few minutes later and they headed down 101 to Pismo.

Kit wasn't feeling too hot. She and Carlos had spent most of the previous day drinking beer and followed up with tequila at night. The combination of too much alcohol and not enough Savannah made for a lousy night's sleep. But the idea of surfing brightened her significantly. She loved catching waves. It soothed her soul. It made her feel at one with nature. It would surely be the cure for what ailed her.

The sun was just cresting as she parked her truck. They carried their surfboards down the rocks until they were at the beach.

"You ready for some fun?" Carlos said.

"You know it."

They paddled out in the cold water to join the few other surfers who had braved the cold morning. Kit straddled her board and looked out to sea, hoping to see some swells approaching. There were none. She cursed herself for not checking the surf site online. But sunrise was always a good time to surf.

A few small waves rolled in and she missed most of them. Disgusted and still hungover, she motioned to Carlos to head to shore. They'd been out three hours and it had been a bust. Just like everything in Kit's life. She needed to catch a break. God knew she deserved it.

Feeling defeated and sorry for herself, Kit slipped out of her wetsuit and dried off. She dressed in gray sweats and a Cal Poly hoodie for warmth. Carlos dressed similarly.

"What's the plan now, Kit?"

"Breakfast. I need something to absorb the rest of the alcohol."
Carlos laughed.

"And a little hair of the dog?"

"I don't know about that. We'll see."

He laughed again, patted her on the back, and climbed into the truck. Kit was grateful for Carlos. They'd been buddies for years and she knew she could trust him with her life. He was a stay-at-home husband. His husband, Reynaldo, had a great job as an architect, and while he was always talking about designing the perfect house for them, he hadn't yet, so they remained living in Kit's three-thousand-square-foot guesthouse. It worked for all involved. Especially Kit, who didn't know what she'd do without Carlos right then.

Neither Carlos nor Reynaldo knew of Kit's thievery. And if she had her way, they'd never find out. How would they? Besides, those days were long over. Right?

Kit drew herself back to the present as she parked at the restaurant. It was mostly empty, so she and Carlos took a booth and perused the menu. Pancakes. That's what Kit wanted. Big, fluffy, buttermilk pancakes to absorb the tequila. Perfect.

"So what are you going to do?" Carlos said.

"About?" In her drunken stupor the previous night, Kit had told Carlos about Savannah. Everything except the jewel thefts and Savannah's FBI affiliation.

"You know what. Her. The love of your life. How are you going to get her back?"

Kit shook her head.

"I can't. She won't text me back. I'm floundering here. But let's not talk about her. Let's talk about something else."

Carlos shook his head.

"I don't think it's healthy for you. You need to go get her."

"How?"

"Go to her house in Maine? Where was it again?"

"Maryland. And I don't know where in Maryland."

"Google her."

"I don't know her last name. Now, please drop it. I say we finish breakfast then go for a ride."

"Yeah? Where to?"

"Oceano."

"That's not much of a ride," Carlos said.

"No, but they have horses. And that's the kind of ride I want to go on."

"Whoa there, Kit. I don't mind caring for the horses you own, but I don't know about riding any on the beach."

"That's right. You're not crazy about horses, are you? I'll drop you back at the house and I'll go by myself."

"You're talking crazy. I'm not going to let you be alone right now. I'll buck up and ride the damned horse on the beach."

The ride was beautiful. Kit loved horseback riding and loved the ocean. So riding horses along the beach was just the therapy she needed. She stayed focused on the horse under her, not allowing her mind to wander to Savannah too many times. When the ride was over, she was sore but rejuvenated. She felt like a new woman. She was ready to make decisions about what to do with her life. She was also ready for a shower.

Kit dried off after her shower and slipped into cotton shorts and an old Pink Floyd T-shirt. She went to the kitchen to get some iced tea and found Carlos with a pitcher of margaritas.

"You're shitting me," Kit said.

"I shit you not. Here. Have a glass."

He poured her a glass of the frozen concoction. She took a sip. It was delicious.

"Yum. But only one, Carlos. I don't need to get drunk."

"Why not?" Carlos said. "You got plans?"

"You know I don't. But I wanted to spend some time, sober time, trying to figure out what I'm going to do next with my life."

"Funny you should mention that. I have just the idea."

Kit was almost afraid to ask.

"Oh, you do? And what, pray tell, might that be?"

"Take one of those lesbian cruises. You'd have your pick of women. Hell, you could sleep your way right through the whole passenger list."

The thought of being on a ship made Kit feel claustrophobic. And bumping into women after she'd seduced them didn't sound very appealing either.

"Nice thought," she said. "But that's not really for me."

"Okay. Well, the only thing I know for sure is that we've got to get you laid."

Kit's mind went immediately to Savannah. She'd been with a woman she truly cared about. She didn't want random sex. Those days were over. All she wanted was Savannah.

"I don't know about that, Carlos."

"What's not to know? You're infamous for your seductions."

"It wouldn't feel right." Nothing felt right. She was tossing along on the waves of life with no direction.

"Damn. You've really got it bad."

"That I do, Carlos. That I do."

CHAPTER TWENTY-SEVEN

Savannah still had a week to go on her hiatus. There had been radio silence from headquarters. Nothing. Zilch. Nada. She couldn't help but fear this was a bad sign. Or was it? Outside of missing Kit like crazy, time away from a job had been rather nice. If only Kit was with her.

She'd tried to keep busy, but there was only so much to do in Hampstead. She'd rearranged her house, painted the shutters, and worked in the yard. But she was lonely. So very lonely. The Goldens had had her over for dinner and tried to lift her spirits, but between not knowing about her job and missing Kit, her spirits didn't seem to want to be lifted.

To cheer herself up, she took a day and went into Baltimore. She took in some museums and shopped for clothes and had lunch. Normally, she didn't mind doing things by herself, but that day she felt alone. More so than ever in her life. She longed to have someone to share her life with. She'd honestly thought that person would be Kit. But she'd given Kit her walking papers and was sure Kit didn't even remember her as anything more than a pleasant fling. If that. Sure, she'd texted once, but Savannah hadn't heard from her since then. She was sure she'd moved on and was tripping the light fantastic with any woman she could find. The thought made Savannah ill. She fought tears as she drove back to her house.

When she arrived at her house, Savannah poured herself a glass of wine and decided a soak in the tub would be just what she needed.

She filled the tub with hot lavender scented water and climbed in. She sipped her wine and tried to relax, but her mind kept drifting to her nights at the casinos of the world. She retraced every step she took and played over every interview she'd given. What had she missed? Had her affair with Kit disrupted her investigating abilities? No. She couldn't believe that. And, once she'd slept with Kit and Kit hadn't stolen from her, should she have moved on?

But Savannah knew that wouldn't have been possible. Kit had meant something to her. She'd fallen hard for Kit and didn't regret it. She only regretted that things had had to end.

The water was tepid when she finally got out of the bath. She dried off, slid into her nightie, and climbed into bed. But sleep escaped her. As was the norm, she couldn't turn her brain off. Thoughts tumbled over each other in her head leaving her confused and awake. She finally sat up and grabbed her phone. She'd read for a while. That would help.

But she couldn't concentrate on the words before her. She started reading a romance, but that was too painful. So she switched to a mystery. But a whodunit only reminded her of her failings as an agent. So she settled on a sci-fi book and that's when she gave up. She couldn't read. It was no use.

She flipped over to the messages on her phone. She read the last text from Kit. Did she still miss her? Did she ever think about her? Before she could talk herself out of it, she sent Kit a text.

Where are you? Are you winning big?

Her heart thudded heavily in her chest. Would Kit respond? She stared at the phone, chest heaving, waiting for a response. None came. She didn't know where Kit was, what casino she was playing in. It might be the middle of the night where she was. She might be sound asleep. Or she might be in bed with a woman. Savannah threw her phone across the room, snuggled under the cover, and cried herself to sleep.

It was ten o'clock in the morning when Savannah woke. She heard the vacuum and knew Mrs. Dennis was there. She smiled. At least she wouldn't be alone. For a few hours anyway. She got up and put on a robe. She waved to Mrs. Dennis who turned off the vacuum and followed Savannah to the kitchen.

"You're up late again," Mrs. Dennis said. "Trouble sleeping?"

Savannah felt the tears roll down her cheeks. She didn't try to stop them. She nodded and poured herself a cup of coffee.

"Oh. Sit down, sweetheart. I'll fix your coffee for you."

Savannah sat and gratefully took the cup Mrs. Dennis handed her.

"Are you ready to talk about her yet? I've been patiently waiting, but it's eating you up inside. Obviously. I think it's time you tell me all about her."

Savannah sobbed as she shared her story of her time with Kit. She didn't leave anything out, including the fact that Kit was one of the main suspects in the jewel thefts.

"So that's what's on my mind." She took a deep breath. "That's why I'm so miserable."

"And have you reached out to this Kit woman? Since you've been home?"

"I texted her last night. She didn't answer."

Mrs. Dennis placed her weathered hand over Savannah's.

"You should call her."

"I can't. If she still cared, she'd text back. I don't know what time zone she's in or what she's doing. I can't call her. It could be the middle of the night where she is. Or she could be with someone." She started sobbing again.

"Sh now. You mustn't think that way. I understand your reasons for not calling. I get that you're afraid. But I think that's your best bet."

Savannah took a shaky breath and nodded.

"Maybe I'll do that. I'll think about it anyway. Thanks for listening."

She poured another cup of coffee and went upstairs to get dressed. She went to check her phone, but it wasn't on the nightstand. That's right. She'd thrown it across the room. She found it behind the wastebasket. Her hands shook when she saw she had a message. It was from Kit.

I gave up globetrotting. I'm in California. Are you still in Maryland? Is everything okay?

Savannah couldn't have wiped the smile off her face for a million dollars. Sure, it was one text, but at least Kit was still speaking to her. Life was looking up.

Kit woke early and reached for her phone. There was another text from Savannah. She couldn't stop smiling.

I'm okay. Still dealing with some stuff. Why did you go back to California?

What kind of stuff could she be dealing with? And why didn't she let Kit share the load? Kit had to offer.

Kit: *Can I help? I'm still here for you. No matter what.*

Savannah: *Aw. You're still so sweet. But I have to deal with this on my own.*

Kit: *If you insist. Want to talk about it?*

Savannah: *No thanks. I want to know why you're in California.*

Kit: *Traveling wasn't the same without you, Savannah.*

Savannah: *I'm sorry. For everything.*

Kit: *Can we give it another try?*

Several minutes passed with no response. Kit was afraid she'd blown it.

Savannah: *Maybe. I don't know. I should have answers in a week or so.*

Kit: *So maybe in a week I can come see you?*

Savannah: *Maybe. I don't know.*

Kit: *Can I call you, Savannah? I'd love to hear your voice.*

Savannah: *Not yet. Give me a week, okay?*

Kit: *As long as you don't shut me out again.*

Savannah: *I don't want to, Kit. God, I miss you.*

Kit: *So after a week you may tell me to hit the road again?*

Savannah: *I'll know more how we can proceed. I need you in my life.*

Kit: *I need to be in your life. So that's a good thing.*

Savannah: *I need to go now, Kit. Text me later?*
Kit: *Count on it.*
Kit stared at her phone, but the connection, tenuous though it was, was broken. What the hell was Savannah going through? Did it have to do with work? Was she going to get another assignment? If so, would she leave Kit in the dust again? Kit wondered if she should tell Savannah she knew she was an FBI agent. Maybe that would make her open up to Kit. But no. That needed to come from Savannah. She needed to be honest with Kit. About everything. Even though Kit would take her own secret to the grave.

With a spring in her step, Kit walked to the kitchen to make breakfast. She was hungry. Carlos was at the kitchen table drinking coffee.

"What's with the big smile, my friend? Did you get lucky last night?"

Kit laughed.

"Not exactly. I just finished texting with Savannah."

"What? Really? That's great. How did that happen? Are you back together? Are you flying to Maine?"

"Maryland. It's Maryland. And she texted me last night. I responded and then she texted me back this morning. So we had an actual conversation. Something's up. I don't know what. But I guess we'll have answers in a week or so."

"So you're going to get back together?"

"It's too soon to tell, but God, I hope so."

"That's awesome, Kit. I'm really happy for you."

"Thanks. Let's go to the beach and get some breakfast. Or have you eaten?"

"I have not. Get dressed. Let's go."

They drove to Avila Beach and had Bloody Marys with breakfast. They walked along the beach after and Kit took her shoes off and walked in the cool water. It was already warm out which was unusual for the Central Coast. It promised to be a hot one. Kit had work to do around the ranch, but she wanted to stay inside and text Savannah again. But no, she'd brave the heat and take care of business. Just knowing Savannah was somewhat back in her life made life worth living again.

Kit finished her chores and took a cool shower. She grabbed a beer and texted Savannah.

How was your day?

She waited. And waited. There was no reply. She had just set her phone on the table when it buzzed.

Savannah: *Low-key. How was yours?*

Kit: *Good. I started my day with you. How could it not be good?*

Savannah: *You're so sweet. But please remember I can't commit to anything for a week.*

Kit: *And then? Maybe you'll commit to me?*

Savannah: *Maybe. But I can't say for sure.*

Kit: *What happens in a week?*

Kit knew better than to ask. But she couldn't resist. She needed to know.

Savannah: *Don't worry about it. You'll be the first to know. I promise.*

Kit: *I hope so. I miss you so much.*

Savannah: *I miss you, too, Kit. So very much.*

Kit: *I could fly out to see you. Just to pass the time.*

Savannah: *It would be better if we wait. Please trust me, Kit.*

Kit: *Of course I trust you.*

Savannah: *Thank you. I need to go now. I'll talk to you tomorrow.*

Kit: *Sleep well, Savannah.*

Savannah: *You, too.*

"Hey, Kit." Carlos came in. "Reynaldo and I are heading into SLO for dinner. You wanna come with?"

"Sure. Where are we going? What's the dress code?"

"Dress nice. I'll be back in half an hour."

Kit showered and put on gray linen slacks and a long-sleeved black shirt. She wore it open at the collar without a tie. San Luis wasn't a fancy town. She figured she looked nice enough.

They went to an Italian restaurant that served deliciously authentic food. The wine was very good as well and Kit and Carlos went through two bottles. Reynaldo was the designated driver, as usual.

Kit was in fine spirits when they arrived back at the ranch. She said good night to the boys and poured herself a whiskey. She wasn't ready to call it a night. She didn't want the day to end. She would forever think of this day as the day she and Savannah got back together. She just hoped it wouldn't be temporary. She wasn't sure what was happening in a week, but she'd keep her fingers crossed for it to work out in her favor. She needed to see Savannah. To be with Savannah. To kiss her and hold her and make love to her. Her fingers were crossed. One week. She could make it.

CHAPTER TWENTY-EIGHT

Savannah sat cooling her heels in the director's waiting room. She'd been there an hour and a half and had no idea when she'd be called in. Her stomach was in knots, her palms sweaty, and her heart raced. She had made up her mind about how she wanted to live her life. She just needed to tell Director Bremer. She was curious as to what the director would have to say to her. She wondered what his investigation had turned up. She knew in her heart of hearts it couldn't have turned up anything, but she knew how those investigations went sometimes.

The door to the director's office opened and there stood Director Bremer.

"Come in, Brown." He was curt, cool, and definitely uninviting.

She walked into his office and sat in the chair he motioned to.

"Tell me about the blue-eyed woman," he said without preamble.

Savannah felt the heat rush to her face. *Stay cool. Don't give anything away.*

"What would you like to know about her?"

"She's the one you investigated personally, no?"

"Yes, sir. We even set up a sting to catch her. But she didn't take the bait."

"Do you still believe she was guilty?"

Savannah thought for a minute. How to answer? Even if Kit had been the thief, she was out of the business now.

"No, sir."

"Who do you think is the thief?"

"I think he's a bold, charming, middle-aged man who seduces women then steals their jewels."

"A man? According to your notes, and Agent Nguyen, you believed it was a woman."

"Yes, sir," Savannah said. "I did. I believed that's why the women were too embarrassed to admit what happened. But I never ruled out the possibility that it was a man. Nguyen ran headlong into the suspect one night and couldn't tell me if it was a man or a woman. So I think it was a masculine woman or a middle-aged man."

"I see. Do you realize that since I've pulled you from the case there hasn't been another robbery?"

"I didn't know that. No, sir."

"How easy would it have been for you to rob these women?"

Savannah couldn't believe her ears.

"Sir! That's not in my nature."

He waved her off.

"Be that as it may, I'm reassigning you. I'm not sure what your new assignment will be. I'll let you know as soon as I decide where we need you."

He stood and Savannah forced herself to stay seated. She took a deep breath.

"You're serious about not assigning me to the jewel thief case again?"

"I am. You squandered department money and took an extended vacation. You were too busy enjoying yourself to fully do your job."

"Sir. That's not true!"

He put out his hand, palm up.

"It's how I see it. Do what you need to with your life now, Brown. I'll let you know as soon as I have another assignment."

Savannah took a deep breath and wiped her palms on her skirt. She was about to make the biggest move of her life. She just hoped to God it was the right thing. She'd enjoyed her downtime once the shock had worn off. And if she wanted to pursue something with Kit, she couldn't be jetting here and there solving crimes.

"Actually, sir." She took a piece of paper out of her briefcase. "I've decided to resign. I think it's time."

"Are you certain? I'm sure I'll have a new assignment for you shortly."

"Thank you. But I really want to go back to being an average citizen. I've enjoyed my time off. Besides, it's time to think about my future. And I don't think my future includes the Bureau. Thank you for everything, Director."

Director Bremer sat heavily in his leather chair.

"So your mind's made up?"

"Yes, sir."

"I'm sorry to see your career end on such a sour note. But if it's time, then I respect your wishes. Your badge and firearm, please."

Savannah handed her things to the director. She was conflicted. It was the right thing to do. But it seemed so final. She wanted to cry at the enormity of it. But she wouldn't cry. Not now. Not in front of him.

"May I reapply in the future?" she said.

"Certainly. If you don't though, have a good life."

She wasn't sure her legs would support her, but she managed to stand and walk out of his office. She left the building for the last time. She was unemployed and, by extension, had no identity. It was surreal. Everything in the city seemed to be moving in slow motion. She watched people walk by as if it was just another day. As if her whole world hadn't just begun anew.

Savannah sat in her car taking deep breaths. She'd done it. And she wouldn't second-guess herself. She was going to move on with Kit. If that's what Kit truly wanted. Tears of fear threatened again. What if she'd just made a colossal mistake? But, she couldn't cry. Not if she was going to drive the hour and a half home. She could cry when she got there. Not before. She started her car and pulled out of the lot, leaving the FBI building and her life in the rearview mirror.

She had stopped shaking by the time she arrived at her house. She was excited instead. She'd been the best agent she knew how to be and had been spiraling upward in the organization. And now? Well, now she was unemployed. And free. She mustn't focus on the negative. She was free to do whatever with whomever. Life was good.

She went into her kitchen and found a pitcher of Bloody Marys with a note from Mrs. Dennis.

"To celebrate or drown your sorrows. Enjoy. I'll see you tomorrow."

Savannah poured herself a glass and sat at her kitchen table. She took a sip. They were good. Damned good. She could drink herself into oblivion. That sounded like a wonderful idea.

As she drank, her mind went back to Director Bremer's words. There'd been no more robberies. Kit was back in the States. Was there a correlation? God, she didn't want to believe that. She had to be able to trust Kit. Could she?

Kit. There was the reason she'd retired. She could spend forever with Kit now. Forever. That was a long time. Was that truly what she wanted? She didn't hesitate. Yes. She wanted forever with Kit. But would Kit be able to give up her thieving ways to spend forever with Savannah? Was it a compulsion to rob? Or was she over it? Was she ever actually involved in it? Savannah was sure she'd never know. She had to accept Kit's innocence in order to move forward with her life. And it was time to do just that.

How's it going?

She sent the text and held her breath waiting for a reply.

Kit: *I'm good. How are you?*

Savannah: *I've had better days.*

Kit: *I'm sorry. What can I do to help?*

Savannah: *Come see me, Kit. Please?*

Kit: *Are you serious? I'd love to. When?*

Savannah: *Yesterday?*

Kit: *LOL So, like now?*

Savannah: *Let's make it tomorrow.*

Kit: *You got it. Where should I fly into?*

Savannah: *Baltimore. Fly into BWI.*

Kit: *What time?*

Savannah: *Whenever. Just book your flight and let me know what time to pick you up.*

Kit: *You got it. I'm off to do that right now. I'll get back to you.*

Savannah: *Sounds good.*

Kit was coming to see her. Would they make it in ordinary life away from the excitement and glitter of the world's most famous casinos? Would Kit find Hampstead, Savannah's little slice of heaven, boring and too mundane? Where did she live in California? She'd never said. Probably somewhere with bright lights and lots of action. Damn. What was Savannah thinking inviting her to Hampstead?

Kit couldn't believe what was happening. She was going to see Savannah. It was like a dream come true. She checked flights to Baltimore. There were layovers on every one. She didn't want to wait that long. She called her private pilot and told him she wanted to leave at eight the next morning. He agreed and she texted Savannah.

I should be there around two tomorrow afternoon. Can't wait to see you.

She waited but there was no response. Frustrated and worried, she sent another text.

Babe? You okay?

Still no reply. She had no idea what was going on on the other side of the country but needed to hear from Savannah.

Are you getting my texts?

No answer. She slipped her phone in her pocket and went down the hall to her bedroom to pack.

What's the weather like there? How long should I pack for?

Maybe Savannah was in the shower. Maybe? She couldn't still her concerns no matter how hard she tried. She thought about calling her, but reasoned Savannah would reply when she could.

Kit googled Baltimore weather. It seemed similar to San Luis Obispo, so she packed cargo shorts and golf shirts with a couple of short-sleeved oxfords. She threw in two pairs of linen slacks and a couple of ties and felt ready to go. She'd packed for a week. She hoped to be there longer. Much longer. But for the time being, a week's worth of clothes would have to suffice.

She looked at her phone again. Nothing from Savannah. She needed to do something, so she texted Carlos to see if he wanted to go surfing. He was in her kitchen ten minutes later in his wetsuit. She changed into hers and they headed for Pismo Beach.

Kit was just getting out of her truck when her phone buzzed.

Sorry. I took a nap. Are you around?

"Give me a few, Carlos," Kit said. "You can head down to the water."

Carlos rolled his eyes but started the trek down the hill.

Kit: *I'm here. I'm glad you're okay. I was worried.*

Savannah: *Sorry to worry you. I'm excited that you'll be here tomorrow afternoon.*

Kit: *I'm excited, too. I'm all packed.*

Savannah: *It's been warm here. In the nineties.*

Kit: *I packed accordingly. I packed for a week. Hope that's okay.*

Savannah: *That's perfect. You may hate it here. LOL*

Kit: *I couldn't hate it there. You're there. That's all that matters.*

Savannah: *Thank you, Kit. I can't wait to see you.*

Kit: *Ditto.*

Savannah: *What are you doing now?*

Kit: *Getting ready to catch some waves.*

Savannah: *Oh good. Enjoy. Text me when you get home?*

Kit: *You got it.*

She stared at her phone but there were no more messages. Kit placed her phone in her glove compartment, grabbed her board, and practically floated down to the water.

Kit felt on top of the world as she rode wave after wave to the shore. Several hours later, exhausted but exhilarated, Kit and Carlos stowed their boards and went to a local dive for beer and burgers.

"So what's the deal with lover girl?" Carlos said.

"I'm going to see her tomorrow."

"And when did you plan on telling me I'd be house sitting again?"

"I'm telling you now."

"Well, good for you. How long will you be gone?"

"I don't know. At least a week."

Carlos nodded.

"I'm happy for you, Kit. It's about time you moved on."

"Thanks, man. I'm so excited."

"You really think she's the one, huh?"

Kit smiled so wide her face hurt.

"I do."

"What does she do again?"

Kit felt her smile fade.

"Well, I think she's independently wealthy, but I also think she may be an FBI agent."

Carlos grew serious.

"Kit, you don't like the law."

It was true. Outside of her extracurricular activities that Carlos knew nothing about, the woman who had crushed Kit's heart had been a cop.

"I know. But I can make an exception. Savannah is wonderful."

"I sure hope you know what you're doing, my friend."

"I can't deny my heart, Carlos. I can't do it."

"I'm not telling you to. I just want you to protect that heart of yours."

"I've protected it long enough. It's time to let it feel again."

"Please be careful," Carlos said.

"Too late."

When they got back to the ranch, Kit hopped in the shower and washed off the salt and sand. She dressed in ratty shorts and a Tubes T-shirt then grabbed her phone and lay on her bed.

Kit: *I'm home. Are you around?*

Savannah: *I am. How was surfing?*

Kit: *Awesome. How's your day going?*

Savannah: *Quiet.*

Kit: *Are you okay?*

Savannah: *I will be. Especially knowing you're coming tomorrow.*

Kit: *I'm like a little kid at Christmas.*

Savannah: *Me, too. I can't wait to see you.*

Kit: *Can I call you, Savannah? I'd love to hear your voice.*

Savannah: *No. Let's just wait until we see each other tomorrow.*

Kit: *But that's so far away.*

Savannah: *LOL. Not really.*

Kit: *Really. But, okay. I'll respect your wishes.*

Savannah: *Thank you.*

Kit searched her mind for something, anything to write. She needed to keep the conversation going.

Kit: *Will you pick me up from the airport?*

Savannah: *Of course. Okay, Kit. It's getting late here. I need to turn in.*

Kit: *No!*

Savannah: *LOL. Yes. It's time. Enjoy the rest of your evening and I'll see you tomorrow.*

Kit: *Sweet dreams, Savannah.*

She waited impatiently but there was no response. She leaned back against her headboard and let out a long sigh. She couldn't wait to see Savannah, couldn't wait to taste her lips again. Were they on the same page? Surely Savannah was thinking the same thing, or she wouldn't have invited Kit to spend time with her. But she'd kicked Kit to the curb once before already. What was to stop her from doing it again?

She needed to get out of her head. She needed to stop that train of thought. She heard noise coming from down the hall and went to investigate. Carlos was rearranging her living room.

"What are you doing?" Kit asked.

"I figured this house is as good as mine now, so I thought I'd arrange it how I want it."

"Very funny. Stop moving my furniture and make a pitcher of margaritas. I need you to get me out of my head."

"Are you having second thoughts?"

"Yes and no. I'm in this one hundred percent. I just hope she is, too."

"Why would she invite you out if she's not?"

"I don't know."

"Damn you. Stop thinking and just go with it."

"What happened to protecting my heart?"

"You said yourself that it's too late."

"It is. But damn, Carlos. I don't want to get hurt again."

"Then don't go. Stay here and forget her."

"I wish I could. I need to go. I miss her so much. But if she dumps me again, I don't know that I'll be able to bounce back," Kit said.

"And conversely? If she doesn't hurt you?"

"I'll be the happiest woman on earth."

CHAPTER TWENTY-NINE

Kit's MO was to have a few cocktails then sleep on the flight. Not that flying scared her. It's just what she did. But she didn't have any cocktails the following morning. She wanted to be sharp when she saw Savannah again. And she couldn't sleep. She was too keyed up. Too excited. So the flight was long and she was about to climb the walls when her pilot finally announced he was beginning his descent.

The butterflies that had taken up residence in her stomach began to flutter with a vengeance. She wiped her palms on her shorts. And then wiped them again. She took some deep breaths, but nothing seemed to calm her down. Her future depended on these next few days, and she realized how important they were. But, she reasoned, Savannah wouldn't have invited her to Baltimore if she wasn't really into Kit. If she never wanted to hear from her again, she could have texted that to her. Or she could have just not responded to Kit. So she must like her. Right?

She took another deep breath as she felt the plane touch down. She was here. In Maryland. Would this be her new home? God, she hoped so.

Kit got off the plane, collected her bags, and headed to the front of the terminal. She didn't know what kind of car Savannah drove so searched the vehicles for her face.

"Kit?" She turned to see Savannah standing behind her. "How did you get past me?"

Damn, Savannah was a sight for sore eyes. She was wearing a green sundress that clung to her curves and made her eyes sparkle.

"Sorry. I took a private jet. No baggage claim for me."

"Nice. Well it sure is good to see you."

"You, too. You look amazing."

Kit wanted to take Savannah in her arms and kiss her right there. But she didn't. She wasn't sure how friendly Baltimore was and she certainly wasn't looking for trouble.

"So do you, Kit. It's so good to see you."

She enveloped Kit in a warm hug that sent Kit's senses reeling. Every nerve ending in Kit's body responded to the feel of Savannah pressed against her. She was let down when Savannah finally stepped back.

"Are you hungry?" Savannah said.

For you.

"Sure. Now that you mention it."

"Great. I thought we'd grab some lunch on the way home."

"Great idea."

Though Kit didn't want to stop. She wanted to get to Savannah's house where they could be alone, and she could reclaim Savannah as hers and only hers. But she knew she had to let Savannah set the pace.

"What's it like living in Baltimore?" Kit asked as she followed Savannah to her car.

"I don't actually live in Baltimore. No worries though. You'll see where I live soon enough." Curiouser and curiouser. "How was your flight?"

"It was good. Long though. Damn, it's a long way across this country of ours."

Savannah laughed. It was music to Kit's ears.

"Yes. Flying coast to coast is a drag. I'll give you that. I'm glad you chartered a private jet. Otherwise the trip would have really dragged out."

"Yeah. Commercial airlines all had a couple of layovers."

"Which airport did you fly out of? I don't even know which part of California you live in."

"I live in the Central Coast. So I flew out of San Luis Obispo."

"San Luis? I love it there. So beautiful."

"Indeed," Kit said. "It's a slice of heaven there."

"I have to admit, I thought you'd live somewhere with bright lights. Like a big city."

"Nope. That's not for me. I love to visit places like that, but my home is my sanctuary. I have a ranch in See Canyon. It's about fifteen minutes from San Luis and about five from the beach."

Savannah reached over and patted Kit's thigh. Her touch seared through Kit's shorts and burned her.

"Good," Savannah said. "Then you might like my little slice of heaven, too. I live in a small town of about six thousand."

"That sounds wonderful."

"It really is. And, while I don't live on a ranch, my three quarters of an acre suits me just fine."

"I can't wait to see your place, Savannah."

Savannah smiled at her before turning her attention back to the road.

"So how far are you from Baltimore?"

"About a half hour to forty-five minutes."

"Nice."

Kit swallowed hard before she asked her next question.

"Are you far from DC?"

"About an hour and a half. So it's a trek, but not bad."

Kit simply nodded. Her mind was a whirlwind of thought, questions, and fears. Yes, she was legit now. And, no, she didn't think she'd ever be caught. But still…the thought that Savannah had been trying to catch her loomed large in her mind. She needed to change her train of thought. Even if Savannah had originally been investigating Kit, surely her feelings had grown. Or was this still part of her investigation? Kit suddenly felt sick.

Savannah drove down a quaint street with colonial buildings.

"Welcome to Hampstead," she said. "It's not much, but it's home."

"It's adorable," Kit said. "Absolutely adorable. I love it."

"Are you ready for lunch?"

Kit wasn't. She didn't know if she could eat. She needed to quit thinking and just enjoy Savannah. Maybe over lunch she'd press her into admitting she was an FBI agent.

"Sure," she lied. "Lead the way."

"You'd better be telling the truth because the portions here will make your head swim."

Kit made herself laugh. She'd have a beer or two. Relax. She needed to lose the tension. She followed Savannah inside a lovely restaurant that smelled delicious. Her stomach responded. She hadn't eaten all day and food would be good for her.

"What's good here?" She picked up her menu and looked at all the restaurant had to offer.

"Anything and everything. I'll be having the crab cakes because they're my favorite."

Kit set her menu down.

"Good enough for me."

Savannah reached across the table and gave Kit's hands a squeeze.

"I've missed you so much, Kit."

"I've missed you, too. But you're okay?"

Savannah nodded and drew a shaky breath.

"I'm getting there."

Kit nodded. She mustered all her courage and looked Savannah in the eye.

"What happened, Savannah? Why did you have to fly home? Why all the secrecy? Why did I have to wait another week? Talk to me, babe."

"I don't know where to begin. Though I know you deserve the truth."

Savannah's stomach tightened. How much should she tell? Would she scare Kit off with the truth? It was her greatest fear. But Kit deserved to know. Their relationship had been founded on lies. If Kit knew the truth would she stay with Savannah?

"Start at the beginning," Kit said.

"Okay." Savannah nodded. "I guess the beginning would mean confessing I wasn't out gambling my way around the world for fun."

"So there's no rich ex who left you a shitload of money?"

"Oh, there was. That part was true. Everything I told you about my life was true. I just left out some important information."

"I'm listening."

"Yes. Lucinda left me with plenty of money. I truly am independently wealthy. But I got bored. I missed her so and needed something to do to occupy my mind and my hours."

"Okay," Kit said.

"I became an FBI agent."

"That sounds exciting."

Kit showed no sign of distress. She sipped her beer and watched Savannah. But she didn't seem in the least bit disturbed by this revelation. Maybe she wasn't a criminal after all.

"Oh, Kit. It was. It was such an awesome job. I got to travel and catch bad guys. It was an incredible job."

"You speak of it in the past tense."

Savannah nodded.

"Right. I'll get to that."

"Okay. Carry on."

Savannah wasn't sure how to phrase the next part. She decided to just forge ahead and watch Kit's reaction.

"I'm not sure if you were aware, but there was a series of jewel heists in the casinos we were at."

"I read something about one or two thefts, but I didn't realize there was a series of them." Kit sounded calm, collected. She showed no signs of guilt. What had Savannah expected? A confession? She pressed onward.

"I was on duty that whole time. I was tasked with finding the thief."

"And did you?"

Savannah shook her head.

"I did not. And then I was pulled from the assignment."

"I'm sorry, Savannah. I'm sure you were the best damned agent they had."

Savannah chuckled wryly.

"I liked to think so. But the director thought otherwise. So I was pulled stateside, put on hiatus for two weeks, and when I met with him again, he had no assignment for me. So I resigned. I'm officially retired now."

"That sounds like a good thing. Why so melancholy?"

Savannah nodded slowly.

"I'll miss it. In some ways. In a lot of ways. But it also freed me up to pursue our relationship. To be with you. If you'll still have me."

"Of course I'll still have you. You were on the job. You couldn't tell me. I get that. I totally get that. But no more hiding things from me, okay? You can tell me anything. You can trust me with your deepest, darkest secrets. Okay?"

"Okay." Savannah released a rush of air. She hadn't realized she'd been holding her breath. "And you? Anything nefarious in your history that I need to know about?"

Kit laughed and shook her head.

"Nope. I've got nothing you need to know. I'm pretty much an open book." She paused. "Well, wait. There is one thing you should know."

Savannah's heart raced.

"What's that?"

"The woman who shattered my heart was in law enforcement. So I do tend to shy away from the law. As in avoid cops and such with a passion. But I'll make an exception for you."

"Oh, thank you, Kit. I'm not about to hurt your heart. Or any part of you. I really want to make this work."

"As do I, Savannah. As do I."

They finished their lunches and took a leisurely stroll along Main Street. Savannah felt a million pounds lighter having told Kit the whole truth. Well, mostly the whole truth. Of course, she hadn't mentioned that Kit had been a prime suspect. Kit need never know that. Savannah would see to that.

"I love your little town," Kit said.

Savannah beamed with pride.

"I'm so glad. Are you ready to see my house now?"

"I'm beyond ready."

Savannah took Kit's hand and they walked back to the parking lot. They drove to Savannah's house and she parked in the driveway.

"Here we are. We're home."

"I love it. I love old Victorian homes."

"Thanks. So do I. It's all modern on the inside though."

"And do you have a yard service? Or do you keep this up on your own?"

"I have a couple of women who see to most of it. But I do love working in my flower beds."

"It shows," Kit said. "It really does show."

"Shall we go inside?"

"I'm ready."

Savannah popped the back door and Kit got her bags. Savannah hurried to open the front door. She stepped out of the way so Kit could enter. And then she held her breath. She needed Kit's approval more than she'd realized.

"Wow. You've really made a home here. It's beautiful, Savannah."

"Thank you."

"Where shall I put my bags?"

"My bedroom is upstairs. So just leave them there by the stairs for now."

Savannah's phone buzzed. She looked at it, wondering who could be texting her. It was Nadine.

Who's the woman?

Savannah laughed.

"What?" Kit said.

"Just the neighbors wanting to know who you are."

"And what will you tell them?"

"What should I tell them?"

"You tell me," Kit said.

"I'll tell them you're the number one woman in my life. But I won't text it to them. Come on. I'll introduce you."

CHAPTER THIRTY

It was a pleasure meeting you." Kit told the Goldens as they left their house. And she meant it. Frank and Nadine were lovely people and Kit had enjoyed having drinks with them and hearing stories about Savannah.

But she'd had enough socializing. She was beyond ready for some serious alone time with Savannah. It had been too long since she'd heard Savannah scream her name. Too long since she'd tasted her unique flavor. Too long since she'd felt her soft, silky skin beneath her. She was beyond ready to prove to her how much she cared.

When they were back at Savannah's house Kit took Savannah in her arms.

"Do you even remember the last time I kissed you?"

"It's been too long," Savannah said. "Far too long."

"I'm glad you feel that way. I was beginning to wonder if you were avoiding me."

"Never, Kit. I need you like I need the air I breathe. I've missed you so these past few weeks."

Kit nuzzled Savannah's neck.

"Mm. Has it only been a few weeks? It feels like forever."

"It really does. You're driving me mad, Kit. Stop messing around and kiss me already."

Kit didn't need to be asked twice. She kissed Savannah softly, tenderly. The emotion behind Savannah's response made her head spin. Kit allowed her tongue to meander into Savannah's mouth and when their tongues met, her heart surged. It galloped in her chest and she couldn't wait for the next step.

"Show me your bedroom," Kit murmured against Savannah's lips.

"Right this way."

She took Kit's hand and led her up the stairs and down the hallway. The beauty of the old house wasn't lost on Kit, but she could wait for the grand tour. The only thing that mattered at that moment was making love to Savannah.

Kit kissed Savannah again. This time she made sure Savannah could feel all her pent up passion. There was no pretense of tenderness. It was a kiss fueled by need and urgency. She thought her head would explode from the blood pounding in it. And then the blood shifted. It was all between her legs. She was throbbing and aching with a pain only Savannah could soothe.

"I love kissing you," Savannah said. "But I need more."

Kit chuckled.

"Impatient much?"

"I am impatient. I need you, Kit. It's been far too long. I need to know I'm the only one for you. Show me, please."

Kit stepped back and absorbed Savannah's words. Did she mean them? Kit felt warm all over.

"Do you mean that?"

"That I need you? Of course."

"No," Kit said. "The other part."

"What other part?"

"The bit about you being the only one for me?"

Savannah's eyes grew large. She looked terrified.

"I mean, if that's what you want."

"No, Savannah. I'm asking if that's what you want."

Savannah moved out of Kit's reach. She sat on the bed and rested her face in her hands. Kit placed a hand gently on Savannah's shoulder.

"Savannah?"

"I know I can't ask that of you. You're a world traveler. You've probably got a woman in every port."

Kit smiled. She'd definitely had a woman pretty much everywhere she'd touched down. But she wanted to put those days behind her. She wanted to commit to Savannah and make a life with her. But she needed to be sure that was what Savannah wanted as well.

"Just answer the question, Savannah. Is that what you want?"

Savannah looked up at Kit and Kit saw her eyes were red and wet.

"Yes, okay? I'd love that, but—"

"No buts, babe. That's what I want, too."

Savannah visibly relaxed. Kit watched the tension leave her body.

"You do?"

Kit genuflected in front of Savannah.

"I don't have a ring...yet...but, Savannah, will you marry me?"

"Are you serious?"

"Dead."

"Oh yes. A million times yes. It would be an honor."

Kit released a long, worried breath. She smiled up at Savannah.

"Most excellent." She stood. "Now that that's settled, let's get to bed."

Kit was frantic for Savannah. She took her quickly and hurriedly. When Savannah claimed she'd had enough, Kit slowed the pace. She took her time and explored every inch of Savannah. She never wanted to leave her again and she wanted Savannah to feel that commitment in every touch, every kiss. She tasted everything Savannah had to offer and relished her flavors, her scents, everything about her.

Savannah arched off the bed and froze, screaming Kit's name. When she'd relaxed in a heap on the mattress, Kit kissed her way back up Savannah's body and held her close.

"I love you, Savannah," she whispered against Savannah's silky locks.

Savannah rolled over and faced her.

"Do you mean that?"

"I'm going to marry you, aren't I?"

"Say it again."

"I'm going to marry you, aren't I?"

They both burst out laughing.

"That's not what I meant and you know it."

"I love you, Savannah. I'll say it as many times as you'd like. I'll shout it from the rooftops. I love you."

"You're the best, Kit. I don't know what I did to deserve you."

"You were born."

"I love you, too, Kit. So very much."

Savannah's phone rang on the bedside table.

"Ignore it," Kit said.

"Don't worry. I'm too busy to answer the phone."

"Good answer."

Kit kissed Savannah then and felt her passion surge. The phone finally stopped, and she could concentrate on Savannah.

"Kit?" Savannah said tentatively.

"Yes, my love?"

"Are you stone?"

Kit laughed. She definitely was not stone.

"No. Not at all. I just derive more pleasure from giving than receiving."

Savannah's phone started ringing again.

"I wonder if I should answer."

"No. Now why did you ask if I was stone?"

"Because. I want to make love to you, Kit. I want to please you as you've pleased me."

Kit stroked Savannah's hair and bare back. She was so soft. All over.

"I'd like that, babe. If you're sure it's what you want to do."

"Oh, thank you. I'm so nervous though. Tell me what you like."

"It's easier to tell you what I don't like. While your mouth on me would feel amazing, you need to know it won't make me climax."

"But it's okay if I taste you?"

"You can do whatever you'd like, lover."

Savannah's heart soared. Even as her stomach tightened with nerves. She wanted to make Kit feel good. What if Savannah couldn't do that? It had been a very long time since she'd pleased a woman. What if she forgot how?

"You okay, babe?" Kit said.

Savannah nodded.

"Yes. Just a little overwhelmed. I don't even know where to start."

"I think you should start by kissing me. Then go from there. Do what feels right. Do what feels natural."

"What if I can't make you feel good?"

"Oh, sweetheart. That's not going to happen."

Savannah was still filled with trepidation. But she needed to try. She pushed her nerves aside and kissed Kit. When their tongues met, all fear dissipated. She lost herself in the kiss and eventually ran her hand over Kit's body. Kit moaned into Savannah's mouth. Emboldened, Savannah brought her hand to a stop at Kit's small, firm breasts. She pinched and tugged on one nipple and then the other.

"Oh, my God. That feels so good," Kit groaned.

Savannah smiled as she ran her hand down to where Kit's legs met. She was so soft and warm. And wet. Dear God, Savannah couldn't believe how wet she was.

"You're so ready for me," Savannah said.

"Always, babe. I'm always ready for you."

Savannah slid her fingers deep inside Kit and Kit arched off the bed to take her deeper. Savannah stroked Kit's walls then began plunging in and out. Kit thrashed her head on the pillow and Savannah knew she was close. She ran her thumb across Kit's clit then pressed into it, making slow circles.

"I'm gonna come," Kit growled.

"Please do. Let me know how good I make you feel."

"Yes." Then Kit let out a guttural moan as she rode her orgasm. Savannah slowly and gently removed her fingers then lay next to Kit, whose eyes were at half mast.

"I love you, Kit," Savannah whispered.

"Thank God. I didn't think you were ever going to tell me."

"I think I've been in love with you for a while now. Saying good-bye to you was one of the hardest things I've ever done."

"It sure sucked for me, too. But we'll never have to say good-bye again, my love. Never."

Savannah's phone rang again.

"Who keeps calling me?"

"Ignore it."

"I will. But if they call again I might answer it."

"Fair enough."

"So how are we going to work this?" Savannah said.

"Work what?"

"You live in California. I live here. That poses a bit of a problem, don't you think?"

Kit propped herself on an elbow and looked into Savannah's eyes.

"Why is that a problem?"

"You mean you want to have a long-distance relationship?"

"Hell no. I couldn't handle being away from you."

"So then what?"

"We spend part of the year here and part on my ranch."

"Seriously?"

"Sure. Unless you have a better idea."

"Not really. It will be nice to spend our winters in California."

"Indeed. No snow or bitter cold there."

"You make me so happy, Kit."

"Right back at you."

The shrill ringing of her phone again made Savannah jump.

"Let me just see who it is," she said.

"Fair enough."

Savannah checked her phone. Li. Why was he calling her? What could he want?

"Do you mind if I answer it?"

"Go for it."

Savannah picked up her phone.

"Hello?"

"Boss? It's Li. Where have you been? I've been trying to reach you."

"Sorry. I was busy. What's up?"

"We got him, Savannah," Li said.

"Who?" She sat up straighter.

"The jewel thief. We caught him red-handed in Atlantic City."

Savannah unconsciously cast a glance over her shoulder at Kit.

"You did? That's fantastic."

"So far he's only copped to one robbery but we're trying to pin the rest on him. It's just a matter of proving he was at all the other casinos. Should be easy enough."

"Well, good job, Li. I'm happy for you."

"Thanks. I'll let you go now. I'll keep you posted by text."

"That would be great. Take care, Li."

"You too, boss."

She set the phone down and lay back down next to Kit.

"Who was that?"

"The guy they placed in charge of the investigation they pulled me from."

"Yeah? What did he want?"

"They caught the jewel thief, Kit." Relief coursed through Savannah's body. She fought not to cry happy tears.

Kit arched an eyebrow.

"They did? That's great, babe. Even though you're not part of the team, that has to feel good."

"You have no idea."

Kit laughed.

"Well, I'm happy for you. Who was it?"

"Some guy. I don't know the details. They caught him with the jewels though. In Atlantic City. Oh, Kit. You have no idea how happy this makes me. We should celebrate."

"Lay back, babe. I know just how I want to celebrate."

Savannah smiled up at Kit, joy coursing through her body. It wasn't Kit. It had never been Kit. She could put her suspicions aside and begin her life of love.

Kit took Savannah to places she'd never dreamed she'd go. She came over and over again and finally lay content in Kit's arms.

"We should talk about our wedding," Savannah said.

Kit chuckled.

"You sure you don't want to sleep for a while?"

"I'm too excited to sleep. Where should we get married?"

Kit lay on her back, hands folded behind her head, and looked up at Savannah.

"Anywhere you want, babe."

"I'd love to get married here. But a wedding on a ranch sounds so romantic."

"You're going to love my ranch. But you know what else sounds romantic?"

"What?"

"A wedding on the beach."

"Where?"

"In California. Or anywhere in the world, babe. Dream big. Anything you want, if it's in my power, I'll give it to you."

"What would I do without you, Kit?"

"That, my love, you'll never have to worry about again."

About the Author

MJ Williamz was raised on California's central coast, which she left at age seventeen to pursue an education. She graduated from Chico State, and it was in Chico that she rediscovered her love of writing. It wasn't until she moved to Portland, however, that her writing really took off, with the publication of her first short story in 2003.

MJ is the author of nineteen books, including three Goldie Award winners. She has also had over thirty short stories published, most of them erotica with a few romances and a few horrors thrown in for good measure. She lives in Houston with her wife, fellow author Laydin Michaels, and their fur babies. You can find her on FaceBook or reach her at mjwilliamz@aol.com

Books Available from Bold Strokes Books

Flight to the Horizon by Julie Tizard. Airline captain Kerri Sullivan and flight attendant Janine Case struggle to survive an emergency water landing and overcome dark secrets to give love a chance to fly. (978-1-63555-331-4)

In Helen's Hands by Nanisi Barrett D'Arnuk. As her mistress, Helen pushes Mickey to her sensual limits, delivering the pleasure only a BDSM lifestyle can provide her. (978-1-63555-639-1)

Jamis Bachman, Ghost Hunter by Jen Jensen. In Sage Creek, Utah, a poltergeist stirs to life and past secrets emerge.(978-1-63555-605-6)

Moon Shadow by Suzie Clarke. Add betrayal, season with survival, then serve revenge smokin' hot with a sharp knife. (978-1-63555-584-4)

Spellbound by Jean Copeland and Jackie D. When the supernatural worlds of good and evil face off, love might be what saves them all. (978-1-63555-564-6)

Temptation by Kris Bryant. Can experienced nanny Cassie Miller deny her growing attraction and keep her relationship with her boss professional? Or will they sidestep propriety and give in to temptation? (978-1-63555-508-0)

The Inheritance by Ali Vali. Family ties bring Tucker Delacroix and Willow Vernon together, but they could also tear them, and any chance they have at love, apart. (978-1-63555-303-1)

Thief of the Heart by MJ Williamz. Kit Hanson makes a living seducing rich women in casinos and relieving them of the expensive jewelry most won't even miss. But her streak ends when she meets beautiful FBI agent Savannah Brown. (978-1-63555-572-1)

Date Night by Raven Sky. Quinn and Riley are celebrating their one-year anniversary. Such an important milestone is bound to result in some extraordinary sexual adventures, but precisely how extraordinary is up to you, dear reader. (978-1-63555-655-1)

Face Off by PJ Trebelhorn. Hockey player Savannah Wells rarely spends more than a night with any one woman, but when photographer Madison Scott buys the house next door, she's forced to rethink what she expects out of life. (978-1-63555-480-9)

Hot Ice by Aurora Rey, Elle Spencer, Erin Zak. Can falling in love melt the hearts of the iciest ice queens? Join Aurora Rey, Elle Spencer, and Erin Zak to find out! (978-1-63555-513-4)

Line of Duty by VK Powell. Dr. Dylan Carlyle's professional and personal life is turned upside down when a tragic event at Fairview Station pits her against ambitious, handsome police officer Finley Masters. (978-1-63555-486-1)

London Undone by Nan Higgins. London Craft reinvents her life after reading a childhood letter to her future self and in doing so finds the love she truly wants. (978-1-63555-562-2)

Lunar Eclipse by Gun Brooke. Moon De Cruz lives alone on an uninhabited planet after being shipwrecked in space. Her life changes forever when Captain Beaux Lestarion's arrival threatens the planet and Moon's freedom. (978-1-63555-460-1)

One Small Step by Michelle Binfield. Iris and Cam discover the meaning of taking chances and following your heart, even if it means getting hurt. (978-1-63555-596-7)

Shadows of a Dream by Nicole Disney. Rainn has the talent to take her rock band all the way, but falling in love is a powerful distraction, and her new girlfriend's meth addiction might just take them both down. (978-1-63555-598-1)

Someone to Love by Jenny Frame. When Davina Trent is given an unexpected family, can she let nanny Wendy Darling teach her to open her heart to the children and to Wendy? (978-1-63555-468-7)

Tinsel by Kris Bryant. Did a sweet kitten show up to help Jessica Raymond and Taylor Mitchell find each other? Or is the holiday spirit to blame for their special connection? (978-1-63555-641-4)

Uncharted by Robyn Nyx. As Rayne Marcellus and Chase Stinsen track the legendary Golden Trinity, they must learn to put their differences aside and depend on one another to survive. (978-1-63555-325-3)

Where We Are by Annie McDonald. Can two women discover a way to walk on the same path together and discover the gift of staying in one spot, in time, in space, and in love? (978-1-63555-581-3)

A Moment in Time by Lisa Moreau. A longstanding family feud separates two women who unexpectedly fall in love at an antique clock shop in a small Louisiana town. (978-1-63555-419-9)

Aspen in Moonlight by Kelly Wacker. When art historian Melissa Warren meets Sula Johansen, director of a local bear conservancy, she discovers that love can come in unexpected and unusual forms. (978-1-63555-470-0)

Back to September by Melissa Brayden. Small bookshop owner Hannah Shepard and famous romance novelist Parker Bristow maneuver the landscape of their two very different worlds to find out if love can win out in the end. (978-1-63555-576-9)

Changing Course by Brey Willows. When the woman of your dreams falls from the sky, you'd better be ready to catch her. (978-1-63555-335-2)

Cost of Honor by Radclyffe. First Daughter Blair Powell and Homeland Security Director Cameron Roberts face adversity when their enemies stop at nothing to prevent President Andrew Powell's reelection. (978-1-63555-582-0)

Fearless by Tina Michele. Determined to overcome her debilitating fear through exposure therapy, Laura Carter all but fails before she's even begun until dolphin trainer Jillian Marshall dedicates herself to helping Laura defeat the nightmares of her past. (978-1-63555-495-3)

Not Dead Enough by J.M. Redmann. A woman who may or may not be dead drags Micky Knight into a messy con game. (978-1-63555-543-1)

Not Since You by Fiona Riley. When Charlotte boards her honeymoon cruise single and comes face-to-face with Lexi, the high school love she left behind, she questions every decision she has ever made. (978-1-63555-474-8)

Not Your Average Love Spell by Barbara Ann Wright. Four women struggle with who to love and who to hate while fighting to rid a kingdom of an evil invading force. (978-1-63555-327-7)

Tennessee Whiskey by Donna K. Ford. Dane Foster wants to put her life on pause and ask for a redo, a chance for something that matters. Emma Reynolds is that chance. (978-1-63555-556-1)

30 Dates in 30 Days by Elle Spencer. A busy lawyer tries to find love the fast way—thirty dates in thirty days. (978-1-63555-498-4)

Finding Sky by Cass Sellars. Skylar Addison's search for a career intersects with her new boss's search for butterflies, but Skylar can't forgive Jess's intrusion into her life. (978-1-63555-521-9)

Hammers, Strings, and Beautiful Things by Morgan Lee Miller. While on tour with the biggest pop star in the world, rising musician Blair Bennett falls in love for the first time while coping with loss and depression. (978-1-63555-538-7)

Heart of a Killer by Yolanda Wallace. Contract killer Santana Masters's only interest is her next assignment—until a chance meeting with a beautiful stranger tempts her to change her ways. (978-1-63555-547-9)

Leading the Witness by Carsen Taite. When defense attorney Catherine Landauer reluctantly becomes the key witness in prosecutor Starr Rio's latest criminal trial, their hearts, careers, and lives may be at risk. (978-1-63555-512-7)

No Experience Required by Kimberly Cooper Griffin. Izzy Treadway has resigned herself to a life without romance because of her bipolar illness but wonders what she's gotten herself into when she agrees to write a book about love. (978-1-63555-561-5)

One Walk in Winter by Georgia Beers. Olivia Santini and Hayley Boyd Markham might be rivals at work, but they discover that lonely hearts often find company in the most unexpected of places. (978-1-63555-541-7)

The Inn at Netherfield Green by Aurora Rey. Advertising executive Lauren Montgomery and gin distiller Camden Crawley don't agree on anything except saving the Rose & Crown, the old English pub that's brought them together. (978-1-63555-445-8)

Top of Her Game by M. Ullrich. When it comes to life on the field and matters of the heart, losing isn't an option for pro athletes Kenzie Shaw and Sutton Flores. (978-1-63555-500-4)

Vanished by Eden Darry. A storm is coming, and Ellery and Loveday must find the chosen one or humanity won't survive it. (978-1-63555-437-3)

All She Wants by Larkin Rose. Marci Jones and Tessa Dalton get more than they bargained for when their plans for a one-night stand turn into an opportunity for love. (978-1-63555-476-2)

Beautiful Accidents by Erin Zak. Stevie Adams and Bernadette Thompson discover that sometimes the best things in life happen purely by accident. (978-1-63555-497-7)

Before Now by Joy Argento. Can Delany and Jade overcome the betrayal that spans the centuries to reignite a love that can't be broken? (978-1-63555-525-7)

Breathe by Cari Hunter. Paramedic Jemima Pardon's chronic bad luck seems to be improving when she meets police officer Rosie Jones. But they face a battle to survive before they can find love. (978-1-63555-523-3)

Double-Crossed by Ali Vali. Hired thief and killer Reed Gable finds something in her scope that will change her life forever when she gets a contract to end casino accountant Brinley Myers's life. (978-1-63555-302-4)

False Horizons by CJ Birch. Jordan and Ash struggle with different views on the alien agenda and must find their way back to each other before they're swallowed up by a centuries-old war. (978-1-63555-519-6)

Legacy by Charlotte Greene. When five women hike to a remote cabin deep inside a national park, unsettling events suggest that they should have stayed home. (978-1-63555-490-8)

Royal Street Reveillon by Greg Herren. Someone is killing the stars of a reality show, and it's up to Scotty Bradley and the boys to find out who. (978-1-63555-545-5)

Somewhere Along the Way by Kathleen Knowles. When Maxine Cooper moves to San Francisco during the summer of 1981, she learns that wherever you run, you cannot escape yourself. (978-1-63555-383-3)

BOLDSTROKESBOOKS.COM

Looking for your next great read?

Visit BOLDSTROKESBOOKS.COM
to browse our entire catalog of paperbacks, ebooks,
and audiobooks.

Want the first word on what's new?
Visit our website for event info,
author interviews, and blogs.

Subscribe to our free newsletter for sneak peeks,
new releases, plus first notice of promos
and daily bargains.

SIGN UP AT
BOLDSTROKESBOOKS.COM/signup

Bold Strokes Books
Quality and Diversity in LGBTQ Literature

*Bold Strokes Books is an award-winning publisher
committed to quality and diversity in LGBTQ fiction.*